BLACK
SPRING

WORKS BY HENRY MILLER
Published by Grove Press

Black Spring
Quiet Days in Clichy
The Rosy Crucifixion (3 vols.)
   Sexus
   Plexus
   Nexus
Tropic of Cancer
Tropic of Capricorn
Under the Roofs of Paris
   (Opus Pistorum)
Crazy Cock
Moloch

Henry Miller

BLACK SPRING

GROVE PRESS
New York

Grove Press
841 Broadway
New York, NY 10003-4793

"Into the Night Life" and "Jabberwhorl Cronstadt" from *New Directions in Prose and Poetry 1936,* copyright New Directions 1936; "Walking Up and Down in China" from *New Directions in Prose and Poetry 1937,* copyright 1937 by New Directions; "The Tailor Shop" from *The Cosmological Eye,* copyright 1939 by New Directions; "The Angel Is My Watermark" from *Stand Still Like the Hummingbird,* copyright 1962 by Henry Miller.

ISBN: 0-8021-3182-4
Library of Congress Catalog Card Number: 63-11077

Manufactured in the United States of America

First Grove Press Edition 1963

10   9   8   7   6   5

TO
ANAÏS NIN

Can I be as I believe myself or as others believe me to be? Here is where these lines become a confession in the presence of my unknown and unknowable me, unknown and unknowable for myself. Here is where I create the legend wherein I must bury myself.

MIGUEL DE UNAMUNO

The Fourteenth Ward

What is not in the open street is false, derived, that is to say, *literature*.

I am a patriot—of the Fourteenth Ward, Brooklyn, where I was raised. The rest of the United States doesn't exist for me, except as idea, or history, or literature. At ten years of age I was uprooted from my native soil and removed to a cemetery, a *Lutheran* cemetery, where the tombstones were always in order and the wreaths never faded.

But I was born in the street and raised in the street. "The post-mechanical open street where the most beautiful and hallucinating iron vegetation," etc. . . . . Born under the sign of Aries which gives a fiery, active, energetic and somewhat restless body. *With Mars in the ninth house!*

To be born in the street means to wander all your life, to be free. It means accident and incident, drama, movement. It means above all dream. A harmony of irrelevant facts which gives to your wandering a metaphysical certitude. In the street you learn what human beings really are; otherwise, or afterwards, you invent them. What is not in the open street is false, derived, that is to say, *literature*. Nothing of what is called "adventure" ever approaches the flavor of the street. It doesn't matter whether you fly to the Pole, whether you sit on the floor of the ocean with a pad in your hand, whether you pull up nine cities one after the other, or whether, like Kurtz, you sail up the river and go mad. No matter how exciting, how intolerable the situation, there are always exits, always ameliorations, comforts, compensations, newspapers, religions. But once there was none of this. Once you were free, wild, murderous. . . .

The boys you worshiped when you first came down into the street remain with you all your life. They are the only real heroes. Napoleon, Lenin, Capone—all fiction. Napoleon is nothing to me in comparison with Eddie Carney, who gave me my first black eye. No man I have ever met seems as princely, as regal, as noble, as Lester Reardon who, by the mere act of walking down the street, inspired fear and admiration. Jules Verne never led me to the places that Stanley Borowski had up his sleeve when it came dark. Robinson Crusoe lacked imagination in comparison with Johnny Paul. All these boys of the Fourteenth Ward have a flavor about them still. They were not invented or imagined: they were real. Their names ring out like gold coins— Tom Fowler, Jim Buckley, Matt Owen, Rob Ramsay, Harry Martin, Johnny Dunne, to say nothing of Eddie Carney or the great Lester Reardon. Why, even now when I say Johnny Paul the names of the saints leave a bad taste in my mouth. Johnny Paul was the living Odyssey of the Fourteenth Ward; that he later became a truck driver is an irrelevant fact.

Before the great change no one seemed to notice that the streets were ugly or dirty. If the sewer mains were opened you held your nose. If you blew your nose you found snot in your handkerchief and not your nose. There was more of inward peace and contentment. There was the saloon, the race track, bicycles, fast women and trot horses. Life was still moving along leisurely. In the Fourteenth Ward, at least. Sunday mornings no one was dressed. If Mrs. Gorman came down in her wrapper with dirt in her eyes to bow to the priest—"Good morning, Father!" "Good morning, Mrs. Gorman!"—the street was purged of all sin. Pat McCarren carried his handkerchief in the tailflap of his frock coat; it was nice and handy there, like the shamrock in his buttonhole. The foam was on the lager and people stopped to chat with one another.

In my dreams I come back to the Fourteenth Ward as a paranoiac returns to his obsessions. When I think of those steel-gray battleships in the Navy Yard I see them lying there in some astrologic dimension in which I am the gunnersmith, the chemist, the dealer in high explosives, the undertaker, the coroner, the cuckold, the sadist, the lawyer and contender, the scholar, the restless one, the jolt-head, and the brazen-faced.

Where others remember of their youth a beautiful garden, a fond mother, a sojourn at the seashore, I remember, with a vividness as if it were etched in acid, the grim, soot-covered walls and chimneys of the tin factory opposite us and the bright, circular pieces of tin that were strewn in the street, some bright and gleaming, others rusted, dull, copperish, leaving a stain on the fingers; I remember the ironworks where the red furnace glowed and men walked toward the glowing pit with huge shovels in their hands, while outside were the shallow wooden forms like coffins with rods through them on which you scraped your shins or broke your neck. I remember the black hands of the ironmolders, the grit that had sunk so deep into the skin that nothing could remove it, not soap, nor elbow grease, nor money, nor love, nor death. Like a black mark on them! Walking into the furnace like devils with black hands—and later, with flowers over them, cool and rigid in their Sunday suits, not even the rain can wash away the grit. All these beautiful gorillas going up to God with swollen muscles and lumbago and black hands. . . .

For me the whole world was embraced in the confines of the Fourteenth Ward. If anything happened outside it either didn't happen or it was unimportant. If my father went outside that world to fish it was of no interest to me. I remember only his boozy breath when he came home in the evening and opening the big green basket spilled the squirming, goggle-eyed monsters on the floor. If a man went off to the war I remember only that he came back of a Sunday afternoon and standing in front of the minister's house puked up his guts and then wiped it up with his vest. Such was Rob Ramsay, the minister's son. I remember that everybody liked Rob Ramsay—he was the black sheep of the family. They liked him because he was a good-for-nothing and he made no bones about it. Sundays or Wednesdays made no difference to him: you could see him coming down the street under the drooping awnings with his coat over his arm and the sweat rolling down his face; his legs wobbly, with that long, steady roll of a sailor coming ashore after a long cruise; the tobacco juice dribbling from his lips, together with warm, silent curses and some loud and foul ones too. The utter indolence, the insouciance of the man, the obscenities, the sacrilege. Not a man of God, like his father. No, a man who inspired love! His frailties were human frailties and he wore them jauntily, tauntingly, flauntingly, like banderillas. He would come down the warm open street with the gas mains bursting and the air full of sun and shit and oaths and maybe his fly would be open and his suspenders undone, or maybe his vest bright with vomit. Sometimes he came charging down the street, like a bull skidding on all fours, and then the street cleared magically, as if the manholes had opened up and swallowed their offal. Crazy Willy Maine would be standing on the shed over the paint shop, with his pants down, jerking away for dear life. There they stood in the dry electrical crackle of the open street with the gas mains bursting. A tandem that broke the minister's heart.

That was how he was then, Rob Ramsay. A man on a perpetual spree. He came back from the war with medals, and with fire in his guts. He puked up in front of his own door and he wiped up his puke with his own vest. He could clear the street quicker than a machine gun. *Faugh a balla!* That was his way. And a little later, in his warmheartedness, in that fine, careless way he had, he walked off the end of a pier and drowned himself.

I remember him so well and the house he lived in. Because it was on the doorstep of Rob Ramsay's house that we used to congregate in the warm summer evenings and watch the goings-on over the saloon across the street. A coming and going all night long and nobody bothered to pull down the shades. Just a stone's throw away from the little burlesque house called The Bum. All around The Bum were the saloons, and Saturday nights there was a long line outside, milling and pushing and squirming to get at the ticket window. Saturday nights, when the Girl in Blue was in her glory, some wild tar from the Navy Yard would be sure to jump out of his seat and grab off one of Millie de Leon's garters. And a little later that night they'd be sure to come strolling down the street and turn in at the family entrance. And soon they'd be standing in the bedroom over the saloon, pulling off their tight pants and the women yanking off their corsets and scratching themselves like monkeys, while down below they were scuttling the suds and biting each other's ears off, and such a wild, shrill laughter all bottled up inside there, like dynamite evaporating. All this from Rob Ramsay's doorstep, the old man upstairs saying his prayers over a kerosene lamp, praying like an obscene nanny goat for an end to come, or when he got tired of praying coming down in his nightshirt, like an old leprechaun, and belaying us with a broomstick.

From Saturday afternoon on until Monday morning it was a period without end, one thing melting into another. Saturday morning already—how it happened God only knows—you could *feel* the war vessels lying at anchor in the big basin. Saturday mornings my heart was in my mouth. I could see the decks being scrubbed down and the guns polished and the weight of those big sea monsters resting on the dirty glass lake of the basin was a luxurious weight on me. I was already dreaming of running away, of going to far places. But I got only as far as the other side of the river, about as far north as Second Avenue and Twenty-eighth Street, via the Belt Line. There I played the Orange Blossom Waltz and in the entr'actes I washed my eyes at the iron sink. The piano stood in the rear of the saloon. The keys were very yellow and my feet wouldn't reach to the pedals. I wore a velvet suit because velvet was the order of the day.

Everything that passed on the other side of the river was sheer lunacy: the sanded floor, the argand lamps, the mica pictures in which the snow never melted, the crazy Dutchmen with steins in their hands, the iron sink that had grown such a mossy coat of slime, the woman from Hamburg whose ass always hung over the back of the chair, the courtyard choked with sauer-kraut. . . . Everything in three-quarter time that goes on forever. I walk between my parents, with one hand in my mother's muff and the other in my father's sleeve. My eyes are shut tight, tight as clams which draw back their lids only to weep.

All the changing tides and weather that passed over the river are in my blood. I can still feel the slipperiness of the big handrail which I leaned against in fog and rain, which sent through my cool forehead the shrill blasts of the ferryboat as she slid out of the slip. I can still see the mossy planks of the ferry slip buckling as the big round prow grazed her sides and the green, juicy water sloshed through the heaving, groaning planks of the slip. And overhead the sea gulls wheeling and diving, making a dirty noise with their dirty beaks, a hoarse, preying sound of inhuman feasting, of mouths fastened down on refuse, of scabby legs skimming the green-churned water.

One passes imperceptibly from one scene, one age, one life to another. Suddenly, walking down a street, be it real or be it a dream, one realizes for the first time that the years have flown, that all this has passed forever and will live on only in memory; and then the memory turns inward with a strange, clutching brilliance and one goes over these scenes and incidents perpetually, in dream and reverie, while walking a street, while lying with a woman, while reading a book, while talking to a stranger . . . suddenly, but always with terrific insist-ence and always with terrific accuracy, these memories intrude, rise up like ghosts and permeate every fiber of one's being. Henceforward everything moves on shift-ing levels—our thoughts, our dreams, our actions, our whole life. A parallelogram in which we drop from one platform of our scaffold to another. Henceforward we walk split into myriad fragments, like an insect with a hundred feet, a centipede with soft-stirring feet that drinks in the atmosphere; we walk with sensitive filaments that drink avidly of past and future, and all things melt into music and sorrow; we walk against a united world, asserting our dividedness. All things, as we walk, splitting with us into a myriad iridescent fragments. The great fragmentation of maturity. The great change. In youth we were whole and the terror and pain of the world penetrated us through and through. There was no sharp separation between joy and sorrow: they fused into one, as our waking life fuses with dream and sleep. We rose one being in the morning and at night we went down into an ocean, drowned out completely, clutching the stars and the fever of the day.

And then comes a time when suddenly all seems to be reversed. We live in the mind, in ideas, in fragments. We no longer drink in the wild outer music of the streets—we *remember* only. Like a monomaniac we relive the drama of youth. Like a spider that picks up the thread over and over and spews it out according to some obsessive, logarithmic pattern. If we are stirred by a fat bust it is the fat bust of a whore who bent over on a rainy night and showed us for the first time the wonder of the great milky globes; if we are stirred by the reflections on a wet pavement it is because at the age of seven we were suddenly speared by a premonition of the life to come as we stared unthinkingly into that bright, liquid mirror of the street. If the sight of a swinging door intrigues us it is the memory of a summer's evening when all the doors were swinging softly and where the light bent down to caress the shadow there were golden calves and lace and glittering parasols and through the chinks in the swinging door, like fine sand sifting through a bed of rubies, there drifted the music and the incense of gorgeous unknown bodies. Perhaps when that door parted to give us a choking glimpse of the world, perhaps then we had the first intimation of the great impact of sin, the first intimation that here over little round tables spinning in the light, our feet idly scraping the sawdust, our hands touching the cold stem of a glass, that here over these little round tables which later we are to look at with such yearning and reverence, that here, I say, we are to feel in the years to come the first iron of love, the first stains of rust, the first black, clawing hands of the pit, the bright circular pieces of tin in the streets, the gaunt soot-colored chimneys, the bare elm tree that lashes out in the summer's lightning and screams and shrieks as the rain beats down, while out of the hot earth the snails scoot away miraculously and all the air turns blue and sulphurous. Here over these tables, at the first call, the first touch of a hand, there is to come the bitter, gnawing pain that gripes at the bowels; the wine turns sour in our bellies and a pain rises from the soles of the feet and the round tabletops whirl with the anguish and the fever in our bones at the soft, burning touch of a hand. Here there is buried legend after legend of youth and melancholy, of savage nights and mysterious bosoms dancing on the wet mirror of the pavement, of women chuckling softly as they scratch themselves, of wild sailors' shouts, of long queues standing in front of the lobby, of boats brushing each other in the fog and tugs snorting furiously against the rush of tide while up on the Brooklyn Bridge a man is standing in agony, waiting to jump, or waiting to write a poem, or waiting for the blood to leave his vessels because if he advances another foot the pain of his love will kill him.

The plasm of the dream is the pain of separation. The dream lives on after the body is buried. We walk the streets with a thousand legs and eyes, with furry antennae picking up the slightest clue and memory of the past. In the aimless to and fro we pause now and then, like long, sticky plants, and we swallow whole the live morsels of the past. We open up soft and yielding to drink in the night and the oceans of blood which drowned the sleep of our youth. We drink and drink with an insatiable thirst. We are never whole again, but living in fragments, and all our parts separated by thinnest membrane. Thus when the fleet maneuvers in the Pacific it is the whole saga of youth flashing before your eyes, the dream of the open street and the sound of gulls wheeling and diving with garbage in their beaks; or it's the sound of the trumpet and flags flying and all the unknown parts of the earth sailing before your eyes without dates or meaning, wheeling like the tabletop in an iridescent sheen of power and glory. Day comes when you stand on the Brooklyn Bridge looking down into black funnels belching smoke and the gun barrels gleam and the buttons gleam and the water divides miraculously under the sharp, cutting prow, and like ice and lace, like a breaking and a smoking, the water churns green and blue with a cold incandescence, with the chill of champagne and burnt gills. And the prow cleaves the waters in an unending metaphor: the heavy body of the vessel moves on, with the prow ever dividing, and the weight of her is the unweighable weight of the world, the sinking down into unknown barometric pressures, into unknown geologic fissures and caverns where the waters roll melodiously and the stars turn over and die and hands reach up and grasp and clutch and never seize nor close but clutch and grasp while the stars die out one by one, myriads of them, myriads and myriads of worlds sinking down into cold incandescence, into fuliginous night of green and blue with broken ice and the burn of champagne and the hoarse cry of gulls, their beaks swollen with barnacles, their foul garbaged mouths stuffed forever under the silent keel of the ship.

One looks down from the Brooklyn Bridge on a spot of foam or a little lake of gasoline or a broken splinter or an empty scow; the world goes by upside down with pain and light devouring the innards, the sides of flesh bursting, the spears pressing in against the cartilage, the very armature of the body floating off into nothingness. Passes through you crazy words from the ancient world, signs and portents, the writing on the wall, the chinks of the saloon door, the cardplayers with their clay pipes, the gaunt tree against the tin factory, the black hands stained even in death. One walks the street at night with the bridge against the sky like a harp and the festered eyes of sleep burn into the shanties, deflower the walls; the stairs collapse in a smudge and the rats scamper across the ceiling; a voice is nailed against the door and long creepy things with furry antennae and thousand legs drop from the pipes like beads of sweat. Glad, murderous ghosts with the shriek of night-wind and the curses of warm-legged men; low, shallow coffins with rods through the body; grief-spit drooling down into the cold, waxen flesh, searing the dead eyes, the hard, chipped lids of dead clams. One walks around in a circular cage on shifting levels, stars and clouds under the escalator, and the walls of the cage revolve and there are no men and women without tails or claws, while over all things are written the letters of the alphabet in iron and permanganate. One walks round and round in a circular cage to the roll of drum-fire; the theater burns and the actors go on mouthing their lines; the bladder bursts, the teeth fall out, but the wailing of the clown is like the noise of dandruff falling. One walks around on moonless nights in the valley of craters, valley of dead fires and whitened skulls, of birds without wings. Round and round one walks, seeking the hub and nodality, but the fires are burned to ash and the sex of things is hidden in the finger of a glove.

And then one day, as if suddenly the flesh came undone and the blood beneath the flesh had coalesced with the air, suddenly the whole world roars again and the very skeleton of the body melts like wax. Such a day it may be when first you encounter Dostoevski. You remember the smell of the tablecloth on which the book rests; you look at the clock and it is only five minutes from eternity; you count the objects on the mantelpiece because the sound of numbers is a totally new sound in your mouth, because everything new and old, or touched and forgotten, is a fire and a mesmerism. Now every door of the cage is open and whichever way you walk is a straight line toward infinity, a straight, mad line over which the breakers roar and great rocs of marble and indigo swoop to lower their fevered eggs. Out of the waves beating phosphorescent step proud and prancing the enameled horses that marched with Alexander, their tight-proud bellies glowing with calcium, their nostrils dipped in laudanum. Now it is all snow and lice, with the great band of Orion slung around the ocean's crotch.

It was exactly five minutes past seven, at the corner of Broadway and Kosciusko Street, when Dostoevski first flashed across my horizon. Two men and a woman were dressing a shop window. From the middle of the upper legs down the mannikins were all wire. Empty shoe boxes lay banked against the window like last year's snow. . . .

That is how Dostoevski's name came in. Unostentatiously. Like an old shoe box. The Jew who pronounced his name for me had thick lips; he could not say Vladivostok, for instance, nor Carpathians—but he could say Dostoevski divinely. Even now, when I say Dostoevski, I see again his big, blubbery lips and the thin thread of spittle stretching like a rubber band as he pronounced the word. Between his two front teeth there was a more than usual space; it was exactly in the middle of this cavity that the word Dostoevski quivered and stretched, a thin, iridescent film of sputum in which all the gold of twilight had collected—for the sun was just going down over Kosciusko Street and the traffic overhead was breaking into a spring thaw, a chewing and grinding noise as if the mannikins in their wire legs were chewing each other alive. A little later, when I came to the land of the Houyhnhnms, I heard the same chewing and grinding overhead and again the spittle in a man's mouth quivered and stretched and shone iridescent in a dying sun. This time it is at the Dragon's Gorge: a man standing over me with a rattan stick and banging away with a wild Arabian smile. Again, as if my brain were a uterus, the walls of the world gave way. The name Swift was like a clear, hard pissing against the tin-plate lid of the world. Overhead the green fire-eater, his delicate intestines wrapped in tar-

paulin; two enormous milk-white teeth champing down
over a belt of black-greased cogs connecting with the
shooting gallery and the Turkish Baths; the belt of cogs
slipping over a frame of bleached bones. The green
dragon of Swift moves over the cogs with an endless
pissing sound, grinding down fine and foreshortened
the human-sized midgets that are sucked in like macaroni. In and out of the esophagus, up and down and
around the scapular bones and the mastoid delta, falling
through the bottomless pit of the viscera, gurgitating
and exgurgitating, the crotch spreading and slipping, the
cogs moving on relentlessly, chewing alive all the fine,
foreshortened macaroni hanging by the whiskers from
the dragon's red gulch. I look into the milk-white smile
of the barker, that fanatical Arabian smile which came
out of the Dreamland fire, and then I step quietly into
the open belly of the dragon. Between the crazy slats of
the skeleton that holds the revolving cogs the land of
the Houyhnhnms spreads out before me; that hissing,
pissing noise in my ears as if the language of men were
made of seltzer water. Up and down over the greasy
black belt, over the Turkish baths, through the house
of the winds, over the sky-blue waters, between the
clay pipes and the silver balls dancing on liquid jets: the
infra-human world of fedoras and banjos, of bandannas
and black cigars; butterscotch stretching from peg to
Winnipeg, beer bottles bursting, spun-glass molasses
and hot tamales, surf-roar and griddle sizzle, foam and
eucalyptus, dirt, chalk, confetti, a woman's white thigh,
a broken oar; the razzle-dazzle of wooden slats, the mec-
cano puzzle, the smile that never comes off, the wild
Arabian smile with spits of fire, the red gulch and the
green intestines. . . .

O world, strangled and collapsed, where are the

strong white teeth? O world, sinking with the silver balls and the corks and the life-preservers, where are the rosy scalps? O glab and glairy, O glabrous world now chewed to a frazzle, under what dead moon do you lie cold and gleaming?

Third or Fourth Day of Spring

To piss warm and drink cold, as Trimalchio says, because our mother the earth is in the middle, made round like an egg, and has all good things in herself, like a honeycomb.

The house wherein I passed the most important years of my life had only three rooms. One was the room in which my grandfather died. At the funeral my mother's grief was so violent that she almost yanked my grandfather out of the coffin. He looked ridiculous, my dead grandfather, weeping with his daughter's tears. As if he were weeping over his own funeral.

In another room my aunt gave birth to twins. When I heard *twins*, she being so thin and barren, I said to myself—why twins? why not triplets? why not quadruplets? why stop? So thin and scraggly she was, and the room so small—with green walls and a dirty iron sink in the corner. Yet it was the only room in the house which could produce twins—or triplets, or jackasses.

The third room was an alcove where I contracted the measles, chicken pox, scarlet fever, diphtheria, et cetera: all the lovely diseases of childhood which make time stretch out in everlasting bliss and agony, especially when Providence has provided a window over the bed with bars and ogres to claw at them and sweat as thick as carbuncles, rapid as a river and sprouting, sprouting as if it were always spring and tropics, with thick tenderloin steaks for hands and feet heavier than lead or light as snow, feet and hands separated by oceans of time or incalculable latitudes of light, the little knob of the brain hidden away like a grain of sand and the toenails rotting blissfully under the ruins of Athens. In this room I heard nothing but inanities. With each fresh, lovely disease my parents became more addlepated. ("Just think, when you were a little baby I took you to the sink and I said baby you don't want to drink from the bottle any more do you and you said No and I smashed the bottle in the sink.") Into this room softly treading ("treading softly," said General Smerdiakov) came Miss Sonowska, spinster of dubious age with a green-black dress. And with her came the smell of old cheese—her sex had turned rancid under the dress. But Miss Sonowska also brought with her the sack of Jerusalem and the nails that so pierced the hands of Jesus that the holes have never disappeared. After the Crusades the Black Death; after Columbus syphilis; after Miss Sonowska schizophrenia.

Schizophrenia! Nobody thinks any more how marvelous it is that the whole world is diseased. No point of reference, no frame of health. God might just as well be typhoid fever. No absolutes. Only light years of deferred progress. When I think of those centuries in which all Europe grappled with the Black Death I realize how radiant life can be if only we are bitten in the right place! The dance and fever in the midst of that corruption! Europe may never again dance so ecstatically. And syphilis! The advent of syphilis! There it was, like a morning star hanging over the rim of the world.

In 1927 I sat in the Bronx listening to a man reading from the diary of a drug addict. The man could scarcely read, he was laughing so hard. Two phenomena utterly disparate: a man lying in luminol, so taut that his feet stretch beyond the window, leaving the upper half of his body in ecstasy; the other man, who is the same man, sitting in the Bronx and laughing his guts out because he doesn't understand.

Aye, the great sun of syphilis is setting. *Low visibility*: forecast for the Bronx, for America, for the whole modern world. Low visibility accompanied by great gales of laughter. No new stars on the horizon. *Catastrophes* . . . only catastrophes!

I am thinking of that age to come when God is born again, when men will fight and kill for God as now and for a long time to come men are going to fight for food. I am thinking of that age when work will be forgotten and books assume their true place in life, when perhaps there will be no more books, just one great big book—a Bible. For me the book is the man and my book is the man I am, the confused man, the negligent man, the reckless man, the lusty, obscene, boisterous, thoughtful, scrupulous, lying, diabolically truthful man that I am. I am thinking that in that age to come I shall not be overlooked. Then my history will become important and the scar which I leave upon the face of the world will have significance. I can not forget that I am making history, a history on the side which, like a chancre, will eat away the other meaningless history. I regard myself not as a book, a record, a document, but as a history of our time—a history of *all* time.

If I was unhappy in America, if I craved more room, more adventure, more freedom of expression, it was because I needed these things. I am grateful to America for having made me realize my needs. I served my sentence there. At present I have no needs. I am a man without a past and without a future. *I am*—that is all. I am not concerned with your likes and dislikes; it doesn't matter to me whether you are convinced that what I say is so or not. It is all the same to me if you drop me here and now. I am not an atomizer from which you can squeeze a thin spray of hope. I see America spreading disaster. I see America as a black curse upon the world. I see a long night settling in and that mushroom which has poisoned the world withering at the roots.

And so it is with a premonition of the end—be it tomorrow or three hundred years hence—that I feverishly write this book. So it is too that my thoughts sputter out now and then, that I am obliged to rekindle the flame again and again, not with courage alone, but with desperation—for there is no one I can trust to say these things for me. My faltering and groping, my search for any and every means of expression, is a sort of divine stuttering. *I am dazzled by the glorious collapse of the world!*

Every evening, after dinner, I take the garbage down to the courtyard. Coming up I stand with empty pail at the staircase window gazing at the Sacré Cœur high up on the hill of Montmartre. Every evening, when I take the garbage down, I think of myself standing out on a high hill in resplendent whiteness. It is no sacred heart that inspires me, no Christ I am thinking of. Something better than a Christ, something bigger than a heart, something beyond God Almighty I think of—MYSELF. *I am a man.* That seems to me sufficient.

I am a man of God and a man of the Devil. To each his due. Nothing eternal, nothing absolute. Before me always the image of the body, our triune god of penis and testicles. On the right, God the Father; on the left and hanging a little lower, God the Son; and between

and above them the Holy Ghost. I can never forget that
this holy trinity is man-made, that it will undergo infinite changes—but as long as we come out of wombs
with arms and legs, as long as there are stars above us
to drive us mad and grass under our feet to cushion the
wonder in us, just so long will this body serve for all
the tunes that we may whistle.

Today it is the third or fourth day of spring and I
am sitting at the Place Clichy in full sunshine. Today,
sitting here in the sun, I tell you it doesn't matter a
damn whether the world is going to the dogs or not; it
doesn't matter whether the world is right or wrong,
good or bad. *It is*—and that suffices. The world is what
it is and I am what I am. I say it not like a squatting
Buddha with legs crossed, but out of a gay, hard wisdom, out of an inner security. This out there and this
in me, all this, *everything*, the resultant of inexplicable
forces. A chaos whose order is beyond comprehension.
Beyond *human* comprehension.

As a human being walking around at twilight, at
dawn, at strange hours, unearthly hours, the sense of
being alone and unique fortifies me to such a degree
that when I walk with the multitude and seem no longer
to be a human being but a mere speck, a gob of spit, I
begin to think of myself alone in space, a single being
surrounded by the most magnificent empty streets, a
human biped walking between the skyscrapers when all
the inhabitants have fled and I am alone walking, singing, commanding the earth. I do not have to look in my
vest pocket to find my soul; it is there all the time,
bumping against my ribs, swelling, inflated with song.
If I just left a gathering where it was agreed that all is
dead, now as I walk the streets, alone and identical with

God, I know that this is a lie. The evidence of death is before my eyes constantly; but this death of the world, a death constantly going on, does not move from the periphery in, to engulf me, this death is at my very feet, moving from me outward, my own death a step in advance of me always. The world is the mirror of myself dying, the world not dying any more than I die, I more alive a thousand years from now than this moment and this world in which I am now dying also more alive then than now though dead a thousand years. When each thing is lived through to the end there is no death and no regrets, neither is there a false springtime; each moment lived pushes open a greater, wider horizon from which there is no escape save living.

The dreamers dream from the neck up, their bodies securely strapped to the electric chair. To imagine a new world is to live it daily, each thought, each glance, each step, each gesture killing and recreating, death always a step in advance. To spit on the past is not enough. To proclaim the future is not enough. One must act *as if* the past were dead and the future unrealizable. One must act *as if* the next step were the last, which it is. Each step forward is the last, and with it a world dies, one's self included. We are here of the earth never to end, the past never ceasing, the future never beginning, the present never ending. The never-never world which we hold in our hands and see and yet is not ourselves. We are that which is never concluded, never shaped to be recognized, all there is and yet not the whole, the parts so much greater than the whole that only God the mathematician can figure it out.

Laughter! counseled Rabelais. For all your ills *laughter!* Jesus but it's hard to take his sane, gay wisdom after all the quack medicines we've poured down our throats. How can one laugh when the lining is worn off his stomach? How can one laugh after all the misery they've poisoned us with, the whey-faced, lantern-jawed, sad, suffering, solemn, serious, seraphic spirits? I understand the treachery that inspired them. I forgive them their genius. But it's hard to free oneself from all the sorrow they've created.

When I think of all the fanatics who were crucified, and those who were not fanatics, but simple idiots, all slaughtered for the sake of ideas, I begin to draw a smile. Bottle up every avenue of escape, I say. Bring the lid down hard on the New Jerusalem! Let's feel each other belly to belly, *without hope!* Washed and unwashed, murderer and evangelist, the whey-faced guys and the three-quarter moons, the weather vanes and the bullet-heads—let them only get closer together, let them stew for a few centuries in this cul-de-sac!

Either the world is too slack or I am not taut enough. If I became unintelligible I would be understood immediately. The difference between understanding and non-understanding is as fine as a hair, *finer*, the difference of a millimeter, a thread of space between China and Neptune. No matter how far out of whack I get, the ratio remains the same; it has nothing to do with clarity, precision, et cetera. (The et cetera is important!) The mind blunders because it is too precise an instrument; the threads break against the mahogany knots, against the cedar and ebony of alien matter. We talk about reality as if it were something commensurable, a piano exercise, or a lesson in physics. The Black Death came with the return of the Crusaders. Syphilis came with the return of Columbus. *Reality will come too! Reality prime*, says my friend Cronstadt. From a poem written on the ocean floor. . . .

To prognosticate this reality is to be off either by a millimeter or by a million light years. The difference is a quantum formed by the intersection of streets. A quantum is a functional disorder created by trying to squeeze oneself into a frame of reference. A reference is a discharge from an old employer, that is to say, a mucopus from an old disease.

These are thoughts born of the street, *genus epileptoid*. You walk out with the guitar and the strings snap —because the idea is not embedded morphologically. To recall the dream one must keep the eyes closed and not budge. The slightest stir and the whole fabric falls apart. In the street I expose myself to the destructive, disintegrating elements that surround me. I let everything wreak its own havoc with me. I bend over to spy on the secret processes, *to obey* rather than to command.

There are huge blocks of my life which are gone forever. Huge blocks gone, scattered, wasted in talk, action, reminiscence, dream. There was never any time when I was living *one* life, the life of a husband, a lover, a friend. Wherever I was, whatever I was engaged in, I was leading multiple lives. Thus, whatever it is that I choose to regard as *my* story is lost, drowned, indissolubly fused with the lives, the drama, the stories of others.

I am a man of the old world, a seed that was transplanted by the wind, a seed which failed to blossom in the mushroom oasis of America. I belong on the heavy tree of the past. My allegiance, physical and spiritual, is with the men of Europe, those who were once

Franks, Gauls, Vikings, Huns, Tatars, what not. The climate for my body and soul is here where there is quickness and corruption. I am proud *not* to belong to this century.

For those stargazers who are unable to follow the act of revelation I append herewith a few horoscopic brushstrokes in the margin of my *Universe of Death*....

I am Chancre, the crab, which moves sideways and backwards and forwards at will. I move in strange tropics and deal in high explosives, embalming fluid, jasper, myrrh, smaragd, fluted snot, and porcupines' toes. Because of Uranus which crosses my longitudinal I am inordinately fond of cunt, hot chitterlings, and water bottles. Neptune dominates my ascendant. That means I am composed of a watery fluid, that I am volatile, quixotic, unreliable, independent, and evanescent. Also quarrelsome. With a hot pad under my ass I can play the braggart or the buffoon as good as any man, no matter what sign he be born under. This is a self-portrait which yields only the missing parts—an anchor, a dinner bell, the remains of a beard, the hind part of a cow. In short, I am an idle fellow who pisses his time away. I have absolutely nothing to show for my labors except my genius. But there comes a time, even in the life of an idle genius, when he has to go to the window and vomit up the excess baggage. If you are a genius you have to do that—if for no other reason than to build a little comprehensible world of your own which will not run down like an eight-day clock! And the more ballast you throw overboard the easier you rise above the esteem of your neighbors. Until you find yourself all alone in the stratosphere. Then you tie a stone around your neck and you jump feet first. That brings about the complete destruction of anagogic dream interpretation together with mercurial stomatitis brought about by inunctions. You have the dream for nighttime and the horse laugh for daytime.

And so, when I stand at the bar of Little Tom Thumb and see these men with three-quarter faces coming up through the trapdoors of hell with pulleys and braces, dragging locomotives and pianos and cuspidors, I say to myself: "Grand! Grand! All this bric-a-brac, all this machinery coming to me on a silver platter! It's grand! It's marvelous! It's a poem created while I was asleep."

What little I have learned about writing amounts to this: *it is not what people think it is*. It is an absolutely new thing each time with each individual. Valparaiso, for example. Valparaiso, when I say it, means something totally different from anything it ever meant before. It may mean an English cunt with all her front teeth gone and the bartender standing in the middle of the street searching for customers. It may mean an angel in a silk shirt running his lacy fingers over a black harp. It may mean an odalisque with a mosquito netting around her ass. It may mean any of these things, or none, but whatever it may mean you can be sure it will be something different, something new. Valparaiso is always five minutes before the end, a little this side of Peru, or maybe three inches nearer. It's the accidental square inch that you do with fever because you've got a hot pad under your ass and the Holy Ghost in your bowels—orthopedic mistakes included. It means "to piss warm and drink cold," as Trimalchio says, "because our mother the earth is in the middle, made round like an egg, and has all good things in herself, like a honeycomb."

And now, ladies and gentlemen, with this little universal can opener which I hold in my hands I am about to open a can of sardines. With this little can opener which I hold in my hands it's all the same—whether you want to open a box of sardines or a drugstore. It's the third or fourth day of spring, as I've told you several times already, and even though it's a poor, shabby, reminiscent spring, the thermometer is driving me crazy as a bedbug. You thought I was sitting at the Place Clichy all the time, drinking an *apéritif* perhaps. As a matter of fact I *was* sitting at the Place Clichy, but that was two or three years ago. And I *did* stand at the bar of Little Tom Thumb, but that was a long time ago and since then a crab has been gnawing at my vitals. All this began in the Metro (first-class) with the phrase —"*l'homme que j'étais, je ne le suis plus.*"

Walking past the railroad yards I was plagued by two fears—one, that if I lifted my eyes a little higher they would dart out of my head; two, that my bunghole was dropping out. A tension so strong that all ideation became instantly rhombohedral. Imagined the whole world declaring a holiday to think about static. On that day so many suicides that there would not be wagons enough to collect the dead. Passing the railroad yards at the Porte I catch the sickening stench from the cattle trains. It's like this: all day today and all day yesterday —three or four years ago, of course—they have been standing there body to body in fear and sweat. Their bodies are saturated with doom. Passing them my mind is terribly lucid, my thoughts crystal clear. I'm in such a hurry to spill out my thoughts that I am running past them in the dark. I too am in great fear. I too am sweating and panting, thirsty, saturated with doom. I'm going by them like a letter through the post. Or not I, but certain ideas of which I am the harbinger. And these ideas are already labeled and docketed, already sealed, stamped and watermarked. They run in series, my ideas, like electric coils. To live *beyond* illusion or *with* it? that's the question. Inside me a terrifying gem which will not wear away, a gem which scratches the windowpanes as I flee through the night. The cattle are lowing and bleating. They stand there in the warm stench of their own dung. I hear again now the music of the A Minor Quartet, the agonized flurries of the strings. There's a madman inside me and he's hacking away, hacking and hacking until he strikes the final discord. *Pure annihilation*, as distinguished from lesser, muddier annihilations. Nothing to be mopped up afterwards. A wheel of light rolling up to the precipice— and over into the bottomless pit. I, Beethoven, I created it! I, Beethoven, I destroy it!

From now on, ladies and gentlemen, you are entering Mexico. From now on everything will be wonderful and beautiful, marvelously beautiful, marvelously wonderful. Increasingly marvelously beautiful and wonderful. From now on no more washlines, no suspenders, no flannel underwear. Always summer and everything true to pattern. If it's a horse it's a horse for all time. If it's apoplexy it's apoplexy, and not St. Vitus's Dance. No early morning whores, no gardenias. No dead cats in the gutter, no sweat and perspiration. If it be a lip it must be a lip that trembles eternally. For in Mexico, ladies and gentlemen, it's always high noon and what glows is fuchsia and what's dead is dead and no feather dusters. You lie on a cement bed and you sleep like an acetylene torch. When you strike it rich it's a bonanza. When you don't strike it rich it's misery, *worse than misery*. No arpeggios, no grace notes, no cadenzas. Either you hold the clue or you don't hold the clue. Either you start with pure melody or you start with listerine. But no Purgatory and no elixir. It's Fourth Eclogue or Thirteenth Arrondissement!

A Saturday Afternoon

This is better than reading Vergil.

It is a Saturday afternoon and this Saturday afternoon is distinct from all other Saturday afternoons, but in no wise like a Monday afternoon or a Thursday afternoon. On this day, as I ride toward the Neuilly Bridge past the little island of Robinson with its temple at the far end and in the temple the little statue like a cotyledon in the mouth of a bell, I have such a sense of being at home that it seems incredible that I was born in America. The stillness of the water, the fishing boats, the iron stakes that mark the channel, the low lying tugs with sluggish curves, the black scows and bright stanchions, the sky never changing, the river bending and twisting, the hills spreading out and ever girdling the valley, the perpetual change of panorama and yet the constancy of it, the variety and movement of life under the fixed sign of the tricolor, all this is the history of the Seine which is in my blood and will go down into the blood of those who come after me when they move along these shores of a Saturday afternoon.

As I cross the bridge at Boulogne, along the road that leads to Meudon, I turn round and roll down the hill into Sèvres. Passing through a deserted street I see a little restaurant in a garden; the sun is beating through the leaves and spangling the tables. I dismount.

What is better than reading Vergil or memorizing Goethe (*alles Vergängliche ist nur ein Gleichnis*, etc.)?

Why, eating outdoors under an awning for eight francs at Issy-les-Moulineaux. *Pourtant je suis à Sèvres*. No matter. I have been thinking lately of writing a *Journal d'un Fou* which I imagine to have found at Issy-les-Moulineaux. And since that *fou* is largely myself I am not eating at Sèvres, but at Issy-les-Moulineaux. And what does the *fou* say when the waitress comes with the big canette of beer? *Don't worry about errors when you're writing. The biographers will explain all errors.* I am thinking of my friend Carl who has spent the last four days getting started on a description of the woman he's writing about. "I can't do it! I can't do it!" he says. Very well, says the *fou*, let *me* do it for you. *Begin!* That's the principal thing. Supposing her nose is not aquiline? Supposing it's a celestial nose? What difference? When a portrait commences badly it's because you're not describing the woman you have in mind: you are thinking more about those who are going to look at the portrait than about the woman who is sitting for you. Take Van Norden—he's another case. He has been trying for two months to get started with his novel. Each time I meet him he has a new opening for his book. It never gets beyond the opening. Yesterday he said: "You see what my problem's like. It isn't just a question of how to begin: the first line decides the cast of the whole book. Now here's a start I made the other day: Dante wrote a poem about a place called H———. H-dash, because I don't want any trouble with the censors."

Think of a book opening with H-dash! A little private hell which mustn't offend the censors! I notice that when Whitman starts a poem he writes: "I, Walt, in my 37th year and in perfect health! . . . I am afoot with my vision. . . . I dote on myself. . . . Walt Whitman, a kosmos, of Manhattan the son, turbulent, fleshy, sensual, eating, drinking and breeding. . . . Unscrew the locks from the doors! Unscrew the doors themselves from their jambs. . . . Here or henceforward it is all the same to me. . . . I exist as I am, that is enough. . . ."

With Walt it is always Saturday afternoon. If the woman be hard to describe he admits it and stops at the third line. Next Saturday, the weather permitting, he may add a missing tooth, or an ankle. Everything can wait, can bide its time. *"I accept Time absolutely."* Whereas my friend Carl, who has the vitality of a bedbug, is pissing in his pants because four days have elapsed and he has only a negative in his hand. "I don't see any reason," says he, "why I should ever die—barring an untoward accident." And then he rubs his hands and closets himself in his room to live out his immortality. He lives on like a bedbug hidden in the wallpaper.

The hot sun is beating through the awning. I am delirious because I am dying so fast. Every second counts. I do not hear the second that has just ticked off —I am clinging like a madman to this second which has not yet announced itself. . . . What is better than reading Vergil? *This!* This expanding moment which has not defined itself in ticks or beats, this eternal moment which destroys all values, degrees, differences. This gushing upward and outward from a hidden source. No truths to utter, no wisdom that can be imparted. A gush and a babble, a speaking to all men at once, everywhere, and in all languages. Now is the thinnest veil between madness and sanity. Now is everything so simple that it mocks one. From this peak of drunkenness one rolls down into the plateau of good health where one reads Vergil and Dante and Montaigne and all the others who spoke only of the moment, the expanding moment that is heard forever. . . . Talking to all men at once. A gush and a babble. This is the moment when I raise the glass to my lips, observing as I do so the fly that has settled on my pinkie; and the fly is as important to this moment as my hand or the glass it holds or the beer that is in the glass or the thoughts that are born of the beer and die with the beer. This is the moment when I know that a sign reading "To Versailles," or a sign reading "To Suresnes," any and all signs pointing to this or that place, should be ignored, that one should always go toward the place for which there is no sign. This is the moment when the deserted street on which I have chosen to sit is throbbing with people and all the crowded streets are empty. This is the moment when any restaurant is the right restaurant so long as it was not indicated to you by somebody. This is the best food, though it is the worst I have ever tasted. This is the food which no one but genius will touch—always within reach, easily digested, and leaving an appetite for more. "The roquefort, was it good?" asks the waitress. *Divine!* The stalest, the wormiest, the lousiest roquefort that was ever fabricated, saturated with the worms of Dante, of Vergil, Homer, Boccaccio, Rabelais, Goethe, all the worms that ever were and have passed on into cheese. To eat this cheese one must have genius. This is the cheese wherein I bury myself, I, Miguel Feodor François Wolfgang Valentine Miller.

The approach to the bridge is paved with cobblestones. I ride so slowly that each cobble sends a separate and distinct message to my spinal column and on up through the vertebrae to that crazy cage in which the medulla oblongata flashes its semaphores. And as I cross the bridge at Sèvres, looking to the right of me and left, crossing any bridge, whether it be over the Seine, the Marne, the Ourcq, the Aude, the Loire, the Lot, the River Shannon or the Liffey, the East River or the Hudson, the Mississippi, the Colorado, the Amazon, the Orinoco, the Jordan, the Tigris, the Iriwaddy, crossing any and every bridge and I have crossed them all, including the Nile, the Danube, the Volga, the Euphrates, crossing the bridge at Sèvres I yell, like that maniac St. Paul—"O death, where is thy sting?" In back of me Sèvres, before me Boulogne, but this that passes under me, this Seine that started up somewhere in a myriad simultaneous trickles, this still jet rushing on from out of a million billion roots, this still mirror bearing the clouds along and stifling the past, rushing on and on and on while between the mirror and the clouds moving transversally I, a complete corporate entity, a universe bringing countless centuries to a conclusion, I and this that passes beneath me and this that floats above me and all that surges through me, I and this, I and that joined up in one continuous movement, this Seine and every Seine that is spanned by a bridge is the miracle of a man crossing it on a bicycle.

This is better than reading Vergil. . . .

Heading back toward St. Cloud, the wheel rolling very slowly, the speedometer in the crazy gray cage clicking like a newsreel. I am a man whose manometer is intact; I am a man on a machine and the machine is in control; I am riding downhill with the brakes on; I could ride just as contentedly on a treadmill and let the mirror pass over me and history under me, or vice versa. I am riding in full sunlight, a man impervious to all except the phenomena of light. The hill of St. Cloud rises up before me on the left, the trees are bending over me to shadow me, the way is smooth and never-ending, the little statue rests in the bell of the temple like a cotyledon. Every Middle Age is good, whether in man or history. It is full sunlight and the roads extend in every direction, and all the roads are downhill. I would not level the road nor remove any of the bumps. Each jolt sends a fresh message to the signal tower. I have marked all the spots in passing: to retrace my thoughts I have only to retrace my journey, re-feel these bumps.

At the St. Cloud bridge I come to a full stop. I am in no hurry—I have the whole day to piss away. I put my bicycle in the rack under the tree and go to the urinal to take a leak. It is all gravy, even the urinal. As I stand there looking up at the house fronts a demure young woman leans out of a window to watch me. How many times have I stood thus in this smiling, gracious world, the sun splashing over me and the birds twittering crazily, and found a woman looking down at me from an open window, her smile crumbling into soft little bits which the birds gather in their beaks and deposit sometimes at the base of a urinal where the water gurgles melodiously and a man comes along with his fly open and pours the steaming contents of his bladder over the dissolving crumbs. Standing thus, with heart and fly and bladder open, I seem to recall every urinal I ever stepped into—all the most pleasant sensations, all the most luxurious memories, as if my brain were a huge divan smothered with cushions and my life one long snooze on a hot, drowsy afternoon. I do not find it so strange that America placed a urinal in the center of the Paris exhibit at Chicago. I think it belongs there and I think it a tribute which the French should appreciate. True, there was no need to fly the tricolor above it. *Un peu trop fort, ça!* And yet, how is a Frenchman to know that one of the first things which strikes the eye of the American visitor, which thrills him, warms him to the very gizzard, is this ubiquitous urinal? How is a Frenchman to know that what impresses the American in looking at a *pissotière*, or a *vespasienne*, or whatever you choose to call it, is the fact that he is in the midst of a people who admit to the necessity of peeing now and then and who know also that to piss one has to use a pisser and that if it is not done publicly it will be done privately and that it is no more incongruous to piss in the street than underground where some old derelict can watch you to see that you commit no nuisance.

I am a man who pisses largely and frequently, which they say is a sign of great mental activity. However it be, I know that I am in distress when I walk the streets of New York. Wondering constantly where the next stop will be and if I can hold out that long. And while in winter, when you are broke and hungry, it is fine to stop off for a few minutes in a warm underground comfort station, when spring comes it is quite a different matter. One likes to piss in sunlight, among human beings who watch and smile down at you. And while the female squatting down to empty her bladder in a china bowl may not be a sight to relish, no man with any feeling can deny that the sight of the male standing behind a tin strip and looking out on the throng with that contented, easy, vacant smile, that long, reminiscent, pleasurable look in his eye, is a good thing. To relieve a full bladder is one of the great human joys.

There are certain urinals I go out of my way to make —such as the battered rattle-trap outside the deaf and

dumb asylum, corner of the Rue St. Jacques and the
Rue de l'Abbé-de-l'Epée, or the Pneu Hutchinson one
by the Luxembourg Gardens, corner Rue d'Assas and
Rue Guynemer. Here, on a balmy night in spring,
through what concatenation of events I do not know
or care, I rediscovered my old friend Robinson Crusoe.
The whole night passed in reminiscence, in pain and
terror, *joyous* pain, *joyous* terror.

"The wonders of this man's life"—so reads the pref-
ace to the original edition—"exceed all that is to be
found extant; the life of one man being scarce capable
of a greater variety." The island now known as Tobago,
at the mouth of the mighty Orinoco, thirty miles north-
west of Trinidad. Where the man Crusoe lived in solitude for eight and twenty years. The footprints in the
sand, so beautifully embossed on the cover. The man
Friday. The umbrella. . . . Why had this simple tale so
fascinated the men of the eighteenth century? *Voici* Larousse:

". . . le récit des aventures d'un homme qui, jeté dans
une île déserte, trouve les moyens de se suffire et même
de se créer un bonheur relatif, que complète l'arrivée
d'un autre être humain, d'un sauvage, Vendredi, que
Robinson a arraché des mains de ses ennemis. . . . L'in-
térêt du roman n'est pas dans la vérité psychologique,
mais dans l'abondance des détails minutieux qui donnent
une impression saisissante de réalité."

So Robinson Crusoe not only found a way of getting
along, but even established for himself a relative happiness! Bravo! One man who was satisfied with a *relative* happiness. So un-Anglo-Saxon! So pre-Christian!
Bringing the story up to date, Larousse to the contrary,
we have here then the account of an artist who wanted
to build himself a world, a story of perhaps the first

genuine neurotic, a man who had himself shipwrecked in order to live outside his time in a world of his own which he could share with another human being, *même un sauvage*. The remarkable thing to note is that, acting out his neurotic impulse, he did find a relative happiness even though alone on a desert island, with nothing more perhaps than an old shot-gun and a pair of torn breeches. A clean slate, with twenty-five thousand years of post-Magdalenian "progress" buried in his neurones. An eighteenth-century conception of relative happiness! And when Friday comes along, though Friday, or *Vendredi*, is only a savage and does not speak the language of Crusoe, the circle is complete. I should like to read the book again—and I will some rainy day. A remarkable book, coming at the culmination of our marvelous Faustian culture. Men like Rousseau, Beethoven, Napoleon, Goethe on the horizon. The whole civilized world staying up nights to read it in ninety-seven different tongues. A picture of reality in the eighteenth century. Henceforward no more desert isles. Henceforward wherever one happens to be born is a desert isle. Every man his own civilized desert, the island of self on which he is shipwrecked: happiness, relative or absolute, is out of the question. Henceforward everyone is running away from himself to find an imaginary desert isle, to live out this dream of Robinson Crusoe. Follow the classic flights, of Melville, Rimbaud, Gauguin, Jack London, Henry James, D. H. Lawrence . . . thousands of them. None of them found happiness. Rimbaud found cancer. Gauguin found syphilis. Lawrence found the white plague. The plague— that's it! Be it cancer, syphilis, tuberculosis, or what not. *The plague!* The plague of modern progress: colonization, trade, free Bibles, war, disease, artificial limbs, factories, slaves, insanity, neuroses, psychoses, cancer, syphilis, tuberculosis, anemia, strikes, lockouts, starvation, nullity, vacuity, restlessness, striving, despair, ennui, suicide, bankruptcy, arterio-sclerosis, megalomania, schizophrenia, hernia, cocaine, prussic acid, stink bombs, tear gas, mad dogs, auto-suggestion, auto-intoxication, psychotherapy, hydrotherapy, electric massages, vacuum cleaners, pemmican, grape nuts, hemorrhoids, gangrene. No desert isles. No Paradise. Not even *relative* happiness. Men running away from themselves so frantically that they look for salvation under the ice floes or in tropical swamps, or else they climb the Himalayas or asphyxiate themselves in the stratosphere. . . .

What fascinated the men of the eighteenth century was the vision of the end. They had enough. They wanted to retrace their steps, climb back into the womb again.

THIS IS AN ADDENDA FOR LAROUSSE. . . .

What impressed me, in the urinal by the Luxembourg, was how little it mattered what the book contained; it was the moment of reading it that counted, the moment that contained the book, the moment that definitely and for all time placed the book in the living ambiance of a room with its sunbeams, its atmosphere of convalescence, its homely chairs, its rag carpet, its odor of cooking and washing, its mother image bulking large and totemlike, its windows giving out on the street and throwing into the retina the jumbled issues of idle, sprawling figures, of gnarled trees, trolley wires, cats on the roof, tattered nightmares dancing from the clotheslines, saloon doors swinging, parasols unfurled, snow clotting, horses slipping, engines racing, the panes frosted, the trees sprouting. The story of Robinson Crusoe owes its appeal—for me, at least—to the moment in which I discovered it. It lives on in an ever-increasing phantasmagoria, a living part of a life filled with phantasmagoria. For me Robinson Crusoe belongs in the same category as certain parts of Vergil—or, *what time is it?* For, whenever I think of Vergil, I think automatically—*what time is it?* Vergil to me is a bald-headed guy with spectacles tilting back in his chair and leaving a grease mark on the blackboard; a bald-headed guy opening wide his mouth in a delirium which he simulated five days a week for four successive years; a big mouth with false teeth producing this strange oracular nonsense: *rari nantes in gurgite vasto*. Vividly I recall the unholy joy with which he pronounced this phrase. A *great* phrase, according to this bald-pated, goggle-eyed son of a bitch. We scanned it and we parsed it, we repeated it after him, we swallowed it like cod liver oil, we chewed it like dyspepsia tablets, we opened wide our mouths as he did and we reproduced the miracle day after day five days in the week, year in and year out, like worn-out records, until Vergil was done for and out of our lives for good and all.

But every time this goggle-eyed bastard opened wide his mouth and the glorious phrase rolled out I heard what was most important for me to hear at that moment—*what time is it?* Soon time to go to Math. Soon time for recess. Soon time to wash up. . . . I am one individual who is going to be honest about Vergil and his fucking *rari nantes in gurgite vasto*. I say without blushing or stammering, without the least confusion, regret or remorse that recess in the toilet was worth a thousand Vergils, always was and always will be. At recess we came alive. At recess we who were Gentile and had no better sense grew delirious: in and out of the cabinets we ran, slamming the doors and breaking the locks. We seemed to have been taken with delirium tremens. As we pelted each other with food and shouted and cursed and tripped each other up, we muttered now and then—*rari nantes in gurgite vasto*. The din we created was so great, and the damage so vast, that whenever we Gentiles went to the toilet the Latin teacher went with us, or if he were eating out that day then the History teacher followed us in. And a wry face they could make, standing in the toilet with delicate, buttered sandwich in hand listening to the pooping and squawking of us brats. The moment they left the toilet to get a breath of fresh air we raised our voices in song, which was not considered reprehensible, but which no doubt was a condition greatly envied by the bespectacled professors who had to use the toilet now and then themselves, learned as they were.

O the wonderful recesses in the toilet! To them I owe my knowledge of Boccaccio, of Rabelais, of Petronius, of *The Golden Ass*. All my good reading, you might say, was done in the toilet. At the worst, *Ulysses*, or a detective story. There are passages in *Ulysses* which can be read only in the toilet—if one wants to extract the full flavor of their content. And this is not to denigrate the talent of the author. This is simply to move him a little closer to the good company of Abelard, Petrarch, Rabelais, Villon, Boccaccio—all the fine, lusty genuine spirits who recognized dung for dung and angels for angels. Fine company, and no *rari nantes in gurgite vasto*. And the more ramshackle the toilet, the more dilapidated it be, the better. (Same for urinals.) To enjoy Rabelais, for example—such a passage as "How to Rebuild the Walls of Paris"—I recommend a plain, country toilet, a little outhouse in the corn patch, with a crescent sliver of light coming through the door. No buttons to push, no chain to pull, no pink toilet paper. Just a rough-carved seat big enough to frame your behind, and two other holes of dimensions suitable for other behinds. If you can bring a friend along and have him sit beside you, excellent! A good book is always more enjoyable in good company. A beautiful half-hour you can while away sitting in the outhouse with a friend—a half-hour which will remain with you all your life, and the book it contained, and the odor thereof.

No harm, I say, can ever be done a great book by taking it with you to the toilet. Only the little books suffer thereby. Only the little books make ass wipers. Such a one is *Little Caesar*, now translated into French and forming one of the *Passions* series. Turning the pages over it seems to me that I am back home again reading the headlines, listening to the goddamned radios, riding tin buggies, drinking cheap gin, buggering virgin harlots with a corn cob, stringing up niggers and burning them alive. Something to give one diarrhoea. And the same goes for the *Atlantic Monthly*, or any other monthly, for Aldous Huxley, Gertrude Stein, Sinclair Lewis, Hemingway, Dos Passos, Dreiser, etc., etc. . . . I hear no bell ringing inside me when I bring these birds to the water closet. I pull the chain and down the sewer they go. Down the Seine and into the Atlantic Ocean. Maybe a year hence they will bob up again— on the shores of Coney Island, or Midland Beach, or Miami, along with dead jelly fish, snails, clams, used condoms, pink toilet paper, yesterday's news, tomorrow's suicides. . . .

No more peeping through keyholes! No more masturbating in the dark! No more public confessions! *Unscrew the doors from their jambs!* I want a world where the vagina is represented by a crude, honest slit, a world that has feeling for bone and contour, for raw, primary colors, a world that has fear and respect for its animal origins. I'm sick of looking at cunts all tickled up, disguised, deformed, idealized. Cunts with nerve ends exposed. I don't want to watch young virgins masturbating in the privacy of their boudoirs or biting their nails or tearing their hair or lying on a bed full of bread crumbs for a whole chapter. I want Madagascan funeral poles, with animal upon animal and at the top Adam and Eve, and Eve with a crude, honest slit between the legs. I want hermaphrodites who are real hermaphrodites, and not make-believes walking around with an atrophied penis or a dried-up cunt. I want a classic purity, where dung is dung and angels are angels. The Bible à la King James, for example. Not the Bible of Wycliffe, not the Vulgate, not the Greek, not the Hebrew, but the glorious, death-dealing Bible that was created when the English language was in flower, when a vocabulary of twenty thousand words sufficed to build a monument for all time. A Bible written in Svenska or Tegalic, a Bible for the Hottentots or the Chinese, a Bible that has to meander through the trickling sands of French is no Bible—it is a counterfeit and a fraud. The King James Version was created by a race of bone-crushers. It revives the primitive mysteries, revives rape, murder, incest, revives epilepsy, sadism, megalomania, revives demons, angels, dragons, leviathans, revives magic, exorcism, contagion, incantation, revives fratricide, regicide, patricide, suicide, revives hypnotism, anarchism, somnambulism, revives the song, the dance, the act, revives the mantic, the chthonian, the arcane, the mysterious, revives the power, the evil, and the glory that is God. All brought into the open on a colossal scale, and so salted and spiced that it will last until the next Ice Age.

A classic purity, then—and to hell with the Post Office authorities! For what is it enables the classics to live at all, if indeed they be living on and not dying as we and all about us are dying? What preserves them against the ravages of time if it be not the salt that is in them? When I read Petronius or Apuleius or Rabelais, how close they seem! That salty tang! That odor of the menagerie! The smell of horse piss and lion's dung, of tiger's breath and elephant's hide. Obscenity, lust, cruelty, boredom, wit. Real eunuchs. Real hermaphrodites. Real pricks. Real cunts. *Real banquets!* Rabelais rebuilds the walls of Paris with human cunts. Trimalchio tickles his own throat, pukes up his own guts, wallows in his own swill. In the amphitheater, where a big, sleepy pervert of a Caesar lolls dejectedly, the lions and the jackals, the hyenas, the tigers, the spotted leopards are crunching real human bones— whilst the coming men, the martyrs and imbeciles, are walking up the golden stairs shouting *Hallelujah!*

When I touch the subject of toilets I relive some of my best moments. Standing in the urinal at Boulogne, with the hill of St. Cloud to the right of me and the woman in the window above me, and the sun beating down on the still river water, I see the strange American I am passing on this quiet knowledge to other Americans who will follow me, who will stand in full sunlight in some charming corner of France and ease their full bladders. And I wish them all well and no gravel in the kidneys.

In passing I recommend certain other urinals which

I know well, where perhaps there may be no woman to smile down at you, but where there is a broken wall, an old belfry, the façade of a palace, a square covered with colored awnings, a horse trough, a fountain, a covey of doves, a bookstall, a vegetable market. . . . Nearly always the French have chosen the right spot for their urinals. Off hand I think of one in Carcassonne which, if I chose the hour well, afforded me an incomparable view of the citadel; so well is it placed that, unless one be burdened and distraught, there must rise up again the same surging pride, the same wonder and awe, the same fierce attachment for this scene as was felt by the weary knight or monk when, pausing at the foot of the hill where now runs the stream that washed away the epidemic, he glanced up to rest his eyes on the grim, battle-stained turrets flung against a wind-swept sky.

And immediately I think of another—just outside the Palais des Papes, in Avignon. A mere stone's throw away from the charming little square which, on a night in spring, seems strewn with velvets and laces, with masks and confetti; so still flows the time that one can hear little horns blowing faint, the past gliding by like a ghost, and then drowned in the deep hammerstroked gongs that smash the voiceless music of the night. Just a stone's throw away from the obscure little quarter where the red lights blaze. There, toward the cool of the evening, you will find the crooked little streets humming with activity, the women, clad in bathing suit or chemise, lounging on the doorsteps, cigarette in mouth, calling to the passers-by. As night falls the walls seem to grow together and from all the little lanes that trickle into the gulch there spills a crowd of curious hungry men who choke the narrow streets, who mill around, dart aimlessly here and there like tailed sperm seeking the ovum, and finally are sucked in by the open maws of the brothels.

Nowadays, as one stands in the urinal beside the Palace, one is hardly aware of this other life. The Palace stands abrupt, cold, tomblike, before a bleak open square. Facing it is a ridiculous-looking building called Institute of Music. There they stand, facing each other across an empty lot. Gone the Popes. Gone the music. Gone all the color and speech of a glorious epoch. Were it not for the little quarter behind the Institute who could imagine what once was that life within the Palace walls? When this tomb was alive I believe that there was no separation between the Palace and the twisted lanes below; I believe that the dirty little hovels, with their rubbled roofs, ran right up to the door of the Palace. I believe that when a Pope stepped out of his gorgeous hive into the glitter of sunlight he communicated instantaneously with the life about him. Some traces of that life the frescoes still retain: the life of outdoors, of hunting, fishing, gaming, of falcons and dogs and women and flashing fish. A large, Catholic life, with intense blues and luminous greens, the life of sin and grace and repentance, a life of high yellows and golden browns, of winestained robes and salmon-colored streams. In that marvelous cubicle in a corner of the Palace, whence one overlooks the unforgettable roofs of Avignon and the broken bridge across the Rhône, in this cubicle where they say the Popes penned their bulls, the frescoes are still so fresh, so natural, so life-breathing, that even this tomb which is the Palace today seems more alive than the world outdoors. One can well imagine a great father of the Church sitting there at his writing table, with a Papal bull before him and a huge tankard at his elbow. And one can also easily imagine a fine, fat wench sitting on his knees, while down below, in the huge kitchen, whole animals are being roasted on the spit, and the lesser dignitaries of the Church, good trenchermen that they were, drinking and carousing to their hearts' content behind the comfort and security of the great walls. No schisms, no hairsplitting, no schizophrenia. When disease came it swept through hovel and castle, through the rich joints of the fathers and the tough joints of the peasants. When the spirit of God descended upon Avignon, it did not stop at the Musical Institute across the way; it penetrated the walls, the flesh, the hierarchies of rank and caste. It flourished as mightily in the red light district as up above on the hill. The Pope could not lift up his skirts and pass untouched. Inside the walls and outside the walls it was one life: faith, fornication, bloodshed. Primary colors. Primary passions. The frescoes tell the story. How they lived each day and the whole day long speaks louder than the books. What the Popes mumbled in their beards is one thing—what they commanded to be painted on their walls is another. Words are dead.

The Angel Is My Watermark!

The object of these pages is to relate the genesis of a masterpiece. The masterpiece is hanging on the wall in front of me; it is dry now. I am putting this down to remember the process, because I shall probably never do another like it.

We must go back a bit. . . . For two whole days I am wrestling with something. If I were to describe it in a word I should say that I have been like a cartridge that's jammed. This is almost deadly accurate, for when I came out of a dream this morning the only image that persisted was that of my big trunk crumpled up like an old hat.

The first day the struggle is undefinable. It is strong enough, however, to paralyze. I put on my hat and go to the Renoir Exhibition and from Renoir I go to the Louvre and from the Louvre I go to the Rue de Rivoli —where it no longer resembles the Rue de Rivoli. There I sit over a beer for three hours, fascinated by the monsters passing me.

The next morning I get up with the conviction that I will do something. There is that fine light tension which augurs well. My notebook lies beside me. I pick it up and riffle the pages absent-mindedly. I riffle them again—this time more attentively. The notes are arranged in cryptic lines: a simple phrase may record a year's struggle. Some of the lines I cannot decipher any more myself—my biographers will take care of them.

I am still obsessed by the idea that I am going to write today. I am merely flipping the pages of my notebook as a warming up exercise. So I imagine. But cursorily and swiftly as I sweep over these notes something fatal is happening to me.

What happens is that I have touched Tante Melia. And now my whole life rushes up in one gush, like a geyser that has just broken through the earth. I am walking home with Tante Melia and suddenly I realize that she is crazy. She is asking me for the moon. "Up there!" she shrieks. "*Up there!*"

It is about ten in the morning when this line shrieks at me. From this moment on—up until four o'clock this morning—I am in the hands of unseen powers. I put the typewriter away and I commence to record what is being dictated to me. Pages and pages of notes, and for each incident I am reminded of where to find the context. All the folders in which my manuscripts are assorted have been emptied on the floor. I am lying on the floor with a pencil, feverishly annotating my work. This continues and continues. I am exultant, and at the same time I am worried. If it continues at this rate I may have a hemorrhage.

About three o'clock I decide to obey no longer. I will go out and eat. Perhaps it will blow over after lunch. I go on my bicycle in order to draw the blood from my head. I carry no notebook with me—purposely. If the dictation starts again, *tant pis*. I'm out for lunch!

At three o'clock you can get only a cold snack. I order cold chicken with mayonnaise. It costs a little more than I usually spend, but that's exactly why I order it. And after a little debate I order a heavy Burgundy instead of the usual *vin ordinaire*. I am hoping that all this will distract me. The wine ought to make me a little drowsy.

I'm on the second bottle and the tablecloth is covered with notes. My head is extraordinarily light. I order cheese and grapes and pastry. Amazing what an appetite I have! And yet, somehow, it doesn't seem to be going down *my* stomach; seems as if some one else were eating all this for me. Well, at least, *I* shall have to pay for it! That's standing on solid ground. . . . I pay and off I go again on the wheel. Stop at a café for a black coffee. Can't manage to get both feet on solid ground. Some one is dictating to me constantly—and with no regard for my health.

I tell you, the whole day passes this way. I've surrendered long ago. O. K., I say to myself. If it's *ideas* today, then it's ideas. *Princesse, à vos ordres.* And I slave away, as though it were exactly what I wanted to do myself.

After dinner I am quite worn out. The ideas are still inundating me, but I am so exhausted that I can lie back now and let them play over me like an electric massage. Finally I am weak enough to be able to pick up a book and rest. It's an old issue of a magazine. Here I will find peace. To my amazement the page falls open on these words: "Goethe and his Demon." The pencil is in my hand again, the margin crammed with notes. It is midnight. I am exhilarated. The dictation has ceased. A free man again. I'm so damned happy that I'm wondering if I shouldn't take a little spin before sitting down to write. The bike is in my room. It's dirty. The bike, I mean. I get a rag and begin cleaning it. I clean every spoke, I oil it thoroughly, I polish the mudguards. She's spick and span. I'll go through the Bois de Boulogne. . . .

As I'm washing my hands I suddenly get a gnawing pain in the stomach. I'm hungry, that's what's the matter. Well, now that the dictation has ceased I'm free to do as I like. I uncork a bottle, cut off a big chunk of bread, bite into a sausage. The sausage is full of garlic. Fine. In the Bois de Boulogne a garlic breath goes unnoticed. A little more wine. Another hunk of bread. This time it's me who's eating and no mistake about it. The other meals were wasted. The wine and the garlic mingle odorously. I'm belching a little.

I sit down for a moment to smoke a cigarette. There's a pamphlet at my elbow, about three inches square. It's called *Art and Madness*. The ride is off. It's getting too late to write anyway. It's coming over me that what I really want to do is to paint a picture. In 1927 or '8 I was on the way to becoming a painter. Now and then, in fits and starts, I do a water color. It comes over you like that: you feel like a water color and you do one. In the insane asylum they paint their fool heads off. They paint the chairs, the walls, the tables, the bedsteads . . . an amazing productivity. If we rolled up our sleeves and went to work the way these idiots do what might we not accomplish in a lifetime!

The illustration in front of me, done by an inmate of Charenton, has a very fine quality about it. I see a boy and girl kneeling close together and in their hands they are holding a huge lock. Instead of a penis and vagina the artist has endowed them with keys, very big keys which interpenetrate. There is also a big key in the lock. They look happy and a little absent-minded. . . . On page 85 there is a landscape. It looks exactly like one of Hilaire Hiler's paintings. In fact, it is better than any of Hiler's. The only peculiar feature of it is that in the foreground there are three miniature men who are deformed. Not badly deformed either—they simply look as if they were too heavy for their legs. The rest of the canvas is so good that one would have to be squeamish indeed to be annoyed at this. Besides, is the world so perfect that there are not three men anywhere who are too heavy for their legs? It seems to me that the insane have a right to their vision as well as we.

I'm very eager to start in. Just the same, I'm at a loss for ideas. The dictation has ceased. I have half a mind to copy one of these illustrations. But then I'm a little ashamed of myself—to copy the work of a lunatic is the worst form of plagiarism.

Well, begin! That's the thing. Begin with a horse! I have vaguely in mind the Etruscan horses I saw in the Louvre. (Note: in all the great periods of art the horse was very close to man!) I begin to draw. I begin naturally with the easiest part of the animal—the horse's ass. A little opening for the tail which can be stuck in afterwards. Hardly have I begun to do the trunk when I notice at once that it is too elongated. Remember, you are drawing a horse—not a liverwurst! Vaguely, vaguely it seems to me that some of those Ionian horses I saw on the black vases had elongated trunks; and the legs began inside the body, delineated by a fine stenciled line which you could look at or not look at according to your anatomical instincts. With this in mind I decide on an Ionian horse. But now fresh difficulties ensue. It's the legs. The shape of a horse's leg is baffling when you have only your memory to rely on. I can recall only about as much as from the fetlock down, which is to say, *the hoof*. To put meat on the hoof is a delicate task, extremely delicate. And to make the legs join the body naturally, not as if they were stuck on with glue. My horse already has five legs: the easiest thing to do is to transform one of them into a phallus erectus. No sooner said than done. And now he's standing just like a terra cotta figure of the sixth century B.C. The tail isn't in yet, but I've left an opening just above the asshole. The tail can be put in any time. The main thing is to get him into action, to make him prance like. So I twist the front legs up. Part of him is in motion, the rest is standing stock still. With the proper kind of tail I could turn him into a fine kangaroo.

During the leg experiments the stomach has become dilapidated. I patch it up as best I can—until it looks like a hammock. Let it go at that. If it doesn't look like a horse when I'm through I can always turn it into a hammock. (Weren't there people sleeping in a horse's stomach on one of the vases I saw?)

Nobody who has not examined the horse's skull attentively can ever imagine how difficult it is to draw. To make it a skull and not a feedbag. To put the eyes in without making the horse laugh. To keep the expression horsey, and not let it grow human. At this point, I admit frankly, I am completely disgusted with my prowess. I have a mind to erase and begin all over again. But I detest the eraser. I would rather convert the horse into a dynamo or a grand piano than erase my work completely.

I close my eyes and try very calmly to picture a horse in my mind's eye. I rub my hands over the mane and the shoulders and the flanks. Seems to me I remember very distinctly how a horse feels, especially that way he has of shuddering when a fly is bothering him. And that warm, squirmy feel of the veins. (In Chula Vista I used to currycomb the jackasses before going to the fields. Thinks I—if only I could make a jackass of him, that would be something!)

So I start all over again—with the mane this time. Now the mane of a horse is something entirely different from a pigtail, or the tresses of a mermaid. Chirico puts wonderful manes on his horses. And so does Valentine Prax. The mane is something, I tell you—it's not just a marcel wave. It has to have the ocean in it, and a lot of mythology. What makes hair and teeth and finger-nails does not make a horse's mane. It's something apart. ... However, when I get into a predicament of this sort I know that I can extricate myself later when it comes time to apply the color. The drawing is simply the ex-cuse for color. The color is the toccata: drawing be-longs to the realm of idea. (Michelangelo was right in despising Da Vinci. Is there anything more ghastly, more sickishly ideational than the "Last Supper"? Is there anything more pretentious than the "Mona Lisa"?

As I say, a little color will put life into the mane. The stomach is still a little out of order, I see. Very well. Where it is convex I make it concave and vice versa. Now suddenly my horse is galloping, his nostrils are snorting fire. But with two eyes he looks still a bit silly, a bit too human. Ergo, rub out an eye. Fine. He's get-ting more and more horsey. He's gotten kind of cute-looking too—like Charley Chase of the movies. . . .

To keep him well within the genus he represents I finally decide to give him stripes. The idea is that if he won't lose his playfulness I can turn him into a zebra. So I put in the stripes. Now, damn it all, he seems to be made of cardboard. The stripes have flattened him out, glued him to the paper. Well, if I close my eyes again I ought to be able to recall the Cinzano horse—he has stripes too, and beautiful ones. Maybe I ought to go down for an *apéritif* and look at a Cinzano. It's getting late for *apéritifs*. Maybe I'll do a little plagiarizing after all. If a lunatic can draw a man on a bicycle he can draw a horse too.

It's remarkable—I find gods and goddesses, devils, bats, sewing machines, flowerpots, rivers, bridges, locks and keys, epileptics, coffins, skeletons—but not a damned horse! If the lunatic who compiled this brochure had wanted to draw a truly profound observation he would have had something to remark about this curious omission. When the horse is missing there is something radically amiss! Human art goes hand in hand with the horse. It's not enough to hint that the symbolists and the imagists are, or were, a little *détraqués*. We want to know, in a study of insanity, what has become of the horse!

Once more I turn to the landscape on page 85. It's an excellent composition despite the geometrical stiffness. (The insane have a terrific obsession for logic and order, as have the French.) I have something to work from now: mountains, bridges, terraces, trees. . . . One of the great merits of insane art is that a bridge is always a bridge and a house a house. The three little men who are balancing themselves on their canes in the foreground are not absolutely necessary to the composition, especially since I already have the Ionian horse which occupies considerable space. I am searching for a setting in which to place the horse and there is something very wistful and very intriguing about this landscape with its crenelated parapets and its sugar-loaf escarpments and the houses with so many windows, as if the inmates were deathly afraid of suffocating. It's very reminiscent of the beginnings of landscape painting— and yet it's completely outside all definitive periods. I should say roughly that it lies in a zone between Giotto and Santos Dumont—with just a faint intimation of the post-mechanical street which is to come. And now, with this as a guide before me, I pick up courage. *Allons-y!*

Right under the horse's ass, where his croup begins and ends, and where Salvador Dali would most likely put a Louis Quinze chair or a watch spring, I begin to draw with free and easy strokes a straw hat, a melon. Beneath the hat I put a face—carelessly, because my ideas are large and sweeping. Wherever the hand falls I do something, following the insinuating deviations of the line. In this manner I take the huge phallus erectus, which was once a fifth leg, and bend it into a man's arm—so! Now I have a man in a big straw hat tickling the horse in the rumps. Fine! Fine and dandy! Should it seem a little grotesque, a little out of keeping with the pseudo-medieval character of the original composition, I can always attribute it to the aberration of the *fou* who inspired me. (Here, for the first time, a suspicion enters my head that I may not be altogether there myself! But on page 366 it says: *"Enfin, pour Matisse, le sentiment de l'objet peut s'exprimer avec toute licence, sans direction intellectuelle ou exactitude visuelle: c'est l'origine de l'expression."* To go on. . . . After a slight difficulty with the man's feet I solve the problem by putting the lower half of his body behind the parapet. He is leaning over the parapet, dreaming most likely, and at the same time he is tickling the horse's ribs. (Along the rivers of France you will often stumble across men leaning over a parapet and dreaming—particularly after they have voided a bagful of urine.)

To shorten my labors, and also to see how much space will be left, I put in a quantity of bold diagonal stripes or planks, for the bridge flooring. This kills at least a third of the picture, as far as composition goes. Now come the terraces, the escarpments, the three trees, the snow-topped mountains, the houses and all the windows that go with them. It's like a jigsaw puzzle. Wherever a cliff refuses to finish properly I make it the side of a house, or the roof of another house which is hidden. Gradually I work my way up toward the top of the picture where the frame happily cuts things short. It remains to put in the trees—and the mountains.

Now trees again are very ticklish propositions. To make a tree, and not a bouquet! Even though I put forked lightning inside the foliage, to lend a hint of structure, it's no go. A few airy clouds, then, to do away with some of the superfluous foliage. (Always a good dodge to simplify your problem by removing it.) But the clouds look like pieces of tissue paper that had blown off the wedding bouquets. A cloud is so light, so less than nothing, and yet it's not tissue paper. Everything that has form has invisible substance. Michelangelo sought it all his life—in marble, in verse, in love, in architecture, in crime, in God. . . . (Page 390: "*Si l'artiste poursuit la création authentique, son souci est ailleurs que sur l'objet, qui peut être sacrifié et soumis aux nécessités de l'invention.*")

I come to the mountain—like Mahomet. By now I am beginning to realize the meaning of liberation. A mountain! What's a mountain? It's a pile of dirt which never wears away, at least, not in historical time. A mountain's too easy. I want a volcano. I want a reason for my horse to be snorting and prancing. Logic, logic! "*Le fou montre un souci constant de logique!*" (*Les Français aussi.*) Well, I'm not a *fou*, especially not a French *fou:* I can take a few liberties, particularly with the work of an imbecile. So I draw the crater first and work down toward the foot of the mountain to join up with the bridgework and the roofs of the houses below. Out of the errors I make cracks in the mountainside—to represent the damage done by the volcano. This is an *active* volcano and its sides are bursting.

When I'm all through I have a shirt on my hands. A shirt, precisely! I can recognize the collar band and the sleeves. All it needs is a Rogers Peet label and size 16 or what have you. . . . One thing, however, stands out unmistakably clear and clean, and that is the bridge. It's strange, but if you can draw an arch the rest of the bridge follows naturally. Only an engineer can ruin a bridge.

It's almost finished, as far as the drawing goes. All the loose ends at the bottom I join up to make cemetery gates. And in the upper left-hand corner, where there is a hole left by the volcano, I draw an angel. It is an object of an original nature, a purely gratuitous invention, and highly symbolic. It is a sad angel with a fallen stomach, and the wings are supported by umbrella ribs. It seems to come down from beyond the *cadre* of my ideas and hover mystically above the wild Ionian horse that is now lost to man.

Have you ever sat in a railway station and watched people killing time? Do they not sit a little like crestfallen angels—with their broken arches and their fallen stomachs? Those eternal few minutes in which they are condemned to be alone with themselves—does it not put umbrella ribs in their wings?

All the angels in religious art are false. If you want to see angels you must go to the Grand Central Depot, or the Gare St. Lazare. Especially the Gare St. Lazare— *Salle des Pas Perdus.*

My theory of painting is to get the drawing done
with as quickly as possible and slap in the color. After
all, I'm a colorist, not a draught horse. *Alors,* out with
the tubes!

I start painting the side of a house, in raw umber.
Not very effective. I put a liberal dash of crimson ali-
zarin in the wall next to it. A little too pretty, too
Italian. All in all, I'm not starting out so well with my
colors. There's a rainy day atmosphere somewhat
reminiscent of Utrillo. I don't like Utrillo's quiet im-
becility, nor his rainy days, nor his suburban streets. I
don't like the way his women stick their behinds out at
you either. . . . I get the bread knife out. May as well
try a loaded impasto. In the act of squeezing out a gen-
erous assortment of colors the impulse seizes me to add
a gondola to the composition. Directly below the bridge
I insert it, which automatically launches it.

And now suddenly I know the reason for the gondola. Among the Renoirs the other day there was a
Venetian scene, and the inevitable gondola of course.
Now what intrigued me, weakly enough, was that the
man who sat in the gondola was so distinctly a man,
though he was only a speck of black, hardly separable
from all the other specks which made up the sunlight,
the choppy sea, the crumbling palaces, the sailboats,
etc. He was just a speck in that fiery combination of
colors—and yet he was distinctly a man. You could
even tell that he was a Frenchman and that he was of
the 1870's or thereabouts. . . .

This isn't the end of the gondola. Two days before
I left for America—1927 or '8—we held a big session
at the house. It was at the height of my water-color
career.

It began in a peculiar way, this water-color mania.

Through hunger, I might say. That and the extreme cold. For weeks I had been hanging out with my friend Joe in poolrooms and comfort stations, wherever there was animal heat and no expense. On our way back to the morgue one evening we noticed a reproduction of Turner's in the window of a department store. That's exactly the way in which it all began. One of the most active, one of the most enjoyable periods of my barren life. When I say that we littered the floor with paintings I am not exaggerating. As fast as they dried we hung them up—and the next day we took them down and hung up another collection. We painted on the backs of old ones, we washed them off, we scraped them with the knife, and in the course of these experiments we discovered, by accident, some astonishing things. We discovered how to get interesting results with coffee grounds and bread crumbs, with coal and arnica; we laid the paintings in the bathtub and let them soak for hours, and then with a loaded brush we approached these dripping omelettes and we let fly at them. Turner started all this—and the severe winter of 1927–'28.

Two nights before my departure, as I was saying, a number of painters come to the house to inspect our work. They are all good eggs and not above taking an interest in the work of amateurs. The water colors are lying about on the floor, as usual, drying. As a last experiment we walk over them, spilling a little wine as we go. Astonishing what effects a dirty heel will produce, or a drop of wine falling from a height of three feet with the best of intentions. The enthusiasm mounts. Two of my friends are working on the walls with chunks of coal. Another is boiling coffee in order to get some nice fresh grounds. The rest of us are drinking.

In the midst of the festivities—about three A.M.—my

wife walks in. She seems a little depressed. Taking me
aside she shows me a steamship ticket. I look at it.
"What's that for?" I said. "You've got to go away," she
answers. "But I don't want to go away," I said. "I'm
quite happy here." "So I see," she says, rather sardon-
ically.

Anyway I go. And when we're pulling up the
Thames the only thought in my mind is to see the
Turner collection at the Tate Gallery. Finally I get
there and I see the famous Turners. And as luck would
have it one of the half-wits there takes a fancy to me.
I find that he's a magnificent water-colorist himself.
Works entirely by lamplight. I really hated to leave
London, he made it so agreeable for me. Anyway,
pulling out of Southampton I thought to myself—"the
circle is complete now: from the department store
window to here."

However, to get on. . . . This gondola is going to
be the *pièce de résistance*! But first I must clean up the
walls. Taking the bread knife and dipping it into the
laque carmine I apply a liberal dose to the windows
of the houses. Holy Jesus! Immediately the houses are
in flames! If I were really mad, and not simulating the
madness of a madman, I'd be putting firemen into the
picture and I'd make ladders out of the bold diagonal
planks of the bridge flooring. But my insanity takes the
form of building a conflagration. I set all the houses on
fire—first with carmine, then with vermilion, and
finally with a bloody concoction of all three. This part
of the picture is clear and decisive: it's a holocaust.

The result of my incendiarism is that I've singed the
horse's back. Now he's neither a horse nor a zebra. He's
become a fire-eating dragon. And where the missing tail
belonged there is now a bunch of fire-crackers, and

with a bunch of fire-crackers up his ass not even an Ionian horse can preserve his dignity. I could, of course, go on to make a real dragon; but this conversion and patching-up is getting on my nerves. If you start with a horse you ought to keep it a horse—or eliminate it entirely. Once you begin to tamper with an animal's anatomy you can go through the whole phylogenetic process.

With a solid opaque green and indigo I blot the horse out. In my mind, to be sure, he's still there. People may look at this opaque object and think—how strange! how curious! But *I* know that at bottom it's a horse. At the bottom of everything there's some animal: that's our deepest obsession. When I see human beings squirming up toward the light like wilted sunflowers, I say to myself: "Squirm, you bastards, and pretend all you like, but at bottom you're a turtle or a guinea-pig." Greece was mad about horses and if they had had the wisdom to remain half horse instead of playing the Titan—well, we might have been spared a great many mythological pains.

When you're an *instinctive* water-colorist everything happens according to God's will. Thus, if you are bidden to paint the cemetery gates a clear gamboge, you do it and you don't grumble about it. Never mind if they are too vivid for such somber portals. Perhaps there is an unknown justification. And truly, when I paint in this bright liquid yellow, this yellow which is to me the finest of all yellows (even yellower than the mouth of the Yangtsze Kiang), I am radiant, radiant. Something dreary, cloying, oppressive has been washed away forever. I would not be surprised if it were the Cypress Hills Cemetery which I passed in disgust and mortification for so many years, which I looked down

on from the bend in the elevated line, which I spat into
from the platform of the train. Or St. John's Cemetery,
with its crazy leaden angels, where I worked as a grave-
digger. Or the Montparnasse Cemetery which in winter
looks as if it had been shellshocked. Cemeteries, cemeteries. . . . By God, I refuse to be buried in a cemetery!
I won't have any imbeciles standing over me with a
sprinkler and looking mournful. I won't have it!

While these thoughts have been passing through my
head I have been inadvertently smearing the trees and
the terraces with a dry brush. The trees gleam now like
a coat of mail, the boughs are studded with silver and
turquoise links. If I had a crucifixion on hand I could
cover the bodies of the martyrs with jeweled pockmarks. On the wall opposite me is a scene from the
wilds of Ethiopia. The body of Christ crucified lies on
the floor covered with smallpox; the bloodthirsty Jews
—black, Ethiopian Jews—are pounding him with iron
quoits. They have a most ferociously gleeful expression.
I bought the picture because of the pockmarks, *why* I
didn't know at the time. It's only now that I've discovered the reason. Only now that I recall a certain picture over a cellar on the Bowery, entitled "Death on
Bugs." Happened I was just coming away from a
lunatic, a professional visit which had not been altogether unpleasant. It's broad afternoon and the dirty
throat of the Bowery is choked with clots of phlegm.
Just below Cooper Square three bums are stretched out
flat beside a lamppost, *à la* Breughel. A penny arcade
is going full blast. A weird, unearthly chant rises up
from the streets, like a man with a cleaver fighting his
way through delirium tremens. And there, over the
slanting cellar door, is this painting called "Death on
Bugs." A naked woman with long flaxen hair lies on the

bed scratching herself. The bed is floating in the middle air and about it dances a man with a squirt gun. He has that same imbecilic air about him as these Jews with the iron quoits. The picture is stippled with pockmarks —to represent that cosmopolitan bloodsucking wingless depressed bug of reddish-brown color and vile odor which infests houses and beds and goes by the formidable name of *Cimex lectularius.*

And here I am now with a dry brush applying the stigmata to the three trees. The clouds are covered with bedbugs, the volcano is belching bedbugs; the bedbugs are scrambling down the steep chalk cliffs and drowning themselves in the river. I am like that young immigrant on the second floor of a poem by some Ivanovich or other who tosses about on the bedsprings haunted by the misery of his starved, wasted life, despairing of all the beauty beyond his grasp. My whole life seems to be wrapped up in that dirty handkerchief, the Bowery, which I walked through day after day, year in and year out—a dose of smallpox whose scars never disappear. If I had a name then it was Cimex Lectularius. If I had a home it was a slide trombone. If I had a passion it was to wash myself clean.

In a fury now I take the brush and dipping it in all the colors successively I commence to smudge the cemetery gates. I smudge and smudge until the lower half of the picture is as thick as chocolate, until the picture actually smells of pigment. And when it is completely ruined I sit there with a vacant enjoyment and twiddle my thumbs.

And then suddenly I get a real inspiration. I take it to the sink and after soaking it well I scrub it with the nail brush. I scrub and scrub and then I hold the picture upside down, letting the colors coagulate. Then gingerly, very gingerly, I flatten it out on my desk. It's a masterpiece, I tell you! I've been studying it for the last three hours. . . .

You may say it's just an accident, this masterpiece, and so it is! But then, so is the Twenty-third Psalm. Every birth is miraculous—and inspired. What appears now before my eyes is the result of innumerable mistakes, withdrawals, erasures, hesitations; it is also the result of certitude. You would like to give the nail brush credit, and the water credit. Do so—by all means. Give everybody and everything credit. Credit Dante, credit Spinoza, credit Hieronymus Bosch. Credit Cash and debit Société Anonyme. Put in the Day Book: *Tante Melia*. So. Draw a balance. Out by a penny, eh? If you could take a penny from your pocket and balance the books you would do so. But you are no longer dealing with actual pennies. There is no machine clever enough to devise, to counterfeit, this penny which does not exist. The world of real and counterfeit is behind us. Out of the tangible we have invented the intangible.

When you can draw up a clean balance you will no longer have a picture. Now you have an intangible, an accident, and you sit up all night with the open ledger cracking your skull over it. You have a minus sign on your hands. All live, interesting data is labeled minus. When you find the plus equivalent you have—*nothing*. You have that imaginary, momentary something called "a balance." A balance never *is*. It's a fraud, like stopping the clock, or like calling a truce. You strike a balance in order to add a hypothetical weight, in order to create a reason for your existence.

I have never been able to draw a balance. I am always *minus* something. I have a reason therefore to go on. I am putting my whole life into the balance in order that it may produce nothing. To get to nothing you have to lay out an infinitude of figures. That's just it: in the living equation the sign for myself is infinity. To get nowhere you must traverse every known universe: you must be everywhere in order to be nowhere. To have disorder you must destroy *every* form of order. To go mad you must have a terrific accumulation of sanities. All the madmen whose works have inspired me were touched by a cold sanity. They have taught me nothing—because the balance sheets which they bequeathed to us have been falsified. Their calculations are meaningless to me—because the figures have been altered. The marvelous gilt-edged ledgers which they handed down have the hideous beauty of plants which are forced in the night.

My masterpiece! It's like a splinter under the nail. I ask you, now that you are looking at it, do you see in it the lakes beyond the Urals? do you see the mad Kotchei balancing himself with a paper parasol? do you see the arch of Trajan breaking through the smoke of Asia? do you see the penguins thawing in the Himalayas? do you see the Creeks and the Seminoles gliding through the cemetery gates? do you see the fresco from the Upper Nile, with its flying geese, its bats and aviaries? do you see the marvelous pommels of the Crusaders and the saliva that washed them down? do you see the wigwams belching fire? do you see the alkali sinks and the mule bones and the gleaming borax? do you see the tomb of Belshazzar, or the ghoul who is rifling it? do you see the new mouths which the Colorado will open up? do you see the starfish lying on their backs and the molecules supporting them? do you see the bursting eyes of Alexander, or the grief that inspired it? do you see the ink on which the squibs are feeding?

No, I'm afraid you don't! You see only the bleak blue angel frozen by the glaciers. You do not even see the umbrella ribs, because you are not trained to look for umbrella ribs. But you see an angel, and you see a horse's ass. And you may keep them: *they are for you!* There are no pockmarks on the angel now—only a cold blue spotlight which throws into relief his fallen stomach and his broken arches. The angel is there to lead you to Heaven, where it is all plus and no minus. The angel is there like a watermark, a guarantee of your faultless vision. The angel has no goiter; it is the artist who has the goiter. The angel is there to drop sprigs of parsley in your omelette, to put a shamrock in your buttonhole. I could scrub the mythology out of the horse's mane; I could scrub the yellow out of the Yangtsze Kiang; I could scrub the date out of the man in the gondola; I could scrub out the clouds and the tissue paper in which were wrapped the bouquets with forked lightning. . . . *But the angel I can't scrub out. The angel is my watermark.*

The Tailor Shop

I've got a motter: *always merry and bright!*

The day used to start like this: "Ask so-and-so for a little something on account, *but don't insult him!*" They were ticklish bastards, all these old farts we catered to. It was enough to drive any man to drink. There we were, just opposite the Olcott, Fifth Avenue tailors even though we weren't on the Avenue. A joint corporation of father and son, with mother holding the boodle.

Mornings, eight A.M. or thereabouts, a brisk intellectual walk from Delancey Street and the Bowery to just below the Waldorf. No matter how fast I walked old man Bendix was sure to be there ahead of me, raising hell with the cutter because neither of the bosses was on the job. How was it we could never get there ahead of that old buzzard Bendix? He had nothing to do, Bendix, but run from the tailor to the shirtmaker and from the shirtmaker to the jeweler's; his rings were either too loose or too tight, his watch was either twenty-five seconds slow or thirty-three seconds fast. He raised hell with everybody, including the family doctor, because the latter couldn't keep his kidneys clear of gravel. If we made him a sack coat in August by October it was too large for him, or too small. When he could find nothing to complain about he would dress on the right side so as to have the pleasure of bawling the pants maker out because he was strangling his, H. W. Bendix's, balls. A difficult guy. Touchy, whimsical, mean, crotchety, miserly, capricious, malevolent. When I look back on it all now, see the old man sitting down to table with his boozy breath and saying *shit why don't some one smile, why do you all look so glum*, I feel sorry for him and for all merchant tailors who have to kiss rich people's asses. If it hadn't been for the Olcott bar across the way and the sots he picked up there God knows what would have become of the old man. He certainly got no sympathy at home. My mother hadn't the least idea what it meant to be kissing rich people's backsides. All she knew how to do was to groan and lament all day, and with her groaning and lamenting she brought on the boozy breath and the potato dumplings grown cold. She got us so damned jumpy with her anxiety that we would choke on our own spittle, my brother and I. My brother was a half-wit and he got on the old man's nerves even more than H. W. Bendix with his "Pastor So-and-so's going to Europe. . . . Pastor So-and-so's going to open a bowling alley," etc. "Pastor So-and-so's an ass," the old man would say, "and why aren't the dumplings hot?"

There were three Bendixes—H. W., the grumpy one, A. F., whom the old man referred to in the ledger as Albert, and R.N., who never visited the shop because his legs were cut off, a circumstance, however, which did not prevent him from wearing out his trousers in due season. R. N. I never saw in the flesh. He was an item in the ledger which Bunchek the cutter spoke of glowingly because there was always a little schnapps about when it came time to try on the new trousers. The three brothers were eternal enemies; they never referred to one another in our presence. If Albert, who was a little cracked and had a penchant for dotted vests, happened to see a cutaway hanging on the rack with the words H. W. Bendix written in green ink on the try-on notice, he would give a feeble little grunt and say—"feels like spring today, eh?" There was not supposed to be a man by the name of H. W. Bendix in existence, though it was obvious to all and sundry that we were not making clothes for ghosts.

Of the three brothers I liked Albert the best. He had arrived at that ripe age when the bones become as brittle as glass. His spine had the natural curvature of old age, as though he were preparing to fold up and return to the womb. You could always tell when Albert was arriving because of the commotion in the elevator —a great cussing and whining followed by a handsome tip which accompanied the process of bringing the floor of the elevator to a dead level with the floor of our tailor shop. If it could not be brought to within a quarter of an inch exactitude there was no tip and Albert with his brittle bones and his bent spine would have a devil of a time choosing the right buttons to go with his dotted vest, his *latest* dotted vest. (When Albert died I inherited all his vests—they lasted me right through the war.) If it happened, as was sometimes the case, that the old man was across the street taking a little nip when Albert arrived, then somehow the whole day became disorganized. I remember periods when Albert grew so vexed with the old man that sometimes we did not see him for three days; meanwhile the vest buttons were lying around on little cards and there was talk of nothing but vest buttons, vest buttons, as if the vest itself didn't matter, only the buttons. Later, when Albert had grown accustomed to the old man's careless ways—they had been growing accustomed to each other for twenty-seven years—he would give us a ring to notify us that he was on the way. And just before hanging up he would add: "I suppose it's all right my coming in at eleven o'clock . . . it won't inconvenience you?" The purport of this little query was twofold. It meant—"I suppose you'll have the decency to be on hand when I arrive and not make me fiddle around for a half-hour while you swill it down with your cronies across the street." *And*, it also meant—"At eleven o'clock I suppose there is little danger of bumping into a certain individual bearing the initials H. W.?" In the twenty-seven years during which we made perhaps 1,578 garments for the three Bendix brothers it so happened that they never met, not in our presence at least. When Albert died R. N. and H. W. both had mourning bands put on their sleeves, on all the left sleeves of their sack coats and overcoats—that is, those which were not black coats—but nothing was said of the deceased, nor even *who* he was. R. N., of course, had a good excuse for not going to the funeral—his legs were gone. H. W. was too mean and too proud to even bother offering an excuse.

About ten o'clock was the time the old man usually chose to go down for his first nip. I used to stand at the window facing the hotel and watch George Sandusky hoisting the big trunks on to the taxis. When there were no trunks to be hoisted George used to stand there with his hands clasped behind his back and bow and scrape to the clients as they swung in and out of the revolving doors. George Sandusky had been scraping and bowing and hoisting and opening doors for about twelve years when I first came to the tailor shop and took up my post at the front window. He was a charming, soft-spoken man with beautiful white hair, and strong as an ox. He had raised this ass-kissing business to an art. I was amazed one day when he came up the elevator and ordered a suit from us. In his off hours he was a gentleman, George Sandusky. He had quiet tastes—always a blue serge or an Oxford gray. A man who knew how to conduct himself at a funeral or a wedding.

After we got to know each other he gave me to understand that he had found Jesus. With the smooth tongue he had, and the brawn, and the active help of said Jesus he had managed to lay aside a nest egg, a little something to ward off the horrors of old age. He was the only man I ever met in that period who had not taken out life insurance. He maintained that God would look after those who were left behind just as He had looked after him, George Sandusky. He had no fear of the world collapsing upon his decease. God had taken care of everybody and everything up to date— no reason to suppose He would fall down on the job after George Sandusky's death. When one day George retired it was difficult to find a man to replace him. There was no one oily or unctuous enough to fill the bill. No one who could bow and scrape like George. The old man always had a great affection for George. He used to try to persuade him to take a drink now and then, but George always refused with that habitual and stubborn politeness which had endeared him to the Olcott guests.

The old man often had moods when he would ask anybody to take a drink with him, even such as George Sandusky. Usually late in the afternoon on a day when things were going wrong, when nothing but bills were coming in. Sometimes a week would pass without a customer showing up, or if one did show up it was only to complain, to ask for an alteration, to bawl the piss out of the coat maker, or to demand a reduction in the price. Things like this would make the old man so blue that all he could do was to put on his hat and go for a drink. Instead of going across the street as usual he would wander off base a bit, duck into the Breslin or the Broztell, sometimes getting as far off the path as the Ansonia where his idol, Julian Legree, kept a suite of rooms.

Julian, who was then a matinée idol, wore nothing but gray suits, every shade of gray imaginable, but only grays. He had that depressingly cheerful demeanor of the beefy-faced English actor who lounges about here and there swapping stories with woolen salesmen, liquor dealers, and others of no account. His accent alone was enough to make men swarm about him; it was English in the traditional stage sense, warm, soapy, glutinous English which gives to even the most insignificant thought an appearance of importance. Julian never said anything that was worth recording but that voice of his worked magic on his admirers. Now and then, when he and the old man were doing the rounds, they would pick up a derelict such as Corse Payton who belonged across the river in the ten-twenty-thirties. Corse Payton was the idol of Brooklyn! Corse Payton was to art what Pat McCarren was to politics.

What the old man had to say during these discussions was always a source of mystery to me. The old man had never read a book in his life, nor had he ever been to a play since the days when the Bowery gave way to Broadway. I can see him standing there at the free lunch counter—Julian was very fond of the caviar and the sturgeon that was served at the Olcott—sponging it up like a thirsty dog. The two matinée idols discussing Shakespeare—whether *Hamlet* or *Lear* was the greatest play ever written. Or else arguing the merits of Bob Ingersoll.

Behind the bar at that time were three doughty Irishmen, three low-down micks such as made the bars of that day the congenial haunts they were. They were so highly thought of, these three, that it was considered a privilege to have such as Patsy O'Dowd, for example, call you a goddamned degenerate cocksucking son of a bitch who hadn't sense enough to button up his fly. And if, in return for the compliment, you asked him if he wouldn't have a little something himself, said Patsy O'Dowd would coldly and sneeringly reply that only such as yourself were fit to pour such rotgut down your throat, and so saying he would scornfully lift your glass by the stem and wipe the mahogany because that was part of his job and he was paid to do it but be damned to you if you thought you could entice such as him to poison his intestines with the vile stuff. The more vicious his insults the more he was esteemed; financiers who were accustomed to having their asses wiped with silk handkerchiefs would drive all the way uptown, after the ticker closed down, in order to have this foulmouthed bastard of an Irish mick call them goddamned degenerate cocksucking sons of bitches. It was the end of a perfect day for them.

The boss of this jaunty emporium was a portly little man with aristocratic shanks and the head of a lion. He always marched with his stomach thrown forward, a little wine cask hidden under his vest. He usually gave a stiff, supercilious nod to the sots at the bar, unless they happened to be guests of the hotel, in which case he would pause a moment, extend three fat little fingers with blue veins and then, with a swirl of his mustache and a gingerly, creaky pirouette, he would whisk away. He was the only enemy the old man had. The old man simply couldn't stomach him. He had a feeling that

Tom Moffatt looked down upon him. And so when Tom Moffatt came round to order his clothes the old man would tack on ten or fifteen per cent to cover the rents in his pride. But Tom Moffatt was a genuine aristocrat: he never questioned the price and he never paid his bills. If we dunned him he would get his accountant to find a discrepancy in our statements. And when it came time to order another pair of flannel trousers, or a cutaway, or a dinner jacket, he would sail in with his usual portly dignity, his stomach well forward, his mustache waxed, his shoes brightly polished and squeaky as always, and with an air of weary indifference, of aloof disdain, he would greet the old man as follows: "Well, have you straightened out that error yet?" Upon which the old man would fly into a rage and palm off a remnant or a piece of American goods on his enemy Tom Moffatt. A long correspondence ensued over the "little error" in our statements. The old man was beside himself. He hired an expert accountant who drew up statements three feet long—but to no avail. Finally the old man hit upon an idea.

Toward noon one day, after he had had his usual portion, after he had stood treat to all the woolen salesmen and the trimmings salesmen who were gathered at the bar, he quietly picked up the bar stubs and taking a little silver pencil which was attached to his watch chain he signed his name to the checks and sliding them across to Patsy O'Dowd he said: "Tell Moffatt to charge them up to my account." Then he quietly moved off and, inviting a few of his select cronies, he took a table in the dining room and commanded a spread. And when Adrian the frog presented the bill he calmly said: "Give me a pencil. There . . . them's

my demi-quivers. Charge it up to my account." Since
it was more pleasant to eat in the company of others
he would always invite his cronies to lunch with him,
saying to all and sundry—"if that bastard Moffatt
won't pay for his clothes then we'll eat them." And so
saying he would commandeer a juicy squab, or a lobster
à la Newburg, and wash it down with a fine Moselle or
any other vintage that Adrian the frog might happen
to recommend.

To all this Moffatt, surprisingly enough, pretended
to pay no heed. He continued to order his usual allot-
ment of clothes for winter, spring, fall and summer,
and he also continued to squabble about the bill which
had become easier to do now since it was complicated
with bar checks, telephone calls, squabs, lobsters, champagne, fresh strawberries, Benedictines, etc., etc. In fact,
the old man was eating into that bill so fast that spindle-
shanks Moffatt couldn't wear his clothes out quickly
enough. If he came in to order a pair of flannel trousers
the old man had already eaten it the next day.

Finally Moffatt evinced an earnest desire to have the
account straightened out. The correspondence ceased.
Patting me on the back one day as I happened to be
standing in the lobby he put on his most cordial manner
and invited me upstairs to his private office. He said he
had always regarded me as a very sensible young man
and that we could probably straighten the matter out
between ourselves, without bothering the old man. I
looked over the accounts and I saw that the old man
had eaten way into the minus side. I had probably eaten
up a few raglans and shooting jackets myself. There
was only one thing to do if we were to keep Tom Moffatt's despised patronage and that was to find an error

in the account. I took a bundle of bills under my arm and promised the old geezer that I would look into the matter thoroughly.

The old man was delighted when he saw how things stood. We kept looking into the matter for years. Whenever Tom Moffatt came round to order a suit the old man would greet him cheerily and say: "Have you straightened out that little error yet? Now here's a fine Barathea weave that I laid aside for you. . . ." And Moffatt would frown and grimace and strut back and forth like a turkey cock, his comb bristling, his thin little legs blue with malice. A half hour later the old man would be standing at the bar swilling it down. "Just sold Moffatt another dinner jacket," he would say. "By the way, Julian, what would you like to order for lunch today?"

It was toward noon, as I say, that the old man usually went down for an appetizer; lunch lasted anywhere from noon till four or five in the afternoon. It was marvelous the companionship the old man enjoyed in those days. After lunch the troupe would stagger out of the elevator, spitting and guffawing, their cheeks aflame, and lodge themselves in the big leather chairs beside the cuspidors. There was Ferd Pattee who sold silk linings and trimmings such as skeins of thread, buttons, chest padding, canvas, etc. A great hulk of a man, like a liner that's been battered by a typhoon, and always walking about in a somnambulistic state; so tired he was that he could scarcely move his lips, yet that slight movement of the lips kept everybody about him in stitches. Always muttering to himself—about cheeses particularly. He was passionate about cheese, about schmierkäse and limburger especially—the moldier the better. In between the cheeses he told stories about

Heine and Schubert, or he would ask for a match just as he was about to break wind and hold it under his seat so that we could tell him the color of the flame. He never said good-by or see you tomorrow; he commenced talking where he had left off the day before, as though there had been no interruption of time. No matter whether it was nine in the morning or six in the evening he walked with the same exasperating slow shambling gait, muttering in his vici-kids, his head down, his linings and trimmings under his arm, his breath foul, his nose purple and translucent. Into the thickest traffic he would walk with head down, schmierkäse in one pocket and limburger in the other. Stepping out of the elevator he would say in that weary monotonous voice of his that he had some new linings and the cheese was fine last night were you thinking of returning the book he had loaned you and better pay up soon if you want more goods like to see some dirty pictures please scratch my back there a little higher that's it excuse me I'm going to fart now have you the time I can't waste all day here better tell the old man to put on his hat it's time to go for a drink. Still mumbling and grumbling he turns on his big scows and presses the elevator button while the old man with a straw hat on the back of his head is making a slide for the home plate from the back of the store, his face lit up with love and gratitude and saying: "Well, Ferd, how are you this morning? It's good to see you." And Ferd's big heavy mask of a face relaxes for a moment into a broad amiable grin. Just a second he holds it and then, lifting his voice he bellows at the top of his lungs—so that even Tom Moffatt across the way can hear it—"BETTER PAY UP SOON WHAT THE HELL DO YOU THINK I'M SELLING THESE THINGS FOR?"

And as soon as the elevator has started down out comes little Rubin from the busheling room and with a wild look in his eye he says to me: "Would you like me to sing for you?" He knows damned well that I would. So, going back to the bench, he picks up the coat that he's stitching and with a wild Cossack shout he lets loose.

If you were to pass him in the street, little Rubin, you would say "dirty little kike," and perhaps he was a dirty little kike but he knew how to sing and when you were broke he knew how to put his hand in his pocket and when you were sad he was sadder still and if you tried to step on him he spat on your shoe and if you were repentant he wiped it off and he brushed you down and put a crease in your trousers like Jesus H. Christ himself couldn't do.

They were all midgets in the busheling room—Rubin, Rapp, and Chaimowitz. At noon they brought out big round loaves of Jewish bread which they smeared with sweet butter and slivers of lox. While the old man was ordering squabs and Rhine wine Bunchek the cutter and the three little bushelmen sat on the big bench among the goose irons and the legs and sleeves and talked earnestly and solemnly about things like the rent or the ulcers that Mrs. Chaimowitz had in her womb. Bunchek was an ardent member of the Zionist party. He believed that the Jews had a happy future ahead of them. But despite it all he could never properly pronounce a word like "screw." He always said: "He *scruled* her." Besides his passion for Zionism Bunchek had another obsession and that was to make a coat one day that would hug the neck. Nearly all the customers were round-shouldered and potbellied, especially the old bastards who had nothing to do all day but run

from the shirtmaker to the tailor and from the tailor
to the jeweler's and from the jeweler's to the dentist
and from the dentist to the druggist. There were so
many alterations to be made that by the time the clothes
were ready to be worn the season had passed and they
had to be put away until next year, and by next year the
old bastards had either gained twenty pounds or lost
twenty pounds and what with sugar in their urine and
water in the blood it was hell to please them even when
the clothes did fit.

Then there was Paul Dexter, a $10,000-a-year man
but always out of work. Once he almost had a job, but
it was $9,000 a year and his pride wouldn't permit him
to accept it. And since it was important to be well
groomed, in the pursuit of this mythical job, Paul felt
it incumbent upon him to patronize a good tailor such
as the old man. Once he landed the job everything
would be settled in full. There was never any question
about that in Paul's mind. He was thoroughly honest.
But he was a dreamer. He came from Indiana. And like
all dreamers from Indiana he had such a lovable disposi-
tion, such a smooth, mellow, honeyed way that if he
had committed incest the world would have forgiven
him. When he had on the right tie, when he had chosen
the proper cane and gloves, when the lapels were softly
rolled and the shoes didn't squeak, when he had a quart
of rye under his belt and the weather wasn't too damp
or dismal then there flowed from his personality such a
warm current of love and understanding that even the
trimmings salesmen, hardened as they were to soft language, melted in their boots. Paul, when all circum-
stances were favorably conjoined, could walk up to a
man, any man on God's green earth and, taking him by
the lapel of his coat, drown him in love. Never did I

see a man with such powers of persuasion, such mag-
netism. When the flood began to rise in him he was invincible.

Paul used to say: "Start with Marcus Aurelius, or
Epictetus, and the rest will follow." He didn't recommend studying Chinese or learning Provençal: he began
with the fall of the Roman Empire. It was my great
ambition in those days to win Paul's approbation, but
Paul was difficult to please. He frowned when I showed
him *Thus Spake Zarathustra*. He frowned when he saw
me sitting on the bench with the midgets trying to ex-
pound the meaning of *Creative Evolution*. Above all,
he loathed the Jews. When Bunchek the cutter ap-
peared, with a piece of chalk and a tape measure slung
around his neck, Paul became excessively polite and
condescending. He knew that Bunchek despised him,
but because Bunchek was the old man's right hand man
he rubbed him down with oil, he larded him with com-
pliments. So that eventually even Bunchek had to admit
that there was something to Paul, some strange mark
of personality which, despite his shortcomings, endeared him to every one.

Outwardly Paul was all cheerfulness. But at bottom
he was morose. Every now and then Cora, his wife,
would sail in with eyes brimming with tears and implore
the old man to take Paul in hand. They used to stand
at the round table near the window conversing in a low
voice. She was a beautiful woman, his wife, tall, statuesque, with a deep contralto voice that seemed to
quiver with anguish whenever she mentioned Paul's
name. I could see the old man putting his hand on her
shoulder, soothing her, and promising her all sorts of
things no doubt. She liked the old man, I could see that.
She used to stand very close to him and look into his

eyes in a way that was irresistible. Sometimes the old
man would put his hat on and the two of them would
go down the elevator together, arm in arm, as if they
were going to a funeral. Off looking for Paul again.
Nobody knew where to find him when he had a drinking fever on. For days on end he would disappear from
sight. And then one day he would turn up, crestfallen,
repentant, humiliated, and beg everybody's forgiveness.
At the same time he would hand in his suit to be dry
cleaned, to have the vomit stains removed, and a bit of
expert repairing done at the knees.

It was after a bout that Paul talked most eloquently.
He used to sit back in one of the deep leather chairs,
the gloves in one hand, the cane between his legs, and
discourse about Marcus Aurelius. He talked even better
when he came back from the hospital, after he had
had the fistula repaired. The way he lowered himself
into the big leather chair made me think then that he
came expressly to the tailor shop because nowhere else
could he find such a comfortable seat. It was a painful
operation either to sit down or to get up. But once
accomplished Paul seemed to be in bliss and the words
rolled off his tongue like liquid velvet. The old man
could listen to Paul all day long. He used to say that
Paul had the gift of gab, but that was only his inarticu-
late way of saying that Paul was the most lovable crea-
ture on God's earth and that he had a fire in his bowels.
And when Paul was too conscience-stricken to order
another suit the old man would coax him into it, saying
to Paul all the while, "Nothing's too good for you,
Paul . . . nothing!"

Paul must have recognized something of a kindred
nature in the old man too. Never have I seen two men
look at each other with such a warm glow of admira-

tion. Sometimes they would stand there looking into each other's eyes adoringly until the tears came. In fact, neither of them was ashamed of showing his tears, something which seems to have gone out of the world now. I can see Paul's homely freckled face and his rather thick, blubbery lips twitching as the old man told him for the thousandth time what a great guy he was. Paul never spoke to the old man about things he wouldn't understand. But into the simple, everyday things which he discoursed about so earnestly he put such a wealth of tenderness that the old man's soul seemed to leave his body and when Paul was gone he was like a man bereaved. He would go then into the little cubbyhole of an office and he would sit there quietly all by himself staring ecstatically at the row of pigeon coops which were filled with letters unanswered and bills unpaid. It used to affect me so, to see him in one of these moods, that I would sneak quietly down the stairs and start to walk home, down the Avenue to the Bowery and along the Bowery to the Brooklyn Bridge, and then over the bridge past the string of cheap flops that extended from City Hall to Fulton Ferry. And if it were a summer's evening, and the entranceways crowded with loungers, I would look among these wasted figures searchingly, wondering how many Pauls there were among them and what it is about life that makes these obvious failures so endearing to men. The others, the successful ones, I had seen with their pants off; I had seen their crooked spines, their brittle bones, their varicose veins, their tumors, their sunken chests, their big breadbaskets which had grown shapeless with years of swilling it. Yes, all the silk-lined duffers I knew well— we had the best families in America on our roster. And what a pus and filth when they opened their dirty traps!

It seemed as though when they had undressed before their tailor they felt compelled to unload the garbage which had accumulated in the plugged-up sinks which they had made of their minds. All the beautiful diseases of boredom and riches. Talked about themselves *ad nauseam*. Always "I," "I." I and my kidneys. I and my gout. I and my liverworts. When I think of Paul's dreadful hemorrhoids, of the marvelous fistula they repaired, of all the love and learning that issued from his grievous wounds, then I think that Paul was not of this age at all but sib brother to Moses Maimonides, he who under the Moors gave us those astounding learned treatises on "hemorrhoids, warts, carbuncles," etc.

In the case of all these men whom the old man so cherished death came quickly and unexpectedly. In Paul's case it happened while he was at the seashore. He was drowned in a foot of water. Heart failure, they said. And so, one fine day Cora came up the elevator, clad in her beautiful mourning garb, and wept all over the place. Never had she looked more beautiful to me, more svelte, more statuesque. Her ass particularly—I remember how caressingly the velvet clung to her figure. Again they stood near the round table at the front window, and this time she wept copiously. And again the old man put on his hat and down the elevator they went, arm in arm.

A short time later the old man, moved by some strange whim, urged me to call on Paul's wife and offer my condolences. When I rang the bell at her apartment I was trembling. I almost expected her to come out stark naked, with perhaps a mourning band around her breasts. I was infatuated with her beauty, with her years, with that somnolent, plantlike quality she had brought from Indiana and the perfume which she bathed in. She greeted me in a low-cut mourning gown, a beautiful clinging gown of black velvet. It was the first time I had ever had a tête-à-tête with a woman bereft, a woman whose breasts seemed to sob out loud. I didn't know what to say to her, especially about Paul. I stammered and blushed, and when she asked me to sit beside her on the couch I almost fell over her in my embarrassment.

Sitting there on the low sofa, the place flooded with soft lights, her big heaving loins rubbing against me, the Malaga pounding my temples and all this crazy talk about Paul and how good he was, I finally bent over and without saying a word I raised her dress and slipped it into her. And as I got it into her and began to work it around she took to moaning like, a sort of delirious, sorrowful guilt punctuated with gasps and little shrieks of joy and anguish, saying over and over again—"I never thought you would do this . . . I never thought you would do this!" And when it was all over she ripped off the velvet dress, the beautiful low-cut mourning gown, and she put my head down on her and she told me to kiss it and with her two strong arms she squeezed me almost in half and moaned and sobbed. And then she got up and she walked around the room naked for a while. And then finally she got down on her knees beside the sofa where I was stretched out and she said in a low tearful voice—"You promise me you'll love me always, won't you? You promise me?" And I said Yes with one hand working around in her crotch. Yes I said and I thought to myself what a sap you've been to wait so long. She was so wet and juicy down there, and so childlike, so trustful, why anybody could have come along and had what's what. She was a push-over.

Always merry and bright! Regularly, every season, there were a few deaths. Sometimes it was a good egg like Paul, or Julian Legree, sometimes a bartender who had picked his nose with a rusty nail—hail and hearty one day, dead the next—but regularly, like the movement of the seasons themselves, the old buzzards dropped off, one by one. *Alors*, nothing to do but draw a red line slantwise down the right-hand side of the ledger and mark "DEAD." Each death brought a little business —a new black suit or else mourning bands on the left sleeve of every coat. Those who ordered mourning bands were cheapskates, according to the old man. And so they were.

As the old 'uns died off they were replaced by young blood. *Young blood!* That was the war cry all along the Avenue, wherever there were silk-lined suits for sale. A fine bloody crew they were, the young bloods. Gamblers, racetrack touts, stockbrokers, ham actors, prize fighters, etc. Rich one day, poor the next. No honor, no loyalty, no sense of responsibility. A fine bunch of gangrened syphilitics they were, most of 'em. Came back from Paris or Monte Carlo with dirty postcards and a string of big blue rocks in their groin. Some of them with balls as big as a lamb's fry.

One of them was the Baron Carola von Eschenbach. He had earned a little money in Hollywood posing as the Crown Prince. It was the period when it was considered riotously funny to see the Crown Prince plastered with rotten eggs. It must be said for the Baron that he was a good double for the Crown Prince. A death's head with arrogant nose, a waspish stride, a corseted waist, lean and ravished as Martin Luther, dour, glum, fanatical, with that brassy, fatuous glare of the Junker class. Before going to Hollywood he was just a nobody, the son of a German brewer in Frankfort. He wasn't even a baron. But afterwards, when he had been knocked about like a medicine ball, when his front teeth had been pushed down his throat and the neck of a broken bottle had traced a deep scar down his left cheek, afterwards when he had been taught to flaunt a red necktie, twirl a cane, clip his mustache short, like Chaplin, then he became somebody. Then he stuck a monocle in his eye and named himself Baron Carola von Eschenbach. And all might have gone beautifully for him had he not fallen for a redhaired walk-on who was rotting away with syphilis. That finished him.

Up the elevator he came one day in a cutaway and spats, a bright red rose in his buttonhole and the monocle stuck in his eye. Blithe and dapper he looked, and the card he took out of his wallet was handsomely engraved. It bore a coat of arms which had been in the family, so he said, for nine hundred years. "The family skeleton," he called it. The old man was highly pleased to have a baron among his clients, especially if he paid cash, as this one promised to do. And then too it was exhilarating to see the baron come sailing in with a pair of soubrettes on his arm—each time a different pair. Even more exhilarating when he invited them into the dressing room and asked them to help him off with his trousers. It was a European custom, he explained.

Gradually he got acquainted with all the old cronies who hung out in the front of the shop. He showed them how the Crown Prince walked, how he sat down, how he smiled. One day he brought a flute with him and he played the Lorelei on it. Another day he came in with a finger of his pigskin glove sticking out of his fly. Each day he had a new trick up his sleeve. He was

gay, witty, amusing. He knew a thousand jokes, some
that had never been told before. He was a riot.

And then one day he took me aside and asked me if
I could lend him a dime—for carfare. He said he
couldn't pay for the clothes he had ordered but he expected a job soon in a little movie house on Ninth
Avenue, playing the piano. And then, before I knew it,
he began to weep. We were standing in the dressing
room and the curtains were drawn, fortunately. I had
to lend him a handkerchief to wipe his eyes. He said he
was tired of playing the clown, that he dropped in to
our place every day because it was warm there and because we had comfortable seats. He asked me if I
couldn't take him to lunch—he had had nothing but
coffee and buns for the last three days.

I took him to a little German restaurant on Third
Avenue, a bakery and restaurant combined. The atmosphere of the place broke him down completely. He
could talk of nothing but the old days, the old days, the
days before the war. He had intended to be a painter,
and then the war came. I listened attentively and when
he got through I proposed that he come to my home for
dinner that evening—perhaps I could put him up with
us. He was overwhelmed with gratitude. Sure, he
would come—at seven o'clock *punkt*. Fine!

At the dinner table my wife was amused by his
stories. I hadn't said anything about his being broke.
Just that he was a baron—the Baron von Eschenbach, a
friend of Charlie Chaplin's. My wife—one of my first
ones—was highly flattered to sit at the same table with
a baron. And puritanical bastard that she was, she never
so much as blushed when he told a few of his risqué
stories. She thought they were delightful—*so Euro-*

pean. Finally, however, it came time to spill the beans. I tried to break the news gently, but how can you be gentle about a subject like syphilis? I didn't call it syphilis at first—I said "venereal disease." *Maladie intime, quoi!* But just that little word "venereal" sent a shudder through my wife. She looked at the cup he was holding to his lips and then she looked at me imploringly, as though to say—"how could you ask a man like that to sit at the same table with us?" I saw that it was necessary to bring the matter to a head at once. "The baron here is going to stay with us for a while," I said quietly. "He's broke and he needs a place to flop." My word, I never saw a woman's expression change so quickly. "*You!*" she said, "*you* ask *me* to do that? And what about the baby? You want us all to have syphilis, is that it? It's not enough that *he* has it—you want the baby to have it too!"

The baron of course was frightfully embarrassed by this outburst. He wanted to leave at once. But I told him to keep his shirt on. I was used to these scenes. Anyway, he got so wrought up that he began to choke over his coffee. I thumped him on the back until he was blue in the face. The rose fell out of his buttonhole on to the plate. It looked strange there, as though he had coughed it up out of his own blood. It made me feel so goddamned ashamed of my wife that I could have strangled her on the spot. He was still choking and sputtering as I led him to the bathroom. I told him to wash his face in cold water. My wife followed us in and watched in murderous silence as he performed his ablutions. When he had wiped his face she snatched the towel from his hands and, flinging the bathroom window open, flung it out. That made me furious. I told her to get the hell out of the bathroom and mind her own business. But the baron stepped between us and flung himself at my wife supplicatingly. "You'll see, my good woman, and you, Henry, you won't have to worry about a thing. I'll bring all my syringes and ointments and I'll put them in a little valise—there, under the sink. You mustn't turn me away, I have nowhere to go. I'm a desperate man. I'm alone in the world. You were so good to me before—why must you be cruel now? Is it my fault that I have the syph? Anybody can get the syph. It's human. You'll see, I'll pay you back a thousand times. I'll do anything for you. I'll make the beds, I'll wash the dishes. . . I'll cook for you. . . ." He went on and on like that, never stopping to take a breath for fear that she would say No. And after he had gotten all through with his promises, after he had begged her forgiveness a hundred times, after he had knelt down and tried to kiss her hand which she drew away abruptly, he sat down on the toilet seat, in his cutaway and spats, and he began to sob, to sob like a child. It was ghastly, the sterile, white-enameled bathroom and the splintering light as if a thousand mirrors had been shattered under a magnifying glass, and then this wreck of a baron, in his cutaway and spats, his spine filled with mercury, his sobs coming like the short puffs of a locomotive getting under way. I didn't know what the hell to do. A man sitting on the toilet like that and sobbing—it got under my skin. Later I became inured to it. I got hard-boiled. I feel quite certain now that had it not been for the two hundred and fifty bed patients whom he was obliged to visit twice a day at the hospital in Lyons, Rabelais would never have been so boisterously gay. I'm sure of it.

Anyhow, apropos the sobs. . . . A little later, when another kid was on the way and no means of getting rid of it, though still hoping, still hoping that something would happen, a miracle perhaps, and her stomach blown up like a ripe watermelon, about the sixth or seventh month, as I say, she used to succumb to fits of melancholy and, lying on the bed with that watermelon staring her in the eye, she would commence to sob fit to break your heart. Maybe I'd be in the other room, stretched out on the couch, with a big, fat book in my hands, and those sobs of hers would make me think of the Baron Carola von Eschenbach, of his gray spats and the cutaway with braided lapels, and the deep red rose in his buttonhole. Her sobs were like music to my ears. Sobbing away for a little sympathy she was, and not a drop of sympathy in the house. It was pathetic. The more hysterical she grew the more deaf I became. It was like listening to the boom and sizzle of surf along the beach on a summer's night: the buzz of a mosquito can drown out the ocean's roar. Anyway, after she had worked herself up to a state of collapse, when the neighbors couldn't stand it any longer and there were knocks on the door, then her aged mother would come crawling out of the bedroom and with tears in her eyes would beg me to go in there and quiet her a bit. "Oh, leave her be," I'd say, "she'll get over it." Whereupon, ceasing her sobs for a moment the wife would spring out of bed, wild, blind with rage, her hair all down and tangled up, her eyes swollen and bleary, and still hiccoughing and sobbing she would commence to pound me with her fists, to lambast me until I became hysterical with laughter. And when she saw me rocking to and fro like a crazy man, when her arms were tired and her fists sore, she would yell like a drunken whore —"Fiend! Demon!"—and then slink off like a weary dog. Afterwards, when I had quieted her down a bit, when I realized that she really needed a kind word or two, I would tumble her on to the bed again and throw a good fuck into her. Blast me if she wasn't the finest piece of tail imaginable after those scenes of grief and anguish! I never heard a woman moan and gibber like she could. "*Do anything* to me!" she used to say. "Do what you want!" I could stand her on her head and blow into it, I could back-scuttle her, I could drag her past the parson's house, as they say, any goddamn thing at all—she was simply delirious with joy. Uterine hysteria, that's what it was! *And I hope God take me*, as the good master used to say, *if I am lying in a single word I say.*

(God, mentioned above, being defined by St. Augustine, as follows: "An infinite sphere, the center of which is everywhere, the circumference nowhere.")

However, *always merry and bright!* If it was before the war and the thermometer down to zero or below, if it happened to be Thanksgiving Day, or New Year's or a birthday, or just any old excuse to get together, then off we'd trot, the whole family, to join the other freaks who made up the living family tree. It always seemed astounding to me how jolly they were in our family despite the calamities that were always threatening. Jolly in spite of everything. There was cancer, dropsy, cirrhosis of the liver, insanity, thievery, mendacity, buggery, incest, paralysis, tapeworms, abortions, triplets, idiots, drunkards, ne'er-do-wells, fanatics, sailors, tailors, watchmakers, scarlet fever, whooping cough, meningitis, running ears, chorea, stutterers, jailbirds, dreamers, storytellers, bartenders—and finally there was Uncle George and Tante Melia. The morgue and the insane asylum. A merry crew and the table loaded with good things—with red cabbage and green spinach, with roast pork and turkey and sauerkraut, with kartoffel-klösze and sour black gravy, with radishes and celery, with stuffed goose and peas and carrots, with beautiful white cauliflower, with apple sauce and figs from Smyrna, with bananas big as a blackjack, with cin-namon cake and Streussel Küchen, with chocolate layer cake and nuts, all kinds of nuts, walnuts, butternuts, almonds, pecans, hickory nuts, with lager beer and bottled beer, with white wines and red, with cham-pagne, kümmel, malaga, port, with schnapps, with fiery cheeses, with dull, innocent store cheese, with flat Holland cheeses, with limburger and schmierkäse, with homemade wines, elderberry wine, with cider, hard and sweet, with rice pudding and tapioca, with roast chest-nuts, mandarins, olives, pickles, with red caviar and black, with smoked sturgeon, with lemon meringue pie, with lady fingers and chocolate eclairs, with macaroons and cream puffs, with black cigars and long thin stogies, with Bull Durham and Long Tom and meerschaums, with corncobs and toothpicks, wooden toothpicks which gave you gum boils the day after, and napkins a yard wide with your initials stitched in the corner, and a blazing coal fire and the windows steaming, every-thing in the world before your eyes except a finger bowl.

Zero weather and crazy George, with one arm bitten off by a horse, dressed in dead men's remnants. Zero weather and Tante Melia looking for the birds she left in her hat. Zero, zero, and the tugs snorting below in the harbor, the ice floes bobbing up and down, and long thin streams of smoke curling fore and aft. The wind blowing down at seventy miles an hour; tons and tons of snow all chopped up into tiny flakes and each one carrying a dagger. The icicles hanging like corkscrews outside the window, the wind roaring, the panes rattling. Uncle Henry is singing "Hurrah for the German Fifth!" His vest is open, his suspenders are down, the veins stand out on his temples. *Hurrah for the German Fifth!*

Up in the loft the creaking table is spread; down below is the warm stable, the horses whinnying in the stalls, whinnying and champing and pawing and stomping, and the fine aromatic smell of manure and horse piss, of hay and oats, of steaming blankets and dry cruds, the smell of malt and old wood, of leather harness and tanbark floats up and rests like incense over our heads.

The table is standing on horses and the horses are standing in warm piss and every now and then they get frisky and whisk their tails and they fart and whinny. The stove is glowing like a ruby, the air is blue with smoke. The bottles are under the table, on the dresser, in the sink. Crazy George is trying to scratch his neck with an empty sleeve. Ned Martini, the ne'er-do-well, is fiddling with the phonograph; his wife Carrie is guzzling it from the tin growler. The brats are downstairs in the stable playing stinkfinger in the dark. In the street, where the shanties begin, the kids are making a sliding pond. It's blue everywhere, with cold and smoke and snow. Tante Melia is sitting in a corner fingering a rosary. Uncle Ned is repairing a harness. The three grandfathers and the two great-grandfathers are huddled near the stove talking about the Franco-Prussian war. Crazy George is lapping up the dregs. The women are getting closer together, their voices low, their tongues clacking. Everything fits together like a jigsaw puzzle—faces, voices, gestures, bodies.

Each one gravitates within his own orbit. The phonograph is working again, the voices get louder and
shriller. The phonograph stops suddenly. I oughtn't to
have been there when they blurted it out, but I was
there and I heard it. I heard that big Maggie, the one
who kept a saloon out in Flushing, well that Maggie
had slept with her own brother and that's why George
was crazy. She slept with everybody—except her own
husband. And then I heard that she used to beat George
with a leather belt, used to beat him until he foamed
at the mouth. That's what brought on the fits. And then
Mele sitting there in the corner—she was another case.
She was queer even as a child. So was the mother, for
that matter. It was too bad that Paul had died. Paul was
Mele's husband. Yes, everything would have been all
right if that woman from Hamburg hadn't shown up
and corrupted Paul. What could Mele do against a
clever woman like that—against a shrewd strumpet!
Something would have to be done about Mele. It was
getting dangerous to have her around. Just the other
day they caught her sitting on the stove. Fortunately
the fire was low. But supposing she took it into her
head to set fire to the house—when they were all
asleep? It was a pity that she couldn't hold a job any
more. The last place they had found for her was such
a nice berth, such a kind woman. Mele was getting lazy.
She had had it too easy with Paul.

The air was clear and frosty when we stepped outdoors. The stars were crisp and sparkly and everywhere, lying over the bannisters and steps and window-
ledges and gratings, was the pure white snow, the driven
snow, the white mantle that covers the dirty, sinful
earth. Clear and frosty the air, pure, like deep draughts
of ammonia, and the skin smooth as chamois. Blue stars,

beds and beds of them, drifting with the antelopes. Such a beautiful, deep silent night, as if under the snow there lay hearts of gold, as if this warm German blood was running away in the gutter to stop the mouths of hungry babes, to wash the crime and ugliness of the world away. Deep night and the river choked with ice, the stars dancing, swirling, spinning like tops. Along the broken street we straggled, the whole family. Walking along the pure white crust of the earth, leaving tracks, foot-stains. The old German family sweeping the snow with a Christmas tree. The whole family there, uncles, cousins, brothers, sisters, fathers, grandfathers. The whole family is warm and winey and no one thinks of the other, of the sun that will come in the morning, of the errands to run, of the doctor's verdict, of all the cruel, ghastly duties that foul the day and make this night holy, this holy night of blue stars and deep drifts, of arnica blossoms and ammonia, of asphodels and carborundum.

No one knew that Tante Melia was going completely off her nut, that when we reached the corner she would leap forward like a reindeer and bite a piece out of the moon. At the corner she leapt forward like a reindeer and she shrieked. "The moon, the moon!" she cried, and with that her soul broke loose, jumped clean out of her body. Eighty-six million miles a minute it traveled. Out, out, to the moon, and nobody could think quick enough to stop it. Just like that it happened. In the twinkle of a star.

And now I'm going to tell you what those bastards said to me. . . .

They said—*Henry, you take her to the asylum tomorrow. And don't tell them that we can afford to pay for her.*

Fine! *Always merry and bright!* The next morning
we boarded the trolley together and we rode out into
the country. If Mele asked where we were going I was
to say—"to visit Aunt Monica." But Mele didn't ask
any questions. She sat quietly beside me and pointed
to the cows now and then. She saw blue cows and green
ones. She knew their names. She asked what happened
to the moon in the daytime. And did I have a piece of
liverwurst by any chance?

During the journey I wept—I couldn't help it. When
people are too good for this world they have to be put
under lock and key. There's something wrong with
people who are too good. It's true Mele was lazy. She
was born lazy. It's true that Mele was a poor housekeeper. It's true Mele didn't know how to hold on to
a husband when they found her one. When Paul ran
off with the woman from Hamburg Mele sat in a corner
and wept. The others wanted her to do something—
put a bullet in him, raise a rumpus, sue for alimony.
Mele sat quiet. Mele wept. Mele hung her head. What
little intelligence she had deserted her. She was like a
pair of torn socks that are kicked around here, there,
everywhere. Always turning up at the wrong moment.

Then one day Paul took a rope and hanged himself.
Mele must have understood what had happened because
now she went completely crazy. The day before they
found her eating her own dung. The day before that
they found her sitting on the stove.

And now she's very tranquil and she calls the cows
by their first name. The moon fascinates her. She has
no fear because I'm with her and she always trusted
me. I was her favorite. Even though she was a half-wit
she was good to me. The others were more intelligent,
but their hearts were bad.

When brother Adolphe used to take her for a carriage ride the others used to say—"Mele's got her eye on him!" But I think that Mele must have talked just as innocently then as she's talking to me now. I think that Mele, when she was performing her marriage duties, must have been dreaming innocently of the beautiful gifts she would give to everybody. I don't think that Mele had any knowledge of sin or of guilt or remorse. I think that Mele was born a half-witted angel. I think Mele was a saint.

Sometimes when she was fired from a job they used to send me to fetch her. Mele never knew her way home. And I remember how happy she was whenever she saw me coming. She would say innocently that she wanted to stay with us. Why couldn't she stay with us? I used to ask myself that over and over. Why couldn't they make a place for her by the fire, let her sit there and dream, if that's what she wanted to do? Why must everybody *work*—even the saints and the angels? Why must half-wits set a good example?

I'm thinking now that after all it may be good for Mele where I'm taking her. No more work. Just the same, I'd rather they had made a corner for her somewhere.

Walking down the gravel path toward the big gates Mele becomes uneasy. Even a puppy knows when it is being carried to a pond to be drowned. Mele is trembling now. At the gate they are waiting for us. The gate yawns. Mele is on the inside, I am on the outside. They are trying to coax her along. They are gentle with her now. They speak to her so gently. But Mele is terror-stricken. She turns and runs toward the gate. I am still standing there. She puts her arms through the bars and clutches my neck. I kiss her tenderly on the forehead.

Gently I unlock her arms. The others are going to take her again. I can't bear seeing that. I must go. I must run. For a full minute, however, I stand and look at her. Her eyes seem to have grown enormous. Two great round eyes, full and black as the night, staring at me uncomprehendingly. No maniac can look that way. No idiot can look that way. Only an angel or a saint.

Mele wasn't a good housekeeper I said, but she knew how to make fricadellas. Here is the recipe, while I think of it: a distemper composed of a humus of wet bread (from a nice urinal) plus horse meat (the fetlocks only) chopped very fine and mixed with a little sausage meat. Roll in palm of hands. The saloon that she ran with Paul, before the Hamburg woman came along, was just near the bend in the Second Avenue El, not far from the Chinese pagoda used by the Salvation Army.

When I ran away from the gate I stopped beside a high wall and, burying my head in my arms, my arms against the wall, I sobbed as I had never sobbed since I was a child. Meanwhile they were giving Mele a bath and putting her into regulation dress; they parted her hair in the middle, brushed it down flat and tied it into a knot at the nape of the neck. Thus no one looks exceptional. All have the same crazy look, whether they are half crazy or three-quarters crazy, or just slightly cracked. When you say "may I have pen and ink to write a letter" they say "yes" and they hand you a broom to sweep the floor. If you pee on the floor absent-mindedly you have to wipe it up. You can sob all you like but you mustn't violate the rules of the house. A bughouse has to be run in orderly fashion just as any other house.

Once a week Mele would be allowed to receive. For thirty years the sisters had been visiting the bughouse. They were fed up with it. When they were tiny tots they used to visit their mother on Blackwell's Island. The mother always said to be careful of Mele, to watch over her. When Mele stood at the gate with eyes so round and bright her mind must have traveled back like an express train. Everything must have leaped to her mind at once. Her eyes were so big and bright, as if they saw more than they could comprehend. Bright with terror, and beneath the terror a limitless confusion. That's what made them so beautifully bright. You have to be crazy to see things so lucidly, so all at once. If you're great you can stay that way and people will believe in you, swear by you, turn the world upside down for you. But if you're only partly great, or just a nobody, then what happens to you is lost.

Mornings a brisk intellectual walk under the screaming elevated line, walking north from Delancey Street toward the Waldorf where the evening before the old man had been lounging around in Peacock Alley with Julian Legree. Each morning I write a new book, walking from the Delancey Street station north toward the Waldorf. On the fly-leaf of each book is written in vitriol: *The Island of Incest*. Every morning it starts with the drunken vomit of the night before; it makes a huge gardenia which I wear in the buttonhole of my lapel, the lapel of my double-breasted suit which is lined with silk throughout. I arrive at the tailor shop with the black breath of melancholy, perhaps to find Tom

Jordan in the busheling room waiting to have the spots removed from his fly. After having written 369 pages on the trot the futility of saying Good Morning prevents me from being ordinarily polite. I have just this morning finished the twenty-third volume of the ancestral book, of which not even a comma is visible since it was all written extemporaneously without even a fountain pen. I, the tailor's son, am now about to say Good Morning to Endicott Mumford's crack woolen salesman who stand before the mirror in his underwear examining the pouches under his eyes. Every limb and leaf of the family tree dangles before my eyes: out of the crazy black fog of the Elbe there floats this changing island of incest which produces the marvelous gardenia that I wear in my buttonhole each morning. I am just about to say Good Morning to Tom Jordan. It trembles there on my lips. I see a huge tree rising out of the black fog and in the hollow of the trunk there sits the woman from Hamburg, her ass squeezed tightly through the back of the chair. The door is on the latch and through the chink I see her green face, the lips set tight, the nostrils distended. Crazy George is going from door to door with picture post cards, the arm that was bitten off by a horse lost and buried, the empty sleeve flapping in the wind. When all the pages have been torn from the calendar except the last six Crazy George will ring the doorbell and, with icicles in his mustache, he will stand on the threshold, cap in hand, and shout—"Merry Christmas!" This is the craziest tree that ever rose out of the Elbe, with every limb blasted and every leaf withered. This is the tree that shouts regularly once a year—"Merry Christmas!" Despite the calamities, despite the flow of cancer, dropsy, thievery, mendacity, buggery, paralysis, tapeworms, running ears, chorea, meningitis, epilepsy, liver-worts, et cetera.

I am just about to say Good Morning. It trembles there on my lips. The twenty-three volumes of the Domesday Book are written with incestuous fidelity, the covers bound in finest morocco, and a lock and key for each volume. Tom Jordan's bloodshot eyes are pasted on the mirror; they shudder like a horse shaking off a fly. Tom Jordan is always either taking off his pants or putting on his pants. Always buttoning or un-buttoning his fly. Always having the stains removed and a fresh crease put in. Tante Melia is sitting in the cooler, under the shade of the family tree. Mother is washing the vomit stains out of last week's dirty wash. The old man is stropping his razor. The Jews are moving up from under the shadow of the bridge, the days are getting shorter, the tugs are snorting or croaking like bullfrogs, the harbor is jammed with ice cakes. Every chapter of the book which is written in the air thickens the blood; the music of it deafens the wild anxiety of the outer air. Night drops like a boom of thunder, deposits me on the floor of the pedestrian highway leading nowhere eventually, but brightly ringed with gleaming spokes along which there is no turning back nor standing still.

From the shadow of the bridges the mob moves up, closer and closer, like a ringworm, leaving a huge festering sore than runs from river to river along Four-teenth Street. This line of pus, which runs invisibly from ocean to ocean, and age to age, neatly divides the Gentile world that I knew from the ledger from the Jewish world that I am about to know from life. Be-tween these two worlds, in the middle of the pus line that runs from river to river, stands a little flower pot filled with gardenias. This is as far as the mastodons roam, where the buffaloes can graze no more; here the cunning, abstract world rises like a cliff in the midst of which are buried the fires of the revolution. Each morning I cross the line, with a gardenia in my button-hole and a fresh volume written in the air. Each morning I wade through a trench filled with vomit to reach the beautiful island of incest; each day the cliff rises up more toweringly, the window-lines straight as a railroad track and the gleam of them even more dazzling than the gleam of polished skulls. Each morning the trench yawns more menacingly.

I should be saying Good Morning now to Tom Jordan, but it hangs there on my lips tremblingly. What morning is this that I should waste in salutation? Is it *good*, this morning of mornings? I am losing the power to distinguish morning from morning. In the ledger is the world of the fast disappearing buffalo; next door the riveters are sewing up the ribs of the coming skyscrapers. Cunning Oriental men with leaden shoes and glass craniums are plotting the paper world of tomorrow, a world made entirely of merchandise which rises box on box like a paper-box factory, f. o. b. Canarsie. Today there is still time to attend the funeral of the recent dead; tomorrow there will be no time, for the dead will be left on the spot and woe to him who sheds a tear. This is a good morning for a revolution if only there were machine guns instead of firecrackers. This morning would be a splendid morning if yesterday's morning had not been an utter fiasco. The past is galloping away, the trench widens. Tomorrow is further off than it was yesterday because yesterday's horse has run wild and the men with leaden shoes cannot catch up with him. Between

the good of the morning and the morning itself there is
a line of pus which blows a stench over yesterday and
poisons the morrow. This is a morning so confused that
if it were only an old umbrella the slightest sneeze
would blow it inside out.

My whole life is stretching out in an unbroken morning. I write from scratch each day. Each day a new
world is created, separate and complete, and there I
am among the constellations, a god so crazy about himself that he does nothing but sing and fashion new
worlds. Meanwhile the old universe is going to pieces.
The old universe resembles a busheling room in which
pants are pressed and stains removed and buttons sewn
on. The old universe smells like a wet seam receiving
the kiss of a red-hot iron. Endless alterations and re-
pairs, a sleeve lengthened, a collar lowered, a button
moved closer, a new seat put in. But never a new suit
of clothes, never a creation. There is the morning
world, which starts from scratch each day, and the
busheling room in which things are endlessly altered
and repaired. And thus it is with my life through which
there runs the sewer of night. All through the night I
hear the goose irons hissing as they kiss the wet seams;
the rinds of the old universe fall on the floor and the
stench of them is sour as vinegar.

The men my father loved were weak and lovable.
They went out, each and every one of them, like brilliant stars before the sun. They went out quietly and
catastrophically. No shred of them remained—nothing
but the memory of their blaze and glory. They flow
now inside me like a vast river choked with falling stars.
They form the black flowing river which keeps the axis
of my world in constant revolution. Out of this black,
endless, ever-expanding girdle of night springs the con-

tinuous morning which is wasted in creation. Each morning the river overflows its banks, leaving the sleeves and buttonholes and all the rinds of a dead universe strewn along the beach where I stand contemplating the ocean of the morning of creation.

Standing there on the ocean's shore I see Crazy George leaning against the wall of the undertaker's shop. He has on a funny little cap, a celluloid collar and no tie; he sits on the bench beside the coffin, neither sad nor smiling. He sits there quietly, like an angel that has stepped outside of a Jewish painting. The man in the coffin, whose body is still fresh, is decked out in a modest pepper and salt suit just George's size. He has a collar and tie on and a watch in his vest pocket. George takes him out, undresses him and, while he changes his clothes, lays him on the ice. Not wishing to steal the watch he lays the watch on the ice beside the body. The man is lying on the ice with a celluloid collar around his neck. It is getting dark as George steps out of the undertaker's shop. He has a tie now and a good suit of clothes. At the corner drugstore he stops off to buy a joke book which he saw in the window; he memorizes a few jokes standing in the subway. They are Joe Miller's jokes.

At precisely the same hour Tante Melia is sending a Valentine greeting to the relatives. She has a gray uniform on and her hair is parted in the middle. She writes that she is very happy with her new-found friends and that the food is good. She would like them to remember however that she asked for some *Fastnacht Küchen* the last time—could they send some by mail, by parcel post? She says that there are some lovely petunias growing up around the garbage can outside the big kitchen. She says that she took a long walk on Sunday last and saw lots of reindeer and rabbits and ostriches. She says that her spelling is very poor, but that she was never a good hand at writing anyway. Everybody is very kind and there is lots of work to do. She would like some *Fastnacht Küchen* as soon as possible, by air mail if possible. She asked the director to make her some for her birthday but they forgot. She says to send some newspapers because she likes to look at the advertisements. There was a hat she saw once, from Bloomingdale's, she thought, and it was marked down. Maybe they could send the hat along with the *Fastnacht Küchen?* She thanks them all for the lovely cards they sent her last Christmas—she still remembers them, especially the one with the silver stars on it. Everybody thought it was lovely. She says that she will soon be going to bed and that she will pray for all of them because they were always so good to her.

It's growing dusky, always about the same hour, and I'm standing there gazing at the ocean's mirror. Ice-cold time, neither fast nor slow, but a stiff lying on the ice with a celluloid collar—and if only he had an erection it would be marvelous . . . too marvelous! In the dark hallway below Tom Jordan is waiting for the old man to descend. He has two blowsers with him and one of them is fixing her garter; Tom Jordan is helping her to fix her garter. Same hour, toward dusk, as I say, Mrs. Lawson is walking through the cemetery to look once again at her darling son's grave. Her dear boy Jack, she says, though he was thirty-two when he kicked off seven years ago. They said it was rheumatism of the heart, but the fact is the darling boy had knocked up so many venereal virgins that when they drained the pus from his body he stank like a shitpump. Mrs. Lawson doesn't seem to remember that at all. It's her darling boy

Jack and the grave is always tidy; she carries a little
piece of chamois in her handbag in order to polish the
tombstone every evening.

Same dusky time, the stiff lying there on the ice, and
the old man is standing in a telephone booth with the
receiver in one hand and something warm and wet with
hair on it in the other. He's calling up to say not to
hold the dinner, that he's got to take a customer out
and he'll be home late, not to worry. Crazy George is
turning the leaves of Joe Miller's joke book. Down
further, toward Mobile, they're practicing the St. Louis
Blues without a note in front of 'em and people are
getting ready to go crazy when they hear it yesterday,
today, tomorrow. Everybody's getting ready to get
raped, drugged, violated, soused with the new music
that seeps out of the sweat of the asphalt. Soon it'll be
the same hour everywhere, just by turning a dial or
hanging suspended over the earth in a balloon. It's the
hour of the kaffee-klatchers sitting around the family
table, each one operated on for a different thing, the one
with the whiskers and the heavy rings on her fingers
having had a harder time than any one else because she
could afford it.

It's staggeringly beautiful at this hour when every
one seems to be going his own private way. Love and
murder, they're still a few hours apart. Love and murder, I feel it coming with the dusk: new babies coming
out of the womb, soft, pink flesh to get tangled up in
barbed wire and scream all night long and rot like dead
bone a thousand miles from nowhere. Crazy virgins
with ice-cold jazz in their veins egging men on to erect
new buildings and men with dog collars around their
necks wading through the muck up to the eyes so that
the czar of electricity will rule the waves. What's in

the seed scares the living piss out of me: a brand new world is coming out of the egg and no matter how fast I write the old world doesn't die fast enough. I hear the new machine guns and the millions of bones splintered at once; I see dogs running mad and pigeons dropping with letters tied to their ankles.

Always merry and bright, whether north from Delancey Street or south toward the pus line! My two soft hands in the body of the world, ploughing up the warm entrails, arranging and disarranging, cutting them up, sewing them together again. The warm body feeling which the surgeon knows, together with oysters, warts, ulcers, hernias, cancer sprouts, the young kohlrabies, the clips and the forceps, the scissors and tropical growths, the poisons and gases all locked up inside and carefully covered with skin. Out of the leaking mains love gushing like sewer gas: furious love with black gloves and bright bits of garter, love that champs and snorts, love hidden in a barrel and blowing the bunghole night after night. The men who passed through my father's shop reeked with love: they were warm and winey, weak and indolent, fast yachts trimmed with sex, and when they sailed by me in the night they fumigated my dreams. Standing in the center of New York I could hear the tinkle of the cowbells, or, by a turn of the head, I could hear the sweet sweet music of the death rattle, a red line down the page and on every sleeve a mourning band. By twisting my neck just a little I could stand high above the tallest skyscraper and look down on the ruts left by the huge wheels of modern progress. Nothing was too difficult for me if only it had a little grief and anguish in it. *Chez nous* there were all the organic diseases—and a few of the inorganic.

Like rock crystal we spread, from one crime to another. A merry whirl, and in the center of it my twenty-first year already covered with verdigris.

And when I can remember no more I shall always remember the night I was getting a dose of clap and the old man so stinking drunk he took his friend Tom Jordan to bed with him. Beautiful and touching this— to be out getting a dose of clap when the family honor was at stake, when it was *at par*, you might say. Not to be there for the shindig, with mother and father wrestling on the floor and the broomstick flying. Not to be there in the cold morning light when Tom Jordan is on his knees and begging to be forgiven but not being forgiven even on his knees because the inflexible heart of a Lutheran doesn't know the meaning of forgiveness. Touching and beautiful to read in the paper next morning that about the same hour the night before the pastor who had put in the bowling alley was caught in a dark room with a naked boy on his lap! But what makes it excruciatingly touching and beautiful is this, that not knowing these things, I came home next day to ask permission to marry a woman old enough to be my mother. And when I said "get married" the old lady picks up the bread knife and goes for me. I remember, as I left the house, that I stopped by the bookcase to grab a book. And the name of the book was—*The Birth of Tragedy*. Droll that, what with the broomstick the night before, the bread knife, the dose of clap, the pastor caught red-handed, the dumplings growing cold, the cancer sprouts, et cetera. . . . I used to think then that all the tragic events of life were written down in books and that what went on outside was just diluted crap. I thought that a beautiful book was a diseased portion of the brain. I never realized that a whole world could be diseased!

Walking up and down with a package under my arm. A fine bright morning, let's say, and the spittoons all washed and polished. Mumbling to myself, as I step into the Woolworth Building—"Good morning, Mr. Thorndike, fine morning this morning, Mr. Thorndike. Are you interested in clothes, Mr. Thorndike?" Mr. Thorndike is not interested in clothes this morning; he thanks me for calling and throws the card in the waste basket. Nothing daunted I try the American Express Building. "Good morning, Mr. Hathaway, fine morning this morning!" Mr. Hathaway doesn't need a good tailor—he's had one for thirty-five years now. Mr. Hathaway is a little peeved and damned right he is thinks I to myself stumbling down the stairs. A fine, bright morning, no denying that, and so to take the bad taste out of my mouth and also have a view of the harbor I take the trolley over the bridge and call on a cheap skate by the name of Dyker. Dyker is a busy man. The sort of man who has his lunch sent up and his shoes polished while he eats. Dyker is suffering from a nervous complaint brought on by dry fucking. He says we can make him a pepper and salt suit if we stop dunning him every month. The girl was only sixteen and he didn't want to knock her up. Yes, patch pockets, please! Besides, he has a wife and three children. Besides, he will be running for judge soon—judge of the Surrogate Court.

Getting toward matinee time. Hop back to New York and drop off at the Burlesk where the usher knows me. The first three rows always filled with judges and politicians. The house is dark and Margie

Pennetti is standing on the runway in a pair of dirty
white tights. She has the most wonderful ass of any
woman on the stage and everybody knows it, herself
included. After the show I walk around aimlessly, looking at the movie houses and the Jewish delicatessen
stores. Stand awhile in a penny arcade listening to the
siren voices coming through the megaphone. Life is
just a continuous honeymoon filled with chocolate
layer cake and cranberry pie. Put a penny in the slot
and see a woman undressing on the grass. Put a penny
in the slot and win a set of false teeth. The world is
made of new parts every afternoon: the soiled parts
are sent to the dry cleaner, the used parts are scrapped
and sold for junk.

Walk uptown past the pus line and stroll through
the lobbies of the big hotels. If I like I can sit down
and watch other people walking through the lobby.
Everybody's on the watch. Things are happening all
about. The strain of waiting for something to happen
is delirious. The elevated rushing by, the taxis honking,
the ambulance clanging, the riveters riveting. Bellhops
dressed in gorgeous livery looking for people who don't
answer to their names. In the golden toilet below men
standing in line waiting to take a leak; everything made
of plush and marble, the odors refined and pleasant, the
flush flushing beautifully. On the sidewalk a stack of
newspapers, the headlines still wet with murder, rape,
arson, strikes, forgeries, revolution. People stepping
over one another to crash the subway. Over in Brooklyn a woman's waiting for me. Old enough to be my
mother and she's waiting for me to marry her. The son's
got T. B. so bad he can't crawl out of bed any more.
Tough titty going up there to her garret to make love
while the son's in the next room coughing his lungs

out. Besides, she's just getting over an abortion and I
don't want to knock her up again—not right away
anyhow.

The rush hour! and the subway a free for all paradise.
Pressed up against a woman so tight I can feel the hair
on her twat. So tightly glued together my knuckles
are making a dent in her groin. She's looking straight
ahead, at a microscopic spot just under my right eye.
By Canal Street I manage to get my penis where my
knuckles were before. The thing's jumping like mad
and no matter which way the train jerks she's always in
the same position vis-à-vis my dickie. Even when the
crowd thins out she stands there with her pelvis thrust
forward and her eyes fixed on the microscopic spot just
under my right eye. At Borough Hall she gets out, without once giving me the eye. I follow her up to the street
thinking she might turn round and say hello at least, or
let me buy her a frosted chocolate, assuming I could
buy one. But no, she's off like an arrow, without turning her head the eighth of an inch. How they do it
I don't know. Millions and millions of them every day
standing up without underwear and getting a dry fuck.
What's the conclusion—a shower? a rubdown? Ten to
one they fling themselves on the bed and finish the job
with their fingers.

Anyway, it's going on toward evening and me walking up and down with an erection fit to burst my fly.
The crowd gets thicker and thicker. Everybody's got
a newspaper now. The sky's choked with illuminated
merchandise every single article of which is guaranteed
to be pleasant, healthful, durable, tasty, noiseless, rain-
proof, imperishable, the *nec plus ultra* without which
life would be unbearable were it not for the fact that
life is already unbearable because there is no life. Just

about the hour when old Henschke is quitting the tailor shop to go to the card club uptown. An agreeable little job on the side which keeps him occupied until two in the morning. Nothing much to do—just take the gentlemen's hats and coats, serve drinks on a little tray, empty the ash trays and keep the matchboxes filled. Really a very pleasant job, everything considered. Toward midnight prepare a little snack for the gentlemen, should they so desire it. There are the spittoons, of course, and the toilet bowl. All such gentlemen, however, that there's really nothing to it. And then there's always a little cheese and crackers to nibble on, and sometimes a thimbleful of port. Now and then a cold veal sandwich for the morrow. Real gentlemen! No gainsaying it. Smoke the best cigars. Even the butts taste good. Really a very, very pleasant job!

Getting toward dinner time. Most of the tailors have closed shop for the day. A few of them, those who have nothing but brittle old geezers on the books, are waiting to make a try-on. They walk up and down with their hands behind their backs. Everybody has gone except the boss tailor himself, and perhaps the cutter or the bushelman. The boss tailor is wondering if he has to put new chalk marks on again and if the check will arrive in time to meet the rent. The cutter is saying to himself: "Why yes, Mr. So-and-so, why to be sure . . . yes, I think it should be just a little higher there . . . yes, you're quite right . . . it *is* a little off on the left side . . . yes, we'll have that ready for you in a few days . . . yes, Mr. So-and-so . . . , yes, yes, yes, yes, yes, yes. . . ." The finished clothes and the unfinished clothes are hanging on the rack; the bolts are neatly stacked on the tables; only the light in the busheling

room is on. Suddenly the telephone rings. Mr. So-and-
so is on the wire and he can't make it this evening but
he would like his tuxedo sent up right away, the one
with the new buttons which he selected last week, and
he hopes to Christ it doesn't jump off his neck any
more. The cutter puts on his hat and coat and runs
quickly down the stairs to attend a Zionist meeting
in the Bronx. The boss tailor is left to close the shop
and switch out all the lights if any were left on by
mistake. The boy that he's sending up with the tuxedo
right away is himself and it doesn't matter much because he will duck round by the trade entrance and
nobody will be the wiser. Nobody looks more like a
millionaire than a boss tailor delivering a tuxedo to Mr.
So-and-so. Spry and spruce, shoes shined, hat cleaned,
gloves washed, mustache waxed. They start to look
worried only when they sit down for the evening meal.
No appetite. No orders today. No checks. They get
so despondent that they fall asleep at ten o'clock and
when it's time to go to bed they can't sleep any more.

Walking over the Brooklyn Bridge. . . . Is this the
world, this walking up and down, these buildings that
are lit up, the men and women passing me? I watch
their lips moving, the lips of the men and women passing me. What are they talking about—some of them
so earnestly? I hate seeing people so deadly serious
when I myself am suffering worse than any of them.
One life! and there are millions and millions of lives to
be lived. So far I haven't had a thing to say about my
own life. Not a thing. Must be I haven't got the guts.
Ought to go back to the subway, grab a Jane and rape
her in the street. Ought to go back to Mr. Thorndike
in the morning and spit in his face. Ought to stand on

Times Square with my pecker in my hand and piss in
the gutter. Ought to grab a revolver and fire point-
blank into the crowd. The old man's leading the life of
Reilly. He and his bosom pals. And I'm walking up and
down, turning green with hate and envy. And when I
turn in the old woman'll be sobbing fit to break her
heart. Can't sleep nights listening to her. I hate her too
for sobbing that way. The one robs me, the other pun-
ishes me. How can I go into her and comfort her when
what I most want to do is to break her heart?

Walking along the Bowery . . . and a beautiful snot-
green pasture it is at this hour. Pimps, crooks, cokies,
panhandlers, beggars, touts, gunmen, chinks, wops,
drunken micks. All gaga for a bit of food and a place
to flop. *Walking and walking and walking*. Twenty-
one I am, white, born and bred in New York, muscular
physique, sound intelligence, good breeder, no bad
habits, etc., etc. Chalk it up on the board. Selling out
at par. Committed no crime, except to be born here.

In the past every member of our family did something with his hands. I'm the first idle son of a bitch
with a glib tongue and a bad heart.

Swimming in the crowd, a digit with the rest. Tai-
lored and re-tailored. The lights are twinkling—on and
off, on and off. Sometimes it's a rubber tire, sometimes
it's a piece of chewing gum. The tragedy of it is that
nobody sees the look of desperation on my face. Thousands and thousands of us, and we're passing one another without a look of recognition. The lights jigging
like electric needles. The atoms going crazy with light
and heat. A conflagration going on behind the glass and
nothing burns away. Men breaking their backs, men
bursting their brains, to invent a machine which a child
will manipulate. If I could only find the hypothetical

child who's to run this machine I'd put a hammer in its hands and say: Smash it! Smash it!

Smash it! Smash it! That's all I can say. The old man's riding around in an open barouche. I envy the bastard his peace of mind. A bosom pal by his side and a quart of rye under his belt. My toes are blistering with malice. Twenty years ahead of me and this thing growing worse by the hour. It's throttling me. In twenty years there won't be any soft, lovable men waiting to greet me. Every bosom pal that goes now is a buffalo lost and gone forever. Steel and concrete hedging me in. The pavement getting harder and harder. The new world eating into me, expropriating me. Soon I won't even need a name.

Once I thought there were marvelous things in store for me. Thought I could build a world in the air, a castle of pure white spit that would raise me above the tallest building, between the tangible and the intangible, put me in a space like music where everything collapses and perishes but where I would be immune, great, godlike, holiest of the holies. It was *I* imagined this, I the tailor's son! I who was born from a little acorn on an immense and stalwart tree. In the hollow of the acorn even the faintest tremor of the earth reached me: I was part of the great tree, part of the past, with crest and lineage, with pride, *pride*. And when I fell to earth and was buried there I remembered *who* I was, *where* I came from. Now I am lost, *lost*, do you hear? You don't hear? I'm yowling and screaming—don't you hear me? Switch the lights off! Smash the bulbs! Can you hear me now? *Louder!* you say. *Louder!* Christ, are you making sport of me? Are you deaf, dumb, and blind? Must I yank my clothes off? Must I dance on my head?

All right, then! I'm going to dance for you! A merry whirl, brothers, and let her whirl and whirl and whirl! Throw in an extra pair of flannel trousers while you're at it. And don't forget, boys, I dress on the right side. You hear me? Let 'er go! *Always merry and bright!*

Jabberwhorl Cronstadt

This man, this skull, this music . . .

He lives in the back of a sunken garden, a sort of bosky glade shaded by whiffletrees and spinozas, by deodars and baobabs, a sort of queasy Buxtehude diapered with elytras and feluccas. You pass through a sentry box where the concierge twirls his mustache *con furioso* like in the last act of Ouida. They live on the third floor behind a mullioned belvedere filigreed with snaffled spaniels and sebaceous wens, with debentures and megrims hanging out to dry. Over the bell-push it says: "JABBERWHORL CRONSTADT, poet, musician, herbologist, weather man, linguist, oceanographer, old clothes, colloids." Under this it reads: "Wipe your feet and blow your nose!" And under this is a rosette from a second-hand suit.

"There's something strange about all this," I said to my companion whose name is Dschilly Zilah Bey. "He must be having his period again."

After we had pushed the button we heard a baby crying, a squeaky, brassy wail like the end of a horse-knacker's dream.

Finally Katya comes to the door—Katya from Hesse-Kassel—and behind her, thin as a wafer and holding a bisque doll, stands little Pinochinni. And Pinochinni says: "You should go in the drawing room, they aren't dressed yet." And when I asked would they be very long because we're famished she said, "Oh no! They've been dressing for hours. You are to look at the new poem father wrote today—it's on the mantelpiece."

And while Dschilly unwinds her serpentine scarf Pinochinni giggles and giggles, saying oh, dear, what is the matter with the world anyway, everything is so behindtime and did you ever read about the lazy little girl who hid her toothpicks under the mattress? It's very strange, father read it to me out of a large iron book.

There is no poem on the mantelpiece, but there are other things—*The Anatomy of Melancholy*, an empty bottle of Pernod Fils, *The Opal Sea*, a slice of cut plug tobacco, hairpins, a street directory, an ocarina . . . and a machine to roll cigarettes. Under the machine are notes written on menus, calling cards, toilet paper, match boxes . . . "meet the Cuntess Cathcart at four" . . . "the opalescent mucus of Michelet" . . . "defluxions . . . cotyledons . . . phthisical" . . . "if Easter falls in Lady Day's lap, beware old England of the clap" . . . "from the ichor of which springs his successor" . . . "the reindeer, the otter, the marmink, the minkfrog."

The piano stands in a corner near the belvedere, a frail black box with silver candlesticks; the black keys have been bitten off by the spaniels. There are albums marked Beethoven, Bach, Liszt, Chopin, filled with bills, manicure sets, chess pieces, marbles, and dice. When he is in good humor Cronstadt will open an album marked "Goya" and play something for you in the key of C. He can play operas, minuets, schottisches, rondos, sarabands, preludes, fugues, waltzes, military marches; he can play Czerny, Prokofief or Granados, he can even improvise and whistle a Provençal air at the same time. *But it must be in the key of* C.

So it doesn't matter how many black keys are missing

or whether the spaniels breed or don't breed. If the bell gets out of order, if the toilet doesn't flush, if the poem isn't written, if the chandelier falls, if the rent isn't paid, if the water is shut off, if the maids are drunk, if the sink is stopped and the garbage rotting, if dandruff falls and the bed creaks, if the flowers are mildewed, if the milk turns, if the sink is greasy and the wallpaper fades, if the news is stale and calamities fail, if the breath is bad or the hands sticky, if the ice doesn't melt, if the pedals won't work, it's all one and come Christmas because everything can be played in the key of C if you get used to looking at the world that way.

Suddenly the door opens to admit an enormous epileptoid beast with fungoid whiskers. It is Jocatha the famished cat, a big, buggerish brute with a taupe fur and two black walnuts hidden under its kinkless tail. It runs about like a leopard, it lifts its hind leg like a dog, it micturates like an owl.

"I'm coming in a minute," says Jabberwhorl through the sash of the door. "I'm just putting on my pants."

Now Elsa comes in—Elsa from Bad Nauheim—and she places a tray with blood-red glasses on the mantelpiece. The beast is bounding and yowling and thrashing and caterwauling: he has a few grains of cayenne pepper on the soft lilypad of his nose, the butt of his nose soft as a dum-dum bullet. He thrashes about in large Siamese wrath and the bones in his tail are finer than the finest sardines. He claws the carpet and chews the wallpaper, he rolls into a spiral and unrolls like a corolla, he whisks the knots out of his tail, shakes the fungus out of his whiskers. He bites clean through the floor to the bone of the poem. He's in the key of C and mad clean through. He has magenta eyes, like old-fashioned vest buttons; he's mowsy and glaubrous,

brown like arnica and then green as the Nile; he's
quaky and qualmy and queasy and teasey; he chews
chasubles and ripples rasubly.

Now Anna comes in—Anna from Hannover-Minden
—and she brings cognac, red pepper, absinthe and a
bottle of Worcestershire sauce. And with Anna come
the little Temple cats—Lahore, Mysore, and Cawnpore. They are all males, including the mother. They
roll on the floor, with their shrunken skulls, and bugger
each other mercilessly. And now the poet himself appears saying what time is it though time is a word he
has stricken from his list, time, sib to death. Death's the
surd and time's the sib and now there is a little time
between the acts, an oleo in which the straight man
mixes a drink to get his stomach muscles twitching.
Time, time, he says, shaking a little cayenne pepper into
his cognac. A time for everything, though I scarcely
use the word any more, and so saying he examines the
tail of Lahore which has a kink in it and scratching his
own last coccyx he adds that the toilet has just been
done in silver where you'll find a copy of *Humanité*.

"You're very beautiful," he says to Dschilly Zilah
Bey and with that the door opens again and Jill comes
forward in a chlamys of Nile green.

"Don't you think she's beautiful?" says Jab.

Everything has suddenly grown beautiful, even that
big buggerish brute Jocatha with her walnuts brown as
cinnamon and soft as lichee.

Blow the conch and tickle the clavicle! Jab's got a
pain in the belly where his wife ought to have it. Once
a month, regular as the moon, it comes over him and
it lays him low, nor will inunctions do him any good.
Nothing but cognac and cayenne pepper—to start the

stomach muscles twitching. "I'll give you three words," he says, "while the goose turns over in the pan: whimsical, dropsical, phthisical."

"Why don't you sit down?" says Jill. "He's got his period."

Cawnpore is lying on an album of Twenty-Four Preludes. "I'll play you a fast one," says Jab, and flinging back the cover of the little black box he goes *plink, plank, plunk!* "I'll do a tremolo," he says, and employing every finger of his right hand in quick succession he hits the white key C in the middle of the board and the chess pieces and the manicure sets and the unpaid bills rattle like drunken tiddledywinks. "That's technique!" he says, and his eyes are glaucous and rimed with hoarfrost. "There's only one thing travels as fast as light and that's angels. Only angels can travel as fast as light. It takes a thousand light years to get to the planet Uranus but nobody has ever been there and nobody is ever going to get there. Here's a Sunday newspaper from America. Did you ever notice how one reads the Sunday papers? First the rotogravure, then the funny sheet, then the sports column, then the magazine, then the theater news, then the book reviews, then the headlines. Recapitulation. Ontogeny-phylogeny. Define your terms and you'll never use words like time, death, world, soul. In every statement there's a little error and the error grows bigger and bigger until the snake is scotched. The poem is the only flawless thing, provided you know what time it is. A poem is a web which the poet spins out of his own body according to a logarithmic calculus of his own divination. It's always right, because the poet starts from the center and works outward. . . ."

The phone is ringing.

"Pythagoras was right. . . . Newton was right. . . .
Einstein is right. . . ."

"Answer the phone, will you!" says Jill.

"*Hello!* Oui, c'est le Monsieur Cronstadt. Et votre
nom, s'il vous plaît? *Bimberg?* Listen, you speak English, don't you? So do I. . . . *What?* Yes, I've got three
apartments—to rent or to sell. *What?* Yes, there's a
bath and a kitchen and a toilet too. . . . No, a regular
toilet. No, not in the hall—in the apartment. One you
sit down on. Would you like it in silver or in gold leaf?
What? No, the toilet! I've got a man here from
Munich, he's a refugee. *Refugee! Hitler! Hitler! Com-
pris?* Yeah, that's it. He's got a swastika on his chest, in
blue. . . . *What?* No, I'm serious. Are *you* serious?
What? Listen, if you mean business it means cash. . . .
Cash! You've got to lay out *cash. What?* Well, that's
the way things are done over here. The French don't
believe in checks. I had a man last week tried to do me
out of 750 francs. Yeah, an American check. *What?*
If you don't like that one I've got another one for you
with a dumbwaiter. It's out of order now but it could
be fixed. *What?* Oh, about a thousand francs. There's
a billiard room on the top floor. . . . *What?* No . . .
no . . . no. Don't have such things over here. Listen,
Mr. Bimberg, you've got to realize that you're in France
now. Yeah, that's it. . . . When in Rome. . . . Listen, call
me tomorrow morning, will you? I'm at dinner now.
Dinner. I'm eating. *What?* Yeah, *cash* . . . 'bye!"

"You see," he says, hanging up, "that's how we do
things in this house. Fast work, what? Real estate. You
people are living in a fairyland. You think literature is
everything. You *eat* literature. Now in this house we
eat goose, for instance. Yeah, it's almost done now.

Anna! Wie geht es? Nicht fertig? Merde alors! Three girls . . . refugees. I don't know where they come from. Somebody gave them our address. Fine girls. Hale, hearty, buxom, sound as a berry. No room for them in Germany. Einstein is busy writing poems about light. These girls want a job, a place to live. Do you know anybody who wants a maid? Fine girls. They're well educated. But it takes the three of them to make a meal. Katya, she's the best of the lot: she knows how to iron. That one, Anna—she borrowed my typewriter yesterday . . . said she wanted to write a poem. I'm not keeping you here to write poems, I said. In this house *I* write the poems—if there are any to write. You learn how to cook and darn the socks. She looked peeved. Listen, Anna, I said, you're living in an imaginary world. The world doesn't need any more poems. The world needs bread and butter. Can you produce more bread and butter? That's what the world wants. Learn French and you can help me with the real estate. Yeah, people have to have places to live in. Funny. But, that's how the world is now. It was always like that, only people never believed it before. The world is made for the future . . . for the planet Uranus. Nobody will ever visit the planet Uranus, but that doesn't make any difference. People must live places and eat bread and butter. For the sake of the future. That's the way it was in the past. That's the way it will be in the future. *The present?* There's no such thing as the present. There's a word called Time, but nobody is able to define it. There's a past and there's a future, and Time runs through it like an electric current. The present is an imaginary condition, a dream state . . . *an oxymoron*. There's a word for you—I'll make you a present of it. Write a poem about it. I'm too busy . . . real estate presses. Must have goose and cranberry sauce. . . . Listen, Jill, what was that word I was looking up yesterday?"

"Omoplate?" says Jill promptly.

"No, not that. Omo . . . omo . . ."

"Omphalos?"

"No, no. Omo . . . omo . . ."

"I've got it," cries Jill. "*Omophagia!*"

"Omophagia, that's it! Do you like that word? Take it away with you! What's the matter? You're not drinking. Jill, where the hell's that cocktail shaker I found the other day in the dumbwaiter? Can you imagine it—a *cocktail shaker!* Anyway, you people seem to think that literature is something vitally necessary. It ain't. It's just literature. I could be making literature too—if I didn't have these refugees to feed. You want to know what the present is? Look at that window over there. No, not there . . . the one above. *There!* Every day they sit there at that table playing cards—just the two of them. She's always got on a red dress. And he's always shuffling the cards. *That's the present.* And if you add another word it becomes subjunctive. . . ."

"Jesus, I'm going to see what those girls are doing," says Jill.

"No you don't! That's just what they're waiting for —for you to come and help them. They've got to learn that this is a *real* world. I want them to understand that. Afterwards I'll find them jobs. I've got lots of jobs on hand. First let them cook me a meal."

"Elsa says everything's ready. Come on, let's go inside."

"Anna, Anna, bring these bottles inside and put them on the table!"

Anna looks at Jabberwhorl helplessly.

"There you are! They haven't even learned to speak English yet. What am I going to do with them? *Anna . . . hier! 'Raus mit 'em! Versteht?* And pour yourself a drink, you blinking idiot."

The dining room is softly lighted. There is a candelabra on the table and the service glitters. Just as we are sitting down the phone rings. Anna gathers up the long cord and brings the apparatus from the piano to the sideboard just behind Cronstadt. "Hello!" he yells, and unslacking the long cord, "just like the intestines . . . *hello!* Oui! Oui, madame . . . je suis le Monsieur Cronstadt . . . et votre nom, s'il vous plaît? Oui, il y a un salon, un entresol, une cuisine, deux chambres à coucher, une salle de bain, un cabinet . . . oui, madame. . . . Non, ce n'est pas cher, pas cher du tout . . . on peut s'arranger facilement . . . comme vous voulez, madame. . . . A quelle heure? Oui . . . avec plaisir. . . . *Comment?* Que dites-vous? Ah non! Au contraire! Ça sera un plaisir . . . un grand plaisir. . . . Au revoir, madame!" Slamming it up—"Küss die Hand, madame! Would you like your back scratched, madame? Do you take milk with your coffee, madame? Will you . . .?"

"Listen," says Jill, "who the hell was that? You were pretty smooth with her. Oui, madame . . . non, madame! Did she promise to buy you a drink too?" Turning to us—"Can you imagine it, he has an actress up here yesterday while I'm taking a bath . . . some trollop from the Casino de Paris . . . and she takes him out and gets him soused. . . ."

"You don't tell that right, Jill. It's this way . . . I'm showing her a lovely apartment—with a dumbwaiter in it—and she says to me won't you show me your poetry

—*poésie* . . . sounds better in French . . . and so I bring her up here and she says I'll have them printed for you in Belgian."

"Why Belgian, Jab?"

"Because that's what she was, a Belgian—or a Belgianess. Anyway, what difference does it make what language they're printed in? Somebody has to print them, otherwise nobody will read them."

"But what made her say that—so quick like?"

"Ask me! Because they're good, I suppose. Why else would people want to print poems?"

"Baloney!"

"See that! She doesn't believe me."

"Of course I don't! If I catch you bringing any prima donnas up here, or any toe dancers, or any trapeze artists, or anything that's French and wears skirts, there's going to be hell to pay. Especially if they offer to print your poems!"

"There you are," says Jabberwhorl, glaucous and glowbry. "That's why I'm in the real estate business. . . . Go ahead and eat, you people. . . . I'm watching."

He mixes another dose of cognac and pepper.

"I think you've had enough," says Jill. "Jesus, how many of them have you had today?"

"Funny," says Jabberwhorl, "I fixed her up all right a few moments ago—just before you came—but I can't fix myself up. . . ."

"Jesus, where's that goose!" says Jill. "Excuse me, I'm going inside and see what the girls are doing."

"No you don't!" says Jab, pushing her back into her seat. "We're gonna sit right here and wait . . . wait and see what happens. Maybe the goose'll never come. We'll be sitting here waiting . . . waiting forever . . . just like this, with the candles and the empty soup plates and the curtains and . . . I can just imagine us sitting here and some one outside plastering a wall around us. . . . We're sitting here waiting for Elsa to bring the goose and time passes and it gets dark and we sit here for days and days. . . . See those candles? We'd eat 'em. And those flowers over there? Them too. We'd eat the chairs, we'd eat the sideboard, we'd eat the alarm clock, we'd eat the cats, we'd eat the curtains, we'd eat the bills and the silverware and the wallpaper and the bugs underneath . . . we'd eat our own dung and that nice new fetus Jill's got inside her . . . we'd eat each other. . . ."

Just at this moment Pinochinni comes in to say good night. She's hanging her head like and there's a quizzical look in her eye.

"What's the matter with you tonight?" says Jill. "You look worried."

"Oh, I don't know what it is," says the youngster. "There's something I want to ask you about. . . . It's awfully complicated. I don't really know if I can say what I mean."

"What is it, snookums?" says Jab. "Say it right out in front of the lady and the gentleman. You know *him*, don't you? Come on, spit it out!"

The youngster is still holding her head down. Out of the corner of her eye she looks up at her father slyly and then suddenly she blurts out: "Oh, what's it all about? What are we here for anyway? Do we have to have a world? Is this the only world there is and why is it? That's what I want to know."

If Jabberwhorl Cronstadt was somewhat astonished he gave no sign of it. Picking up his cognac nonchalantly, and adding a little cayenne pepper, he answered blithely: "Listen, kid, before I answer that question—

if you *insist* on my answering that question—you'll have to first define your terms."

Just then there came a long shrill whistle from the garden.

"Mowgli!" says Cronstadt. "Tell him to come on up."

"Come up!" says Jill, stepping to the window.

No answer.

"He must have gone," says Jill. "I don't see him any more."

Now a woman's voice floats up. "*Il est saoul . . . complètement saoul.*"

"Take him home! Tell her to take him home!" yells Cronstadt.

"*Mon mari dit qu'il faut rentrer chez vous . . . oui, chez vous.*"

"*Y'en a pas!*" floats up from the garden.

"Tell her not to lose my copy of Pound's *Cantos*," yells Cronstadt. "And don't ask them up again . . . we have no room here. Just enough space for German refugees."

"That's a shame," says Jill, coming back to the table.

"You're wrong again," says Jab. "It's very good for him."

"Oh, you're drunk," says Jill. "Where's that damned goose anyhow? Elsa! Elsa!"

"Never mind the goose, darling! This is a game. We're going to sit here and outlast 'em. The rule is, jam tomorrow and jam yesterday—but never jam today. . . . Wouldn't it be wonderful if you people sat here just like you are and I began to grow smaller and smaller . . . until I got to be just a tiny, weeny little speck . . . so that you had to have a magnifying glass to see me? I'd be a little spot on the tablecloth and I'd be saying—

Timoor . . . *Ti-moor!* And you'd say where is he?
And I'd be saying—*Timoor*, logodaedaly, glycophos-
phates, Billancourt, Ti-*moor* . . . O timbus twaddle
down the brawkish brake . . . and you'd say. . . ."

"Jesus, Jab, you're drunk!" says Jill. And Jabberwhorl glausels with gleerious glitter, his awbrous orbs
atwit and atwitter.

"He'll be getting cold in a minute," says Jill, getting
up to look for the Spanish cape.

"That's right," says Jab. "Whatever she says is right.
You think I'm a very contrary person. *You*," he says,
turning to me, "*you* with your Mongolian verbs, your
transitives and intransitives, don't you see what an
affable being I am? You're talking about China all the
time . . . *this* is China, don't you see that? *This* . . .
this what? Get me the cape, Jill, I'm cold. This is a terrible cold . . . sub-glacial cold. You people are warm,
but I'm freezing. I can feel the ice caps coming down
again. A fact. Everything is rolling along nicely, the
dollar is falling, the apartments are rented, the refugees
are all refuged, the piano is tuned, the bills are paid, the
goose is cooked and what are we waiting for? *For the
next Ice Age!* It's coming tomorrow morning. You'll
go to the window and everything'll be frozen tight. No
more problems, no more history, no more nothing.
Settled. We'll be sitting here like this waiting for Anna
to bring in the goose and suddenly the ice will roll over
us. I can feel the terrible cold already, the bread all
icicled, the butter blenched, the goose gazzled, the walls
wildish white. And that little angel, that bright new
embryo that Jill's got under her belt, that'll be frozen
in the womb, a glairy gawk with ice-cold wings and the
lips of a snail. Jugger, jugger, and everything'll be still
and quiet. Say something warm! My legs are frozen.

Herodotus says that on the death of its father the phoenix embalms the body in an egg made of myrrh and once every five hundred years or so it conveys the little egg embalmed in myrrh from the desert of Arabia to the temple of the sun at Heliopolis. *Do you like that?* According to Pliny there is only one egg at a time and when the bird perceives that its end is near it builds a nest of cassia twigs and frankincense and dies upon it. From the body of the nest is born a little worm which becomes the phoenix. Hence *bennu*, symbol of the resurrection. *How's that?* I need something hotter. Here's another one. . . . The firewalkers in Bulgaria are called *Nistingares*. They dance in the fire on the twenty-first of May during the feast of Saint Helena and Saint Constantine. They dance on the red-hot embers until they're blue in the face, and then they utter prophecies."

"Don't like that at all," says Jill.

"Neither do I," says Jab. "I like the one about the little soul-worms that fly out of the nest for the resurrection. Jill's got one inside her too . . . it's sprouting and sprouting. Can't stop it. Yesterday it was a tadpole, tomorrow it'll be a honeysuckle vine. Can't tell what it's going to be yet . . . not eventually. It dies in the nest every day and the next day it's born again. Put your ear to her belly . . . you can hear the whirring of its wings. Whirrrr . . . whirrrr. Without a motor. Wonderful! She's got millions of them inside her and they're all whirring around in there dying to get out. Whirrrr . . . whirrrr. And if you just put a needle inside and punctured the bag they'd all come whirring out . . . imagine it . . . a great cloud of soul-worms . . . millions of them . . . and so thick the swarm that we wouldn't be able to see each other. . . . A fact! No need to write

about China. Write about *that!* About what's inside
of you . . . the great vertiginous vertebration . . . the
zoospores and the leucocytes . . . the wamroths and
the holenlindens . . . every one's a poem. The jellyfish
is a poem too—the finest kind of poem. You poke him
here, you poke him there, he slithers and slathers, he's
dithy and clabberous, he has a colon and intestines, he's
vermiform and ubisquishous. And Mowgli in the garden whistling for the rent, he's a poem too, a poem with
big ears, a wambly bretzular poem with logamundiddy
of the goo-goo. He has round, auricular daedali, round
robin-breasted ruches that open up like an open barouche. He wambles in the wambhorst whilst the
whelkin winkles . . . he wabbles through the wendish
wikes whirking his worstish wights. . . . Mowgli . . .
owgli . . . whist and wurst. . . ."

"He's losing his mind," says Jill.

"Wrong again," says Jabber. "I've just found my
mind, only it's a different sort of mind than you
imagined. You think a poem must have covers around
it. The moment you write a thing the poem ceases. The
poem is the present which you can't define. You live it.
Anything is a poem if it has time in it. You don't have
to take a ferryboat or go to China to write a poem. The
finest poem I ever lived was a kitchen sink. Did I ever
tell you about it? There were two faucets, one called
Froid and the other Chaud. Froid lived a life *in extenso*,
by means of a rubber hose attached to his schnausel.
Chaud was bright and modest. Chaud dripped all the
time, as if he had the clap. On Tuesdays and Fridays
he went to the Mosque where there was a clinic for
venereal faucets. Tuesdays and Fridays Froid had to do
all the work. He was a bugger for work. It was his
whole world. Chaud on the other hand had to be petted

and coaxed. You had to say "not so fast," or he'd scald
the skin off you. Once in a while they worked in unison, Froid and Chaud, but that was seldom. Saturday
nights, when I washed my feet at the sink, I'd get to
thinking how perfect was the world over which these
twain ruled. Never anything more than this iron sink
with its two faucets. No beginnings and no ends.
Chaud the alpha and Froid the omega. Perpetuity. The
Gemini, ruling over life and death. Alpha-Chaud running out through all degrees of Fahrenheit and Reau-
mur, through magnetic filings and comets' tails, through
the boiling cauldron of Mauna Loa into the dry light of
the Tertiary moon; Omega-Froid running out through
the Gulf Stream into the paludal bed of the Sargasso
Sea, running through the marsupials and the foramini-
fera, through the mammal whales and the Polar fissures,
running down through island universes, through dead
cathodes, through dead bone and dry rot, through the
follicles and tentacles of worlds unformed, worlds untouched, worlds unseen, worlds unborn and forever
lost. Alpha-Chaud dripping, dripping; Omega-Froid
working, working. Hand, feet, hair, face, dishes, vege-
tables, fish washed clean and away; despair, ennui,
hatred, love, jealousy, crime . . . dripping, dripping. I,
Jabberwhorl, and my wife Jill, and after us legions
upon legions . . . all standing at the iron sink. Seeds
falling down through the drain: young canteloupes,
squash, caviar, macaroni, bile, spittle, phlegm, lettuce
leaves, sardines' bones, Worcestershire sauce, stale beer,
urine, bloodclots, Kruschen salts, oatmeal, chew tobacco, pollen, dust, grease, wool, cotton threads, match
sticks, live worms, shredded wheat, scalded milk, castor
oil. Seeds of waste falling away forever and forever
coming back in pure draughts of a miraculous chemical

substance which refuses to be named, classified, labeled, analyzed, or drawn and quartered. Coming back as Froid and Chaud perpetually, like a truth that can't be downed. You can take it hot or cold, or you can take it tepid. You can wash your feet or gargle your throat; you can rinse the soap out of your eyes or drive the grit out of the lettuce leaves; you can bathe the new-born babe or swab the rigid limbs of the dead; you can soak bread for fricadellas or dilute your wine. First and last things. Elixir. I, Jabberwhorl, tasting the elixir of life and death. I, Jabberwhorl, of waste and H_2O composed, of hot and cold and all the intermediate realms, of scum and rind, of finest, tiniest substance never lost, of great sutures and compact bone, of ice fissures and test tubes, of semen and ova fused, dissolved, dispersed, of rubber schnausel and brass spigot, of dead cathodes and squirming infusoria, of lettuce leaves and bottled sunlight . . . I, Jabberwhorl, sitting at the iron sink am perplexed and exalted, never less and never more than a poem, an iron stanza, a boiling follicle, a lost leucocyte. The iron sink where I spat out my heart, where I bathed my tender feet, where I held my first child, where I washed my sore gums, where I sang like a diamond-backed terrapin and I am singing now and will sing forever though the drains clog and the faucets rust, though time runs out and I be all there is of present, past and future. *Sing*, Froid, sing transitive! *Sing*, Chaud, sing intransitive! Sing Alpha and Omega! Sing Hallelujah! Sing out, O sink! Sing while the world sinks . . ."

And singing loud and clear like a dead and stricken swan on the bed we laid him out.

Into the Night Life. . .

A Coney Island of the mind.

Over the foot of the bed is the shadow of the cross. There are chains binding me to the bed. The chains are clanking loudly, the anchor is being lowered. Suddenly I feel a hand on my shoulder. Some one is shaking me vigorously. I look up and it is an old hag in a dirty wrapper. She goes to the dresser and opening a drawer she puts a revolver away.

There are three rooms, one after the other, like a railroad flat. I am lying in the middle room in which there is a walnut bookcase and a dressing table. The old hag removes her wrapper and stands before the mirror in her chemise. She has a little powder puff in her hand and with this little puff she swabs her armpits, her bosom, her thighs. All the while she weeps like an idiot. Finally she comes over to me with an atomizer and she squirts a fine spray over me. I notice that her hair is full of rats.

I watch the old hag moving about. She seems to be in a trance. Standing at the dresser she opens and closes the drawers, one after the other, mechanically. She seems to have forgotten what she remembered to go there for. Again she picks up the powder puff and with the powder puff she daubs a little powder under her armpits. On the dressing table is a little silver watch attached to a long piece of black tape. Pulling off her chemise she slings the watch around her neck; it reaches just to the pubic triangle. There comes a faint tick and then the silver turns black.

In the next room, which is the parlor, all the relatives are assembled. They sit in a semicircle, waiting for me to enter. They sit stiff and rigid, upholstered like the chairs. Instead of warts and wens there is horsehair sprouting from their chins.

I spring out of bed in my nightshirt and I commence to dance the dance of King Kotschei. In my nightshirt I dance, with a parasol over my head. They watch me without a smile, without so much as a crease in their jowls. I walk on my hands for them, I turn somersaults, I put my fingers between my teeth and whistle like a blackbird. Not the faintest murmur of approval or disapproval. They sit there solemn and imperturbable. Finally I begin to snort like a bull, then I prance like a fairy, then I strut like a peacock, and then realizing that I have no tail I quit. The only thing left to do is to read the Koran through at lightning speed, after which the weather reports, the *Rime of the Ancient Mariner* and the Book of Numbers.

Suddenly the old hag comes dancing in stark naked, her hands aflame. Immediately she knocks over the umbrella stand the place is in an uproar. From the upturned umbrella stand there issues a steady stream of writhing cobras traveling at lightning speed. They knot themselves around the legs of the tables, they carry away the soup tureens, they scramble into the dresser and jam the drawers, they wriggle through the pictures on the wall, through the curtain rings, through the mattresses, they coil up inside the women's hats, all the while hissing like steam boilers.

Winding a pair of cobras about my arms I go for the old hag with murder in my eyes. From her mouth, her eyes, her hair, from her vagina even, the cobras are streaming forth, always with that frightful steaming hiss as if they had been ejected fresh from a boiling crater. In the middle of the room where we are locked an immense forest opens up. We stand in a nest of cobras and our bodies come undone.

I am in a strange, narrow little room, lying on a high bed. There is an enormous hole in my side, a clean hole without a drop of blood showing. I can't tell any more who I am or where I came from or how I got here. The room is very small and my bed is close to the door. I have a feeling that some one is standing on the doorsill watching me. I am petrified with fright.

When I raise my eyes I see a man standing at the doorsill. He wears a gray derby cocked on the side of his head; he has a flowing mustache and is dressed in a checkerboard suit. He asks my name, my address, my profession, what I am doing and where I am going and so on and so forth. He asks endless prying questions to which I am unable to respond, first because I have lost my tongue, and second because I cannot remember any longer what language I speak. "Why don't you speak?" he says, bending over me jeeringly, and taking his light rattan stick he jabs a hole in my side. My anguish is so great that it seems I must speak even if I have no tongue, even if I know not who I am or where I came from. With my two hands I try to wrench my jaws apart, but the teeth are locked. My chin crumbles away like dry clay, leaving the jawbone exposed. "Speak!" he says, with that cruel, jeering smile and, taking his stick once again, he jabs another hole through my side.

I lie awake in the cold dark room. The bed almost touches the ceiling now. I hear the rumbling of trains, the regular rhythmic bouncing of the trains over the

frozen trestle, the short, throttled puffs of the locomotive, as if the air were splintered with frost. In my hand
are the pieces of dry clay which crumbled from my
chin. My teeth are locked tighter than ever; I breathe
through the holes in my side. From the window of the
little room in which I lie I can see the Montreal bridge.
Through the girders of the bridge, driven downward
by the blinding blizzard, the sparks are flying. The
trains are racing over the frozen river in wreaths of
fire. I can see the shops along the bridgeway gleaming
with pies and hamburger sandwiches. Suddenly I do
remember something. I remember that just as I was
about to cross the border they asked me what I had to
declare and, like an idiot, I answered: *"I want to declare
that I am a traitor to the human race."* I remember
distinctly now that this occurred just as I was walking
up a treadmill behind a woman with balloon skirts.
There were mirrors all around us and above the mirrors
a balustrade of slats, series after series of slats, one on top
of another, tilted, toppling, crazy as a nightmare. In the
distance I could see the Montreal bridge and below the
bridge the ice floes over which the trains raced. I remember now that when the woman looked around at
me she had a skull on her shoulders, and written into
the fleshless brow was the word sex stony as a lizard. I
saw the lids drop down over her eyes and then the
sightless cavern without bottom. As I fled from her I
tried to read what was written on the body of a car
racing beside me, but I could catch only the tail end
and it made no sense.

At the Brooklyn Bridge I stand as usual waiting for
the trolley to swing round. In the heat of the late afternoon the city rises up like a huge polar bear shaking
off its rhododendrons. The forms waver, the gas chokes

the girders, the smoke and the dust wave like amulets. Out of the welter of buildings there pours a jellywash of hot bodies glued together with pants and skirts. The tide washes up in front of the curved tracks and splits like glass combs. Uuder the wet headlines are the diaphanous legs of the amoebas scrambling on to the running boards, the fine, sturdy tennis legs wrapped in cellophane, their white veins showing through the golden calves and muscles of ivory. The city is panting with a five o'clock sweat. From the tops of the sky-scrapers plumes of smoke soft as Cleopatra's feathers. The air beats thick, the bats are flapping, the cement softens, the iron rails flatten under the broad flanges of the trolley wheels. Life is written down in headlines twelve feet high with periods, commas and semicolons. The bridge sways over the gasoline lakes below. Melons rolling in from Imperial Valley, garbage going down past Hell Gate, the decks clear, the stanchions gleaming, the hawsers tight, the slips grunting, the moss splitting and spelching in the ferry slips. A warm sultry haze ly-ing over the city like a cup of fat, the sweat trickling down between the bare legs, around the slim ankles. A mucous mass of arms and legs, of half-moons and weather vanes, of cock robins and round robins, of shuttlecocks and bright bananas with the light lemon pulp lying in the bell of the peel. Five o'clock strikes through the grime and sweat of the afternoon, a strip of bright shadow left by the iron girders. The trolleys wheel round with iron mandibles, crunching the papier-mâché of the crowd, spooling it down like punched transfers.

As I take my seat I see a man I know standing on the rear platform with a newspaper in his hand. His straw hat is tilted on the back of his head, his arm rests on the motorman's brass brake. Back of his ears the cable web spreads out like the guts of a piano. His straw hat is just on a level with Chambers Street; it rests like a sliced egg on the green spinach of the bay. I hear the cogs slipping against the thick stub of the motorman's toe. The wires are humming, the bridge is groaning with joy. Two little rubber knobs on the seat in front of me, like two black keys on a piano. About the size of an eraser, not round like the end of a cane. Two gummy thingamajigs to deaden the shock. The dull thud of a rubber hammer falling on a rubber skull.

The countryside is desolate. No warmth, no snugness, no closeness, no density, no opacity, no numerator, no denominator. It's like the evening newspaper read to a deaf mute standing on a hat rack with a palmetto leaf in his hand. In all this parched land no sign of human hand, of human eye, of human voice. Only headlines written in chalk which the rain washes away. Only a short ride on the trolley and I am in a desert filled with thorns and cactus.

In the middle of the desert is a bathhouse and in the bathhouse is a wooden horse with a log-saw lying athwart it. By the zinc-covered table, looking out through the cobwebbed window, stands a woman I used to know. She stands in the middle of the desert like a rock made of camphor. Her body has the strong white aroma of sorrow. She stands like a statue saying good-by. Head and shoulders above me she stands, her buttocks swoopingly grand and out of all proportion. Everything is out of proportion—hands, feet, thighs, ankles. She's an equestrian statue without the horse, a fountain of flesh worn away to a mammoth egg. Out of the ballroom of flesh her body sings like iron. Girl of my dreams, what a splendid cage you make! Only where is the little perch for your three-pointed toes? The little perch that swung backward and forward between the brass bars? You stand by the window, dead as a canary, your toes stiff, your beak blue. You have the profile of a line drawing done with a meat-ax. Your mouth is a crater stuffed with lettuce leaves. Did I ever dream that you could be so enormously warm and lopsided? Let me look at your lovely jackal paws; let me hear the croaking, dingy chortle of your dry breath.

Through the cobwebs I watch the nimble crickets, the long, leafy spines of the cactus oozing milk and chalk, the riders with their empty saddlebags, the pommels humped like camels. The dry desert of my native land, her men gray and gaunt, their spines twisted, their feet shod with rowel and spur. Above the cactus bloom the city hangs upside down, her gaunt, gray men scratching the skies with their spurred boots. I clasp her bulging contours, her rocky angles, the strong dolmen breasts, the cloven hoofs, the plumed tail. I hold her close in the choked spume of the canyons under the locked watersheds twisted with golden sands while the hour runs out. In the blinding surge of grief the sand slowly fills my bones.

A pair of blunt, rusty scissors lies on the zinc-covered table beside us. The arm which she raises is webbed to her side. The hoary inflexible movement of her arm is like the dull raucous screech of day closing and the cord which binds us is wired with grit. The sweat stands out on my temples, clots there and ticks like a clock. The clock is running down with nervous wiry sweat. The scissors move between on slow rusty hinges. My nerves race along the teeth of the comb, my spurs bristle, the veins glow. Is all pain dull and bearable like this? Along the scissors' edge I feel the rusty blunt anguish of day closing, the slow webbed movement of hunger satisfied, of clean space and starry sky in the arms of an automaton.

I stand in the midst of the desert waiting for the train. In my heart there is a little glass bell and under the bell there is an edelweiss. All my cares have dropped away. Even under the ice I sense the bloom which the earth prepares in the night.

Reclining in the luxurious leather seat I have a vague feeling that it is a German line on which I am traveling. I sit by the window reading a book; I am aware that some one is reading over my shoulder. It is my own book and there is a passage in it which baffles me. The words are incomprehensible. At Darmstadt we descend a moment while the engines are being changed. The glass shed rises to a nave supported by lacy black girders. The severity of the glass shed has a good deal the appearance of my book—when it lay open on my lap and the ribs showed through. In my heart I can feel the edelweiss blooming.

At night in Germany, when you pace up and down the platform, there is always some one to explain things to you. The round heads and the long heads get together in a cloud of vapor and all the wheels are taken apart and put together again. The sound of the language seems more penetrating than other tongues, as if it were food for the brain, substantial, nourishing, appetizing. Glutinous particles detach themselves and they dissipate slowly, months after the voyage, like a smoker exhaling a fine stream of smoke through his nostrils after he has taken a drink of water. The word *gut* is the longest lasting word of all. *"Es war gut!"* says some one, and his *gut* rumbles in my bowels like a rich pheasant. Surely nothing is better than to take a train at night when all the inhabitants are asleep and to drain from their open mouths the rich succulent morsels of their unspoken tongue. When every one sleeps the mind is crowded with events; the mind travels in a swarm, like summer flies that are sucked along by the train.

Suddenly I am at the seashore and no recollection of the train stopping. No remembrance of it departing even. Just swept up on the shore of the ocean like a comet.

Everything is sordid, shoddy, thin as pasteboard. A Coney Island of the mind. The amusement shacks are running full blast, the shelves full of chinaware and dolls stuffed with straw and alarm clocks and spittoons. Every shop has three balls over it and every game is a ball game. The Jews are walking around in mackintoshes, the Japs are smiling, the air is full of chopped onions and sizzling hamburgers. Jabber, jabber, and over it all in a muffled roar comes the steady hiss and boom of the breakers, a long uninterrupted adenoidal wheeze that spreads a clammy catarrh over the dirty shebang. Behind the pasteboard streetfront the breakers are ploughing up the night with luminous argent teeth; the clams are lying on their backs squirting ozone from their anal orifices. In the oceanic night Steeplechase looks like a wintry beard. Everything is sliding and crumbling, everything glitters, totters, teeters, titters.

Where is the warm summer's day when first I saw the green-carpeted earth revolving and men and women moving like panthers? Where is the soft gurgling music which I heard welling up from the sappy roots of the earth? Where am I to go if everywhere there are trapdoors and grinning skeletons, a world turned inside out and all the flesh peeled off? Where am I to lay my head if there is nothing but beards and mackintoshes and peanut whistles and broken slats? Am I to walk forever along this endless pasteboard street, this pasteboard which I can punch a hole in, which I can blow down with my breath, which I can set fire to with a match? The world has become a mystic maze erected by a gang of carpenters during the night. Everything is a lie, a fake. Pasteboard.

I walk along the ocean front. The sand is strewn with human clams waiting for some one to pry their shells apart. In the roar and hubbub their pissing anguish goes unnoticed. The breakers club them, the lights deafen them, the tide drowns them. They lie behind the pasteboard street in the onyx-colored night and they listen to the hamburgers sizzling. Jabber, jabber, a sneezing and wheezing, balls rolling down the long smooth troughs into tiny little holes filled with bric-a-brac, with chinaware and spittoons and flowerpots and stuffed dolls. Greasy Japs wiping the rubberplants with wet rags, Armenians chopping onions into microcosmic particles, Macedonians throwing the lasso with molasses arms. Every man, woman, and child in a mackintosh has adenoids, spreads catarrh, diabetes, whooping cough, meningitis. Everything that stands upright, that slides, rolls, tumbles, spins, shoots, teeters, sways and crumbles is made of nuts and bolts. The monarch of the mind is a monkey wrench. Sovereign pasteboard power.

The clams have fallen asleep, the stars are dying out. Everything that is made of water snoozes now in the flap-pocket of a hyena. Morning comes like a glass roof over the world. The glassy ocean sways in its depths, a still, transparent sleep.

It is neither night nor day. It is the dawn traveling in short waves with the flir of an albatross's wings. The sounds that reach me are cushioned, gonged, muffled, as if man's labors were being performed under water. I feel the tide ebbing without fear of being sucked in; I hear the waves splashing without fear of drowning. I walk amidst the wrack and debris of the world, but my feet are not bruised. There is no finitude of sky, no division of land and sea. I move through sluice and orifice with gliding slippery feet. I smell nothing, I hear nothing, I see nothing, I feel nothing. Whether on my back or on my belly, whether sidewise like the crab or spiral like a bird, all is bliss downy and undifferentiated.

The white chalk breath of Plymouth stirs the geologic spine; the tip of her dragon's tail clasps the broken continent. Unspeakably brown earth and men with green hair, the old image recreated in soft, milky whiteness. A last wag of the tail in non-human tranquility; an indifference to hope or despair or melancholy. The brown earth and the oxide green are not of air or sky or sight or touch. The peace and solemnity, the far-off, intangible tranquility of the chalk cliffs, distils a poison, a noxious, croaking breath of evil that hangs over the land like the tip of a dragon's tail. I feel the invisible claws that grip the rocks. The heavy, sunken green of the earth is not the green of grass or hope but of slime, of foul, invincible courage. I feel the brown hoods of the martyrs, their matted hair, their sharp talons hidden in scabrous vestments, the brown wool of their hatred, their ennui, their emptiness. I have a tremendous longing for this land that lies at the end of the earth, this irregular spread of earth like an alligator basking. From the heavy, sexless lid of her batted eye there emanates a deceptive, poisonous calm. Her yawning mouth is open like a vision. It is as if the sea and all who had been drowned in it, their bones, their hopes, their dreamy edifices, had made the white amalgam which is England.

My mind searches vainly for some remembrance which is older than any remembrance, for the myth engraved on a tablet of stone which lies buried under a mountain. Under the elevated structure, the windows full of pies and hamburgers, the rails swiftly turning, the old sensations, the old memories invade me again. All that belongs with docks and wharves, with funnels, cranes, pistons, wheels, ties, bridges, all the paraphernalia of travel and hunger repeats itself like a blind mechanism. As I come to the crossroads the living street spreads out like a map studded with awnings and wine shops. The noonday heat cracks the glazed surface of the map. The streets buckle and snap.

Where a rusty star marks the boundary of the past there rises up a clutter of sharp, triangular buildings with black mouths and broken teeth. There is the smell of iodoform and ether, of formaldehyde and ammonia, of fresh tin and wet iron molds. The buildings are sagging, the roofs are crushed and battered. So heavy is the air, so acrid and choking, that the buildings can no longer hold themselves erect. The entrance ways have sunk to below the level of the street. There is something croaking and froglike about the atmosphere. A dank, poisonous vapor envelops the neighborhood, as if a marsh-bog underlay the very foundations.

When I reach my father's home I find him standing at the window shaving, or rather not shaving, but stropping his razor. Never before has he failed me, but now in my need he is deaf. I notice now the rusty blade he is using. Mornings with my coffee there was always the bright flash of his blade, the bright German steel laid against the smooth dull hide of the strop, the splash of lather like cream in my coffee, the snow banked on the window ledge, putting a felt around his words. Now the blade is tarnished and the snow turned to slush; the diamond frost of the window panes trickles in a thin grease that stinks of toads and marsh gas. "Bring me huge worms," he begs, "and we will plough the minnows." Poor, desperate father that I have. I clutch with empty hands across a broken table.

A night of bitter cold. Walking along with head down a whore sidles up to me and putting her arm in mine leads me to a hotel with a blue enamel sign over the door. Upstairs in the room I take a good look at her. She is young and athletic, and best of all, she is ignorant. She doesn't know the name of a single king. She doesn't even speak her own language. Whatever I relate to her she licks up like hot fat. She lards herself with it. The whole process is one of getting warm, of putting on a coat of grease for the winter, as she explains to me in her simple way. When she has extracted all the grease from my marrow bones she pulls back the coverlet and with the most astounding sprightliness she commences her trapezoid flights. The room is like a humming bird's nest. Nude as a berry she rolls herself into a ball, her head tucked between her breasts, her arms pinned to her crotch. She looks like a green berry out of which a pea is about to burst.

Suddenly, in that silly American way, I hear her say: "Look, I can do *this*, but I can't do *that!*" Whereupon she does it. Does what? Why, she commences to flap the lips of her vagina, just like a hummingbird. She has a furry little head with frank doglike eyes. Like a picture of the devil when the Palatinate was in flower. The incongruity of it sledges me. I sit down under a trip-hammer: every time I glance at her face I see an iron slit and behind it a man in an iron mask winking at me. A terrifying drollery because he winks with a blind eye, a blind, teary eye that threatens to turn into a cataract.

If it weren't that her arms and legs were all entangled, if she weren't a slippery, coiling snake strangled by a mask, I could swear that it was my wife Alberta, or if not my wife Alberta then another wife, though I think it's Alberta. I thought I'd always know Alberta's crack, but twisted into a knot with a mask between her legs one crack is as good as another and over every sewer there's a grating, in every pod there's a pea, behind every slit there's a man with an iron mask.

Sitting in the chair by the iron bedstead, with my suspenders down and a trip-hammer pounding the dome of my skull, I begin to dream of the women I have known. Women who deliberately cracked their pelvis in order to have a doctor stick a rubber finger inside them and swab the crannies of their epiglottis. Women with such thin diaphragms that the scratch of a needle sounded like Niagara Falls in their fallen bladders. Women who could sit by the hour turning their womb inside out in order to prick it with a darning needle. Queer doglike women with furry heads and always an alarm clock or a jigsaw puzzle hidden in the wrong place; just at the wrong moment the alarm goes off; just when the sky is blazing with Roman candles and out of the wet sparks crabs and star fish, just then always and without fail a broken saw, a wire snapping, a nail through the finger, a corset rotting with perspiration. Queer dogfaced women in stiff collars, the lips drooping, the eyes twitching. Devil dancers from the Palatinate with fat behinds and the door always on a crack and a spittoon where the umbrella stand should be. Celluloid athletes who burst like ping-pong balls when they shoot through the gaslight. Strange women—and I'm always sitting in a chair beside an iron bedstead. Such skilful fingers they have that the hammer always falls in the dead center of my skull and cracks the glue of the joints. The brain pan is like a hamburger steak in a steaming window.

Passing through the lobby of the hotel I see a crowd gathered around the bar. I walk in and suddenly I hear a child howling with pain. The child is standing on a table in the midst of the crowd. It's a girl and she has a slit in the side of her head, just at the temple. The blood is bubbling from her temple. It just bubbles—it doesn't run down the side of her face. Every time the slit in her temple opens I see something stirring inside. It looks like a chick in there. I watch closely. This time I catch a good glimpse of it. It's a cuckoo! People are laughing. Meanwhile the child is howling with pain.

In the anteroom I hear the patients coughing and scraping their feet; I hear the pages of a magazine closing and the rumble of a milk wagon on the cobblestones outside. My wife is sitting on a white stool, the child's head is against my breast. The wound in her temple is throbbing, throbbing as if it were a pulse laid against my heart. The surgeon is dressed in white; he walks up and down, up and down, puffing at his cigarette. Now and then he stops at the window to see how the weather looks. Finally he washes his hands and puts on the rubber gloves. With the sterilized gloves on his hands he lights a flame under the instruments; then he looks at his watch absent-mindedly and fingers the bills lying on the desk. The child is groaning now; her whole body is twitching with pain. I've got her arms and legs pinned. I'm waiting for the instruments to boil.

At last the surgeon is ready. Seating himself on a little white stool he selects a long, delicate instrument with a red-hot point and without a word of warning he plunges it into the open wound. The child lets out such a blood-curdling scream that my wife collapses on the floor. "Don't pay any attention to *her!*" says the cool, collected surgeon, shoving her body aside with his foot. "Hold tight now!" And dipping his cruelest instrument into a boiling antiseptic he plunges the blade into the temple and holds it there until the wound bursts into flames. Then, with the same diabolical swiftness, he suddenly withdraws the instrument to which there is attached, by an eyelet, a long white cord which changes gradually into red flannel and then into chewing gum and then into popcorn and finally into sawdust. As the last flake of sawdust spills out the wound closes up clean and solid, leaving not even the suggestion of a scar. The child looks up at me with a peaceful smile and, slipping off my lap, walks steadily to the corner of the room where she sits down to play.

"That was excellent!" says the surgeon. "Really quite excellent!"

"Oh, it was, eh?" I scream. And jumping up like a maniac I knock him off the stool and with my knees firmly planted in his chest I grab the nearest instrument and commence to gouge him with it. I work on him like a demon. I gouge out his eyes, I burst his eardrums, I slit his tongue, I break his windpipe, I flatten his nose. Ripping the clothes off him I burn his chest until it smokes, and while the flesh is still raw and quivering from the hot iron I roll back the outer layers and I pour nitric acid inside—until I hear the heart and lungs sizzling. Until the fumes almost keel me over.

The child meanwhile is clapping her hands with glee.

As I get up to look for a mallet I notice my wife sitting in the other corner. She seems too paralyzed with fright to get up. All she can do is to whisper—"Fiend! Fiend!" I run downstairs to look for the mallet.

In the darkness I seem to distinguish a form standing beside the little ebony piano. The lamp is guttering but there is just sufficient light to throw a halo about the man's head. The man is reading aloud in a monotonous voice from a huge iron book. He reads like a rabbi chanting his prayers. His head is thrown back in ecstasy, as if it were permanently dislocated. He looks like a broken street lamp gleaming in a wet fog.

As the darkness increases his chanting becomes more and more monotonous. Finally I see nothing but the halo around his head. Then that vanishes also and I realize that I have grown blind. It is like a drowning in which my whole past rises up. Not only my personal past, but the past of the whole human race which I am traversing on the back of a huge tortoise. We travel with the earth at a snail-like pace; we reach the limits of her orbit and then with a curious lopsided gait we stagger swiftly back through all the empty houses of the zodiac. We see the strange phantasmal figures of the animal world, the lost races which had climbed to the top of the ladder only to fall to the ocean floor. Particularly the soft red bird whose plumes are all aflame. The red bird speeding like an arrow, always to the north. Winging her way north over the bodies of the dead there follows in her wake a host of angelworms, a blinding swarm that hides the light of the sun.

Slowly, like veils being drawn, the darkness lifts and I discern the silhouette of a man standing by the piano with the big iron book in his hands, his head thrown back and the weary monotonous voice chanting the litany of the dead. In a moment he commences pacing back and forth in a brisk, mechanical way, as if he were absent-mindedly taking exercise. His movements obey a jerky, automatic rhythm which is exasperating to witness. He behaves like a laboratory animal from which part of the brain has been removed. Each time he comes to the piano he strikes a few chords at random—plink, plank, plunk! And with this he mumbles something under his breath. Moving briskly toward the east wall he mumbles—"theory of ventilation"; moving briskly toward the west wall he mumbles—"theory of opposites"; tacking north-northwest he mumbles—"fresh air theory all wet." And so on and so forth. He moves like an old four-masted schooner bucking a gale, his arms hanging loosely, his head drooping slightly to one side. A brisk indefatigable motion like a shuttle passing over a loom. Suddenly heading due north he mumbles—"Z for zebra . . . zeb, zut, Zachariah . . . no sign of b for bretzels. . . ."

Flicking the pages of the iron book I see that it is a collection of poems from the Middle Ages dealing with mummies; each poem contains a prescription for the treatment of skin diseases. It is the Day Book of the great plague written by a Jewish monk. A sort of elaborate chronicle of skin diseases sung by the troubadors. The writing is in the form of musical notes representing all the beasts of evil omen or of creeping habits, such as the mole, the toad, the basilisk, the eel, the beetle, the bat, the turtle, the white mouse. Each poem contains a formula for ridding the body of the possessed of the demons which infest the underlayers of the skin.

My eye wanders from the musical page to the wolf hunt which is going on outside the gates. The ground is covered with snow and in the oval field beside the castle walls two knights armed with long spears are worrying the wolf to death. With miraculous grace and dexterity the wolf is gradually brought into position for the death stroke. A voluptuous feeling comes over me watching the long-drawn-out death deal. Just as the spear is about to be hurled the horse and rider are gathered up in an agonizing elasticity: in one simultaneous movement the wolf, the horse, and the rider revolve about the pivot of death. As the spear wings through the body of the wolf the ground moves gently upward, the horizon slightly tilted, the sky blue as a knife.

Walking through the colonnade I come to the sunken streets which lead to the town. The houses are surrounded by tall black chimneys from which a sulphurous smoke belches forth. Finally I come to the box factory from a window of which I catch a view of the cripples standing in line in the courtyard. None of the cripples have feet, few have arms; their faces are covered with soot. All of them have medals on their chest.

To my horror and amazement I slowly perceive that from the long chute attached to the wall of the factory a steady stream of coffins is being emptied into the yard. As they tumble down the chute a man steps forward on his mutilated stumps and pausing a moment to adjust the burden to his back slowly trudges off with his coffin. This goes on ceaselessly, without the slightest interruption, without the slightest sound. My face is streaming with perspiration. I want to run but my feet are rooted to the spot. Perhaps I have no feet. I am so frightened that I fear to look down. I grip the window sash and without daring to look down I cautiously and fearfully raise my foot until I am able to touch the heel of my shoe with my hand. I repeat the experiment with the other foot. Then, in a panic, I look about me swiftly for the exit. The room in which I am standing is littered with empty packing boxes; there are nails and hammers lying about. I thread my way among the empty boxes searching for the door. Just as I find the door my foot stumbles against an empty box. I look down into the empty box and behold, it is not empty! Hastily I cast a glance at the other boxes. None of them are empty! In each box there is a skeleton packed in excelsior. I run from one corridor to another searching frantically for the staircase. Flying through the halls I catch the stench of embalming fluid issuing from the open doors. Finally I reach the staircase and as I bound down the stairs I see a white enamel hand on the landing below pointing to—The Morgue.

It is night and I am on my way home. My path lies through a wild park such as I had often stumbled through in the dark when my eyes were closed and I heard only the breathing of the walls. I have the sensation of being on an island surrounded by rock coves and inlets. There are the same little bridges with their paper lanterns, the rustic benches strewn along the graveled paths; the pagodas in which confections were sold, the brilliant skups, the sunshades, the rocky crags above the cove, the flimsy Chinese wrappers in which the firecrackers were hidden. Everything is exactly as it used to be, even to the noise of the carrousel and the kites fluttering in the tangled boughs of the trees. *Except that now it is winter*. Midwinter, and all the roads covered with snow, a deep snow which has made the roads almost impassable.

At the summit of one of the curved Japanese bridges I stand a moment, leaning over the handrail, to gather

my thoughts. All the roads are clearly spread out before
me. They run in parallel lines. In this wooded park
which I know so well I feel the utmost security. Here
on the bridge I could stand forever, sure of my destina-
tion. It hardly seems necessary to go the rest of the
way for now I am on the threshold, as it were, of my
kingdom and the imminence of it stills me. How well
I know this little bridge, the wooded clump, the stream
that flows beneath! Here I could stand forever lost in
a boundless security, lulled and forever rapt by the
lapping murmur of the stream. Over the mossy stones
the stream swirls endlessly. A stream of melting snow,
sluggish above and swift below. Icy clear under the
bridge. So clear that I can measure the depth of it with
my eye. Icy clear to the neck.

And now, out of the dark-clustered wood, amidst
the cypresses and evergreens, there comes a phantom
couple arm in arm, their movements slow and languid.
A phantom couple in evening dress—the woman's low-
necked gown, the man's gleaming shirt studs. Through
the snow they move with airy steps, the woman's feet
so soft and dry, her arms bare. No crunch of snow, no
howling wind. A brilliant diamond light and rivulets
of snow dissolving in the night. Rivulets of powdered
snow sliding beneath the evergreens. No crunch of jaw,
no moan of wolf. Rivulets and rivulets in the icy light
of the moon, the rushing sound of white water and
petals lapping the bridge, the island floating away in
ceaseless drift, her rocks tangled with hair, her glens
and coves bright black in the silver gleam of the stars.

Onward they move in the phantasmal flux, onward
toward the knees of the glen and the white-whiskered
waters. Into the clear icy depths of the stream they
walk, her bare back, his gleaming shirt studs, and from

afar comes the plaintive tinkle of glass curtains brushing the metal teeth of the carrousel. The water rushes down in a thin sheet of glass between the soft white mounds of the banks; it rushes below the knees, carrying the amputated feet forward like broken pedestals before an avalanche. Forward on their icy stumps they glide, their bat wings spread, their garments glued to their limbs. And always the water mounting, higher, higher, and the air growing colder, the snow sparkling like powdered diamonds. From the cypresses above a dull metallic green sweeps down, sweeps like a green shadow over the banks and stains the clear icy depths of the stream. The woman is seated like an angel on a river of ice, her wings spread, her hair flown back in stiff glassy waves.

Suddenly, like spun-glass under a blue flame, the stream quickens into tongues of fire. Along a street flaming with color there moves a dense equinoctial throng. It is the street of early sorrows where the flats string out like railroad cars and all the houses flanked with iron spikes. A street that slopes gently toward the sun and then forward like an arrow to lose itself in space. Where formerly it curved with a bleak, grinding noise, with stiff, pompous roofs and blank dead walls, now like an open switch the gutter wheels into place, the houses fall into line, the trees bloom. Time nor goal bothers me now. I move in a golden hum through a syrup of warm lazy bodies.

Like a prodigal son I walk in golden leisure down the street of my youth. I am neither bewildered nor disappointed. From the perimeter of the six extremes I have wandered back by devious routes to the hub where all is change and transformation, a white lamb continually shedding its skin. When along the mountain ridges

I howled with pain, when in the sweltering white valleys I was choked with alkali, when fording the sluggish streams my feet were splintered by rock and shell, when I licked the salty sweat of the lemon fields or lay in the burning kilns to be baked, *when was all this that I never forgot what is now no more?*

When down this cold funereal street they drove the hearse which I hailed with joy had I already shed my skin? I was the lamb and they drove me out. I was the lamb and they made of me a striped tiger. In an open thicket I was born with a mantle of soft white wool. Only a little while did I graze in peace, and then a paw was laid upon me. In the sultry flame of closing day I heard a breathing behind the shutters; past all the houses I wandered slowly, listening to the thick flapping of the blood. And then one night I awoke on a hard bench in the frozen garden of the South. Heard the mournful whistle of the train, saw the white sandy roads gleaming like skull tracks.

If I walk up and down the world without joy or pain it's because in Tallahassee they took my guts away. In a corner against a broken fence they reached inside me with dirty paws and with a rusty jackknife they cut away everything that was mine, everything that was sacred, private, taboo. In Tallahassee they cut my guts out; they drove me round the town and striped me like the tiger. Once I whistled in my own right. Once I wandered through the streets listening to the blood beating through the filtered light of the shutters. Now there's a roar inside me like a carnival in full blast. My sides are bursting with a million barrel-organ tunes. I walk down the street of early sorrows with the carnival going full blast. I rub my way along spilling the tunes I have learned. A glad, lazy depravity swinging from curb to curb. A skein of human flesh that swings like a heavy rope.

By the spiral-hung gardens of the casino where the cocoons are bursting a woman slowly mounting the flowerpath pauses a moment to train the full weight of her sex on me. My head swings automatically from side to side, a foolish bell stuck in a belfry. As she moves away the sense of her words begins to make itself manifest. *The cemetery*, she said. *Have you seen what they did to the cemetery?* Moseying along in the warm wine press, the blinds all thrown open, the stoops swarming with children, I keep thinking of her words. Moseying along with light niggerish fancy, bare necked, splayfooted toes spread, scrotum tight. A warm southern fragrance envelops me, a good-natured ease, the blood thick as molasses and flapping with condors' wings.

What they have done for the street is what Joseph did for Egypt. What *they* have done? No *you* and no *they* any more. A land of ripe golden corn, of red Indians and black bucks. Who *they* are or were I know not. I know only that they have taken the land and made it smile, that they have taken the cemetery and made of it a fertile, groaning field. Every stone has been removed, every wreath and cross has vanished. Hard by my home now there lies a huge sunken checkerboard groaning with provender; the loam is rich and black, the sturdy, patient mules sink their slender hoofs into the wet loam which the plough cuts through like soft cheese. The whole cemetery is singing with its rich fat produce. Singing through the blades of wheat, the corn, the oats, the rye, the barley. The cemetery is bursting with things to eat, the mules are switching

their tails, the big black bucks are humming and chanting and the sweat rolls down their shanks.

The whole street is living now off the cemetery
grounds. Plenty for everybody. More than enough. The
excess provender goes off in steam, in song and dance,
in depravity and recklessness. Who would have dreamed
that the poor dead flat-chested buggers rotting under
the stone slabs contained such fertilizing wisdom? Who
would have thought that these bony Lutherans, these
spindle-shanked Presbyterians, had such good fat meat
left on their bones, that they could make such a marvelous harvest of corruption, such nestsful of worms? Even
the dry epitaphs which the stonecutters chiseled out
have worked their fecundating power. Quietly there
under the cool sod these lecherous, fornicating ghouls
are working their power and glory. Nowhere in the
whole wide world have I seen a cemetery blossom like
this. Nowhere in the whole wide world such rich,
steaming manure. Street of early sorrows, I embrace
you! No more pale white faces, no Beethoven skulls,
no crossbones, no spindle shanks. I see nothing but corn
and maize, and goldenrods and lilacs; I see the common
hoe, the mule in his traces, flat broad feet with toes
spread and rich silky loam of earth sloshing between
the toes. I see red handkerchiefs and faded blue shirts
and broad sombreros glistening with sweat. I hear flies
droning and the drone of lazy voices. The air hums
with careless, reckless joy; the air hums with insects
and their powdered wings spread pollen and depravity.
I hear no bells, no whistles, no gongs, no brakes grinding; I hear the clink of the hoe, the drip of water dripping, the buzz and quiet pandemonium of toil. I hear
the guitar and the harmonica, a soft tam-tam, a patter

of slippered feet; I hear the blinds being lowered and the braying of a jackass deep in his oats.

No pale white faces, thanks be to Christ! I see the coolie, the black buck, the squaw. I see chocolate and cinnamon shades, I see a Mediterranean olive, a tawny Hawaiian gold; I see every pure and every cross shade, *but no white.* The skull and crossbones have disappeared with the tombstones; the white bones of a white race have yielded their harvest. I see that everything pertaining to their name and memory has faded away, and *that,* that makes me wild with joy. In the buzz of the open field, where once the earth was humped into crazy little sods, I mosey along down the sunken wet furrows with thirsty tinkling toes; right and left I spatter the juicy cabbage loam, the mud pressed by the wheel, the broad green leaves, the crushed berries, the tart juice of the olive. Over the fat worms of the dead, squashing them back into the sod, I walk in benediction. Like the drunken sailor man I reel from side to side, my feet wet, my hands dry. I look through the wheat toward the puffs of cloud; my eye travels along the river, her low-laden dhows, her slow drift of sail and mast. I see the sun shooting down its broad rays, sucking gently at the river's breast. On the farther shore the pointed poles of wigwams, the lazy curl of smoke. I see the tomahawk sailing through the air to the sound of familiar bloodcurdling yells. I see painted faces, bright beads, the soft moccasin dance, the long flat teats and the braided papoose.

Delaware and Lackawanna, Monongahela, the Mohawk, the Shenandoah, Narragansett, Tuskegee, Oskaloosa, Kalamazoo, Seminole and Pawnee, Cherokee, the great Manitou, the Blackfeet, the Navaho range: like a huge red cloud, like a pillar of fire, a vision of the out-lawed magnificence of our earth passes before my eyes. I see no Letts, Croats, Finns, Danes, Swedes; no micks, no wops, no chinks, no polacks, no frogs, no heinies, no kikes. I see the Jews sitting in their crows' nests, their parched faces dry as leather, their skulls shriveled and boneless.

Once more the tomahawk gleams, scalps fly, and out of the river bed there rolls a bright billowy cloud of blood. From the mountain sides, from the great caves, from the swamps and Everglades pours a flood of blood-flecked men. From the Sierras to the Appalachians the land smokes with the blood of the slain. My scalp is cut away, the gray meat hangs over my ears in shreds; my feet are burned away, my sides pierced with arrows. In a pen against a broken fence I lie with my bowels beside me; all mangled and gory the beautiful white temple that was stretched with skin and muscle. The wind roars through my broken rectum, howls like sixty white lepers. A white flame, a jet of blue ice, a torchspray spins in my hollow guts. My arms are yanked from their sockets. My body is a sepulcher which the ghouls are rifling. I am full of raw gems that bleed with icy brilliance. Like a thousand pointed lances the sun pierces my wounds, the gems flame, the gizzards shriek. Night or day I know not which; the tent of the world collapses like a gasbag. In a flame of blood I feel the cold touch of a tong: through the river gorge they drag me, blind and helpless, choking, gasping, shrieking with impotence. Far away I hear the rush of icy water, the moan of jackals neath the evergreens; through the dark green forest a stain of light spreads, a vernal, prussic light that stains the snow and the icy depths of the stream. A pleasant, choking gurgle, a quiet pandemonium as when the angel with her wings outstretched floated legless under the bridge.

The gutters are choked with snow. It is winter and the sun glares down with the low bright glint of noon. Going down the street past the flats. For an hour or two, while the sun lasts, everything turns to water, everything flows, trickles, gurgles. Between the curbs and the snow banks a freshet of clear blue water rises. Within me a freshet that chokes the narrow gorge of my veins. A clear, blue stream inside me that circulates from my toes to the roots of my hair. I am completely thawed out, choking with an ice-blue gaiety.

Going down the street past the flats, an ice-blue gaiety in my narrow, choking veins. The winter's snow is melting, the gutters are swimming over. Sorrow gone and joy with it, melted, trickling away, pouring into the sewer. Suddenly the bells begin to toll, wild funereal bells with obscene tongues, with wild iron clappers that smash the glass hemorrhoids of the veins. Through the melting snow a carnage reigns: low Chinese horses hung with scalps, long finely jointed insects with green mandibles. In front of each house an iron railing spiked with blue flowers.

Down the street of early sorrows comes the witch mother stalking the wind, her wide sails unfurled, her dress bulging with skulls. Terrified we flee the night, perusing the green album, its high decor of frontal legs, the bulging brow. From all the rotting stoops the hiss of snakes squirming in the bag, the cord tied, the bowels knotted. Blue flowers spotted like leopards, squashed, blood-sucked, the earth a vernal stain, gold, marrow, bright bone dust, three wings aloft and the march of the white horse, the ammonia eyes.

The melting snow melts deeper, the iron rusts, the leaves flower. On the corner, under the elevated, stands a man with a plug hat, in blue serge and linen spats, his white mustache chopped fine. The switch opens and out rolls all the tobacco juice, the golden lemons, the elephant tusks, the candelabras. Moishe Pippik, the lemon dealer, fowled with pigeons, breeding purple eggs in his vest pocket and purple ties and watermelons and spinach with short stems, stringy, marred with tar. The whistle of the acorns loudly stirring, flurry of floozies bandaged in lysol, ammonia and camphor patches, little mica huts, peanut shells triangled and corrugated, all marching triumphantly with the morning breeze. The morning light comes in creases, the window panes are streaked, the covers are torn, the oilcloth is faded. Walks a man with hair on end, not running, not breathing, a man with a weathervane that turns the corners sharply and then bolts. A man who thinks not how or why but just to walk in lusterless night with all stars to port and loaded whiskers trimmed. Gowselling in the grummels he wakes the plaintiff night with pitfalls tuning left to right, high noon on the wintry ocean, high noon all sides aboard and aloft to starboard. The weathervane again with deep oars coming through the portholes and all sounds muffled. Noiseless the night on all fours, like the hurricane. Noiseless with loaded caramels and nickel dice. Sister Monica playing the guitar with shirt open and laces down, broad flanges in either ear. Sister Monica streaked with lime, gum wash, her eyes mildewed, craped, crapped, crenelated.

The street of early sorrows widens, the blue lips

blubber, the albatross wings ahead, her gory neck un-
hinged, her teeth agibber. The man with the bowler hat
creaks his left leg, two notches further down to the
right, under the gunwales, the Cuban flag spliced with
noodles and mock oranges, with wild magnolias and
young palmetto shoots chaffed with chalk and green
slaver. Under the silver bed the white geranium bowl,
two stripes for the morning, three for the night. The
castors crooning for blood. The blood comes in white
gulps, white choking gulps of clay filled with broken
teeth, with mucilage and wasted bones. The floor is
slippery with the coming and going, with the bright
scissors, the long knives, the hot and cold tongs.

In the melting snow outside the menagerie breaks
loose, first the zebras with gorgeous white planks, then
the fowling birds and rooks, then the acacias and the
diamond backs. The greenery yawns with open toes,
the red bird wheels and dives below, the scrum-tuft
breaks a beak, the lizard micturates, the jackal purrs,
the hyenas belch and laugh and belch again. The whole
wide cemetery safely sprinkled cracks its joints in the
night. The automatons crack too with mighty suits of
armor encumbered and hinges rusted and bolts un-
locked, abandoned by the tin trust. The butter blossoms
out in huge fan wreaths, fat, oleandrous butter marked
with crow's feet and twice spliced by the hangman
John the Crapper. The butter yowsels in the mortuary,
pale shafts of moonbeam trickling through, the estuaries
clogged, the freights ashudder, the sidings locked.
Brown beagled bantams trimmed with red craw and
otter's fur browse the bottom lands. The larkspur does
a hemorrhage. The magnesia wells ignite, the eagle soars
aloft with a cleaver through the ankle.

Bloody and wild the night with all hawk's feet slashed and trimmed. Bloody and wild the night with all the belfries screeching and all the slats torn and all the gas mains bursting. Bloody and wild the night with every muscle twisted, the toes crossed, the hair on end, the teeth red, the spine cracked. All the world wide awake twittering like the dawn, and a low red fire crawling over the gums. All through the night the combs break, the ribs sing. Twice the dawn breaks, then steals away again. In the trickling snow the oxide fumes. All through the street the hearses pass up and down, up and down, the drivers munching their long whips, their white crapes, their cotton gloves.

North toward the white pole, south toward the red heron, the pulse beats wild and straight. One by one, with bright glass teeth, they cut away the cords. The duck comes with his broad bill and then the low-bellied weasel. One after another they come, summoned from the fungus, their tails afeather, their feet webbed. They come in waves, bent like trolley poles, and pass under the bed. Mud on the floor and strange signs, the windows blazing, nothing but teeth, then hands, then carrots, then great nomadic onions with emerald eyes, comets that come and go, come and go.

East toward the Mongols, west toward the redwoods, the pulse swings back and forth. Onions marching, eggs chattering, the menagerie spinning like a top. Miles high on the beaches lie the red caviar beds. The breakers foam, snap their long whips. The tide roars beneath the green glaciers. Faster, faster spins the earth.

Out of black chaos whorls of light with portholes jammed. Out of the static null and void a ceaseless equilibrium. Out of whalebone and gunnysack this mad thing called sleep that runs like an eight-day clock.

Walking Up and Down in China

Now I am never alone. At the very worst I am with God!

In Paris, out of Paris, leaving Paris or coming back to Paris, it's always Paris and Paris is France and France is China. All that which is incomprehensible to me runs like a great wall over the hills and valleys through which I wander. Within this great wall I can live out my Chinese life in peace and security.

I am not a traveler, not an adventurer. Things happened to me in my search for a way out. Up till now I had been working away in a blind tunnel, burrowing in the bowels of the earth for light and water. I could not believe, being a man of the American continent, that there was a place on earth where a man could be himself. By force of circumstance I became a Chinaman—a Chinaman in my own country! I took to the opium of dream in order to face the hideousness of a life in which I had no part. As quietly and naturally as a twig falling into the Mississippi I dropped out of the stream of American life. Everything that happened to me I remember, but I have no desire to recover the past, neither have I any longings or regrets. I am like a man who awakes from a long sleep to find that he is dreaming. A pre-natal condition—the born man living unborn, the unborn man dying born.

Born and reborn over and over. Born while walking the streets, born while sitting in a café, born while lying over a whore. Born and reborn again and again. A fast pace and the penalty for it is not death simply, but repeated deaths. Hardly am I in heaven, for example, when the gates swing open and under my feet I find cobblestones. *How did I learn to walk so soon? With whose feet am I walking?* Now I am walking to the grave, marching to my own funeral. I hear the clink of the spade, the rain of sods. My eyes are scarcely closed, I have barely time to smell the flowers in which they've smothered me, when *bango!* I've lived out another immortality. Coming back and forth to earth this way puts me on the alert. I've got to keep my body in trim for the worms. Got to keep my soul intact for God.

Afternoons, sitting at La Fourche, I ask myself calmly: "Where do we go from here?" By nightfall I may have traveled to the moon and back. Here at the crossroads I sit and dream back through all my separate and immortal egos. I weep in my beer. Nights, walking back to Clichy, it's the same feeling. Whenever I come to La Fourche I see endless roads radiating from my feet and out of my own shoes there step forth the countless egos which inhabit my world of being. Arm in arm I accompany them over the paths which once I trod alone: what I call the grand obsessional walks of my life and death. I talk to these self-made companions much as I would talk to myself had I been so unfortunate as to live and die only once and thus be forever alone. *Now I am never alone. At the very worst I am with God!*

There is something about the little stretch from the Place Clichy to La Fourche which causes all the grand obsessional walks to bloom at once. It's like moving from one solstice to another. Supposing I have just left the Café Wepler and that I have a book under my arm, a book on Style and Will. Perhaps when I was reading this book I didn't comprehend more than a phrase or two. Perhaps I was reading the same page all evening. Perhaps I wasn't at the Café Wepler at all, but hearing the music I left my body and flew away. *And where am I then?* Why, I am out for an obsessional walk, a short walk of fifty years or so accomplished in the turning of a page.

It's when I'm leaving the Café Wepler that I hear a strange, swishing noise. No need to look behind—I know it's my body rushing to join me. It's at this moment usually that the shit-pumps are lined up along the Avenue. The hoses are stretched across the sidewalk like huge groaning worms. The fat worms are sucking the shit out of the cesspools. It's this that gives me the proper spiritual gusto to look at myself in profile. I see myself bending over the book in the café; I see the whore alongside me reading over my shoulder; I feel her breath on my neck. She waits for me to raise my eyes, perhaps to light the cigarette which she holds in her hand. She is going to ask me what I am doing here alone and am I not bored. The book is on Style and Will and I have brought it to the café to read because it's a luxury to read in a noisy café—and also a protection against disease. The music too is good in a noisy café—it augments the sense of solitude, of loneliness. I see the upper lip of the whore trembling over my shoulder. Just a triangular patch of lip, smooth and silky. It trembles on the high notes, poised like a chamois above a ravine. And now I am running the gauntlet, I and myself firmly glued together. The little stretch from the Place Clichy to La Fourche. From the blind alleys that line the little stretch thick clusters of whores leap out, like bats blinded by the light. They get in my hair, my ears, my eyes. They cling with

bloodsucking paws. All night long they are festering
in the alleyways; they have the smell of plants after a
heavy rain. They make little plantlike sounds, imbecilic
cries of endearment which make the flesh creep. They
swarm over me like lice, lice with long plantlike tendrils
which sponge the sweat of my pores. The whores, the
music, the crowds, the walls, the light on the walls, the
shit and the shit-pumps working valorously, all this
forms a nebula which condenses into a cool, waking
sweat.

Every night, as I head toward La Fourche, I run the
gauntlet. Every night I'm scalped and tomahawked. If
it were not so I would miss it. I come home and shake
the lice out of my clothes, wash the blood from my
body. I go to bed and snore loudly. *Just the right world
for me!* Keeps my flesh tender and my soul intact.

The house in which I live is being torn down. All
the rooms are exposed. My house is like a human body
with the skin peeled off. The wallpaper hangs in tatters,
the bedsteads have no mattresses, the sinks are gone.
Every night before entering the house I stand and look
at it. The horror of it fascinates me. After all, why not
a little horror? Every living man is a museum that
houses the horrors of the race. Each man adds a new
wing to the museum. And so, each night, standing before the house in which I live, the house which is being torn down, I try to grasp the meaning of it. The
more the insides are exposed the more I get to love my
house. I love even the old pisspot which stands under
the bed, and which nobody uses any more.

In America I lived in many houses, but I do not remember what any house was like inside. I had to take
what was happening to me and walk the streets with it.
Once I hired an open barouche and I rode down Fifth

Avenue. It was an afternoon in the fall and I was riding through my own city. Men and women promenading on the sidewalks: curious beasts, half-human, half-celluloid. Walking up and down the Avenue half-crazed, their teeth polished, their eyes glazed. The women clothed in beautiful garbs, each one equipped with a cold storage smile. The men smiled too now and then, as if they were walking in their coffins to meet the Heavenly Redeemer. Smiling through life with that demented, glazed look in the eyes, the flags unfurled, and sex flowing sweetly through the sewers. I had a gat with me and when we got to Forty-second Street I opened fire. Nobody paid any attention. I mowed them down right and left, but the crowd got no thinner. The living walked over the dead, smiling all the while to advertise their beautiful white teeth. It's this cruel white smile that sticks in my memory. I see it in my sleep when I put out my hand to beg—the George C. Tilyou smile that floats above the span-dangled bananas at Steeplechase. America smiling at poverty. It costs so little to smile—why not smile as you ride along in an open barouche? Smile, smile. Smile and the world is yours. Smile through the death rattle—it makes it easier for those you leave behind. Smile, damn you! *The smile that never comes off!*

A Thursday afternoon and I'm standing in the Metro face to face with the homely women of Europe. There's a worn beauty about their faces, as if like the earth itself they had participated in all the cataclysms of nature. The history of their race is engraved on their faces; their skin is like a parchment on which is recorded the whole struggle of civilization. The migrations, the hatreds and persecutions, the wars of Europe—all have left their impress. They are not smiling;

their faces are composed and what is written on them is composed in terms of race, character, history. I see on their faces the ragged, multicolored map of Europe, a map streaked with rail, steamship and airplane lines, with national frontiers, with indelible, ineradicable prejudices and rivalries. The very raggedness of the contours, the big gaps that indicate sea and lake, the broken links that make the islands, the curious mythological hangovers that are the peninsulas, all this strain and erosion indicates the conflict that is going on perpetually between man and reality, a conflict of which this book is but another map. I am impressed, gazing at this map, that the continent is much more vast than it seems, that in fact it is not a continent at all but a part of the globe which the waters have broken into, a land broken into by the sea. At certain weak points the land gave way. One would not have to know a word of geology to understand the vicissitudes which this continent of Europe with its network of rivers, lakes, and inland seas has undergone. One can spot at a glance the titanic efforts that were made at different periods, just as one can detect the abortive, frustrated efforts. One can actually feel the great changes of climate that followed upon the various upheavals. If one looks at this map with the eyes of a cartologist one can imagine what it will look like fifty or a hundred thousand years hence.

So it is that, looking at the sea and land which compose the continents of man, I see certain ridiculous, monstrous formations and others again which bear witness to heroic struggles. I can trace, in the long, winding rivers, the loss of faith and courage, the slipping away from grace, the slow, gradual attrition of the soul. I can see that the frontiers are marked with heavy, natural boundaries and also with light, wavering lines, variable as the wind. I can feel just *where* the climate is going to change, perceive as inevitable that certain fertile regions will wither and other barren places blossom. I am sure that in certain quarters the myth will come true, that here and there a link will be found between the unknown men we were and the unknown men we are, that the confusion of the past will be marked by a greater confusion to come, and that it is only the tumult and confusion which is of importance and that we must get down and worship it. As man we contain all the elements which make the earth, its real substance and its myth; we carry with us everywhere and always our changing geography, our changing climate. The map of Europe is changing before our eyes; nobody knows where the new continent begins or ends.

I am here in the midst of a great change. I have forgotten my own language and yet I do not speak the new language. I am in China and I am talking Chinese. I am in the dead center of a changing reality for which no language has yet been invented. According to the map I am in Paris; according to the calendar I am living in the third decade of the twentieth century. But I am neither in Paris nor in the twentieth century. I am in China and there are no clocks or calendars here. I am sailing up the Yangtsze in a dhow and what food I gather is collected from the garbage dumped overboard by the American gunboats. It takes me all day to prepare a humble meal, but it is a delectable meal and I have a cast-iron stomach.

Coming in from Louveciennes. . . . Below me the valley of the Seine. The whole of Paris thrown up in relief, like a geodetic survey. Looking across the plain that holds the bed of the river I see the city of Paris: ring upon ring of streets; village within village; fortress within fortress. Like the gnarled stump of an old red-wood, solitary and majestic she stands there in the broad plain of the Seine. Forever in the same spot she stands, now dwindling and shrinking, now rising and expanding: the new coming out of the old, the old de-caying and dying. From whatever height, from what-ever distance of time or place, there she stands, the fair city of Paris, soft, gemlike, a holy citadel whose mys-terious paths thread beneath the clustering sea of roofs to break upon the open plain.

In the froth and bubble of the rush hour I sit and dream over an *apéritif*. The sky is still, the clouds mo-tionless. I sit in the dead center of traffic, stilled by the hush of a new life growing out of the decay about me. My feet are touching the roots of an ageless body for which I have no name. I am in communication with the whole earth. Here I am in the womb of time and nothing will jolt me out of my stillness. One more wanderer who has found the flame of his restlessness. Here I sit in the open street composing my song. It's the song I heard as a child, the song which I lost in the new world and which I would never have recovered had I not fallen like a twig into the ocean of time.

For him who is obliged to dream with eyes wide open all movement is in reverse, all action broken into ka-leidoscopic fragments. I believe, as I walk through the horror of the present, that only those who have the courage to close their eyes, only those whose permanent absence from the condition known as reality can affect our fate. I believe, confronted with this lucid wide-awake horror, that all the resources of our civilization will prove inadequate to discover the tiny grain of sand necessary to upset the stale, stultifying balance of our world. I believe that only a dreamer who has fear neither of life nor death will discover this infinitesimal iota of force which will hurtle the cosmos into whack —*instantaneously*. Not for one moment do I believe in the slow and painful, the glorious and logical, ingloriously illogical evolution of things. I believe that the whole world—not the earth alone and the beings which compose it, nor the universe whose elements we have charted, including the island universes beyond our sight and instruments—but the whole world, known and unknown, is out of kilter, screaming in pain and madness. I believe that if tomorrow the means were discovered whereby we might fly to the most remote star, to one of those worlds whose light according to our weird calculus will not reach us until our earth itself be extinguished, I believe that if tomorrow we were transported there in a time which has not yet begun we would find an identical horror, an identical misery, an identical insanity. I believe that if we are so attuned to the rhythm of the stars about us as to escape the miracle of collision that we are also attuned to the fate which is being worked out simultaneously here, there, beyond and everywhere, and that there will be no escape from this universal fate unless simultaneously here, there, beyond and everywhere each and every one, man, beast, plant, mineral, rock, river, tree and mountain *wills* it.

Of a night when there is no longer a name for things I walk to the dead end of the street and, like a man who has come to the end of his tether, I jump the precipice which divides the living from the dead. As I plunge beyond the cemetery wall, where the last dilapidated urinal is gurgling, the whole of my childhood comes to a lump in my throat and chokes me. Wherever I have made my bed I have fought like a maniac to drive out the past. But at the last moment it is the past which rises up triumphantly, the past in which one drowns. With the last gasp one realizes that the future is a sham, a dirty mirror, the sand in the bottom of the hourglass, the cold, dead slag from a furnace whose fires have burned out. Walking on into the heart of Levallois-Perret I pass an Arab standing at the entrance to a blind alley. He stands there under the brilliant arc light as if petrified. Nothing to mark him as human—no handle, no lever, no spring which by a magic touch might lift him out of the trance in which he is sunk. As I wander on and on the figure of the Arab sinks deeper and deeper into my consciousness. The figure of the Arab standing in a stone trance under the brilliant arc light. The figures of other men and women standing in the cold sweat of the streets—figures with human contours standing on little points in a space which has become petrified. Nothing has changed since that day I first came down into the street to take a look at life on my own account. What I have learned since is false and of no use. And now that I have put away the false the face of the earth is even more cruel to me than it was in the beginning. In this vomit I was born and in this vomit I shall die. No escape. No Paradise to which I can flee. The scale is at balance. Only a tiny grain of sand is needed, but this tiny grain of sand it is impossible to find. The spirit and the will are lacking. I think again of the wonder and the terror with which the street first inspired me. I recall the house I lived in, the mask it

wore, the demons which inhabited it, the mystery that
enveloped it; I recall each being who crossed the horizon of my childhood, the wonder that wrapped him
about, the aura in which he floated, the touch of his
body, the odor he gave off; I recall the days of the
week and the gods that ruled over them, their fatality,
their fragance, each day so new and splendorous or else
long and terrifyingly void; I recall the home we made
and the objects which composed it, the spirit which
animated it; I recall the changing years, their sharp
decisive edges, like a calendar hidden away in the trunk
of the family tree; I recall even my dreams, both those
of night and those of day. Since passing the Arab I have
traversed a long straight road toward infinity, or at
least I have the illusion that I am traversing a straight
and endless road. I forgot that there is such a thing as
the geodetic curve, that no matter how wide the devia-
tion, there where the Arab stands, should I keep going,
I shall return again and again. At every crossroads I
shall come upon a figure with human contours standing
in a stone trance, a figure pitted against a blind alley
with a brilliant arc light glaring down upon him.

Today I am out for another grand obsessional walk.
I and myself firmly glued together. Again the sky hangs
motionless, the air stilly hushed. Beyond the great wall
that hems me in the musicians are tuning up. Another
day to live before the debacle! Another day! While
mumbling thus to myself I swing suddenly round past
the cemetery wall into the Rue de Maistre. The sharp
swing to the right plunges me into the very bowels of
Paris. Through the coiling, sliding intestines of Montmartre the street runs like a jagged knife wound. I am

walking in blood, my heart on fire. Tomorrow all this will perish, and I with it. Beyond the wall the devils are tuning up. Faster, faster, my heart is afire!

Climbing the hill of Montmartre, St. Anthony on one side of me, Beelzebub on the other. One stands there on the high hill, resplendent in his whiteness. The surface of the mind breaks into a choppy sea. The sky reels, the earth sways. Climbing up the hill, above the granulated lids of the roofs, above the scarred shutters and the gasping chimney pots. . . .

At that point where the Rue Lepic lies over on its side for a breathing spell, where it bends like a hairpin to renew the steep ascent, it seems as if a flood tide had receded and left behind a rich marine deposit. The dance halls, the bars, the cabarets, all the incandescent lace and froth of the electrical night pales before the seething mass of edibles which girdle the base of the hill. Paris is rubbing her belly. Paris is smacking her lips. Paris is whetting her palate for the feast to come. Here is the body moving always in its ambiance—a great dynamic procession, like the temple friezes of Egypt, like the Etruscan legend, like the morning of the glory of Crete. Everything staggeringly alive, a swarm of differentiated matter. The warm hive of the human body, the grape cluster, the honey stored away like warm diamonds. The streets swarm through my fingers. I gather up the whole of France in my one hand. In the honeycomb I am, in the warm belly of the Sphinx. The sky and the earth they tremble with the live, pleasant weight of humanity. At the very core is the body. Beyond is doubt, despair, disillusionment. The body is the fundament, the imperishable.

Along the Rue d'Orsel, the sun sinking. Perhaps it's the sun sinking, perhaps it's the street itself dismal as a vestibule. My blood is sinking of its own weight into the fragile, glassy hemorrhoids of the nerves. Over the sorrow-bitten façades a thin scum of grease, a thin green film of fadedness, a touch of dementia. And then suddenly, presto! all is changed. Suddenly the street opens wide its jaws and there, like a still white dream, like a dream embedded in stone, the Sacré Cœur rises up. A late afternoon and the heavy whiteness of it is stifling. A heavy, somnolent whiteness, like the belly of a jaded woman. Back and forth the blood ebbs, the contours rounded with soft light, the huge, billowy cupolas taut as savage teats. On the dizzy escarpments the trees stick out like spiny thorns whose fuzzy boughs wave sluggishly above the invisible current that moves trance-like beneath the roots. Pieces of sky still clinging to the tips of the boughs—soft, cottony wisps dyed with an eastern blue. Level above level, the green earth dotted with bread crumbs, with mangy dogs, with little cannibals who leap out of the pouches of kangaroos.

From the bones of the martyrs the white balustrades, the martyred limbs still writhing in agony. Silk legs crossed in Kufic characters, maybe silk sluts, maybe thin cormorants, maybe dead houris. The whole bulging edifice with its white elephant skin and its heavy stone breasts bears down on Paris with a Moorish fatalism.

Night is coming on, the night of the boulevards, with the sky red as hell-fire, and from Clichy to Barbès a fretwork of open tombs. The soft Paris night, like a ladder of toothless gums, and the ghouls grinning between the rungs. All along the foot of the hill the urinals are gurgling, their mouths choked with soft bread. It's in the night that Sacré Cœur stands out in all its stinking loveliness. Then it is that the heavy whiteness of her skin and her humid stone breath clamps down on the blood like a valve. The night and Paris pissing her white fevered blood away. Time rolling out over the xylophones, the moon gonged, the mind gouged. Night comes like an upturned cuspidor and the fine flowers of the mind, the golden jonquils and the chalk poppies, are chewed to slaver. Up on the high hill of Montmartre, under a sky-blue awning, the great stone horses champ noiselessly. The pounding of their hoofs sets the earth trembling north in Spitzbergen, south in Tasmania. The globe spins round on the soft runway of the boulevards. Faster and faster she spins. Faster and faster, while beyond the rim the musicians are tuning up. Again I hear the first notes of the dance, the devil dance with poison and shrapnel, the dance of flaming heartbeats, each heart aflame and shrieking in the night.

On the high hill, in the spring night, alone in the giant body of the whale, I am hanging upside down, my eyes filled with blood, my hair white as worms. One belly, one corpse, the great body of the whale rotting away like a fetus under a dead sun. Men and lice, men and lice, a continuous procession toward the maggot heap. This is the spring that Jesus sang, the sponge to his lips, the frogs dancing. No trace of rust, no stain of melancholy. The head slung down between the crotch in black frenzied dream, the past slowly sinking, the image balled and chained. In every womb the pounding of iron hoofs, in every grave the roar of hollow shells. Womb and shell and in the hollow of the womb a full-grown idiot picking buttercups. Man and horse moving now in one body, the hands soft, the hoofs cloven. On they come in steady procession, with red eyeballs and fiery manes. Spring is coming in the

night with the roar of a cataract. Coming on the wings
of mares, their manes flying, their nostrils smoking.

Up the Rue Caulaincourt, over the bridge of tombs.
A soft spring rain falling. Below me the little white
chapels where the dead lie buried. A splash of broken
shadows from the heavy lattice work of the bridge. The
grass is pushing up through the sod, greener now than
by day—an electric grass that gleams with horsepower
carats. Farther on up the Rue Caulaincourt I come upon
a man and woman. The woman is wearing a straw hat.
She has an umbrella in her hand but she doesn't open it.
As I approach I hear her saying—"*c'est une combinaison!*"—and thinking that *combinaison* means underwear I prick up my ears. But it's a different sort of
combinaison she's talking about and soon the fur is flying. Now I see why the umbrella was kept closed.
"*Combinaison!*" she shrieks, and with that she begins
to ply the umbrella. And all the poor devil can say is—
"*Mais non, ma petite, mais non!*"

The little scene gives me intense pleasure—not because she is plying him with the umbrella, but because
I had forgotten the other meaning of "*combinaison.*" I
look to the right of me and there on a slanting street is
precisely the Paris I have always been searching for.
You might know every street in Paris and not know
Paris, but when you have forgotten where you are and
the rain is softly falling, suddenly in the aimless wandering you come to the street through which you have
walked time and again in your sleep *and this is the street
you are now walking through.*

It was along this very street that I passed one day
and saw a man lying on the sidewalk. He was lying
flat on his back with arms outstretched—as if he had

just been taken down from the cross. Not a soul approached him, not *one*, to see if he were dead or not.
He lay there flat on his back, with arms outstretched,
and there was not the slightest stir or movement of his
body. As I passed close to the man I reassured myself
that he was not dead. He was breathing heavily and
there was a trickle of tobacco juice coming from his
lips. As I reached the corner I paused a moment to see
what would happen. Hardly had I turned round when
a gale of laughter greeted my ears. Suddenly the door-
ways and shopfronts were crowded. The whole street
had become animated in the twinkling of an eye. Men
and women standing with arms akimbo, the tears rolling
down their cheeks. I edged my way through the crowd
which had gathered around the prostrate figure on the
sidewalk. I couldn't understand the reason for this
sudden interest, this sudden spurt of hilarity. Finally I
broke through and stood again beside the body of the
man. He was lying on his back as before. There was a
dog standing over him and its tail was wagging with
glee. The dog's nose was buried in the man's open fly.
That's why everybody was laughing so. I tried to laugh
too. I couldn't. I became sad, frightfully sad, sadder
than I've ever been in all my life. I don't know what
came over me. . . .

All this I remember now climbing the slanting street.
It was just in front of the butcher shop across the way,
the one with the red and white awning. I cross the
street and there on the wet pavement, exactly where the
other man had lain, is the body of a man with arms outstretched. I approach to have a good look at him. It's the
same man, only now his fly is buttoned *and he's dead*.
I bend over him to make absolutely sure that it's the
same man and that he's dead. I make absolutely sure be-

fore I get up and wander off. At the corner I pause a
moment. What am I waiting for? I pause there on one
heel expecting to hear again that gale of laughter which
I remember so vividly. Not a sound. Not a person in
sight. Except for myself and the man lying dead in
front of the butcher shop the street is deserted. Perhaps it's only a dream. I look at the street sign to see if
it be a name that I know, a name I mean that I would
recognize if I were awake. I touch the wall beside me,
tear a little strip from the poster which is pasted to the
wall. I hold the little strip of paper in my hand a moment, then crumple it into a tiny pill and flip it in the
gutter. It bounces away and falls into a gleaming
puddle. I am not dreaming apparently. The moment I
assure myself that I am awake a cold fright seizes me.
If I am not dreaming then I am insane. And what is
worse, if I am insane I shall never be able to prove
whether I was dreaming or awake. But perhaps it isn't
necessary to prove anything, comes the assuring
thought. I am the only one who knows about it. I am
the only one who has doubts. The more I think of it
the more I am convinced that what disturbs me is not
whether I am dreaming or insane but whether the man
on the sidewalk, the man with arms outstretched, was
myself. If it is possible to leave the body in dream, or
in death, perhaps it is possible to leave the body forever, to wander endlessly unbodied, unhooked, a name-
less identity, or an unidentified name, a soul unattached,
indifferent to everything, a soul immortal, perhaps in-
corruptible, like God—who can say?

My body—the places it knew, so many places, and all
so strange and unrelated to *me*. God Ajax dragging me
by the hair, dragging me through far streets in far places
—*crazy places* . . . Quebec, Chula Vista, Brownsville,

Suresnes, Monte Carlo, Czernowitz, Darmstadt, Canarsie, Carcassonne, Cologne, Clichy, Cracow, Budapest, Avignon, Vienna, Prague, Marseilles, London, Montreal, Colorado Springs, Imperial City, Jacksonville, Cheyenne, Omaha, Tucson, Blue Earth, Tallahassee, Chamonix, Greenpoint, Paradise Point, Point Loma, Durham, Juneau, Arles, Dieppe, Aix-la-Chapelle, Aix-en-Provence, Havre, Nîmes, Asheville, Bonn, Herkimer, Glendale, Ticonderoga, Niagara Falls, Spartanburg, Lake Titicaca, Ossining, Dannemora, Narragansett, Nuremberg, Hanover, Hamburg, Lemberg, Needles, Calgary, Galveston, Honolulu, Seattle, Otay, Indianapolis, Fairfield, Richmond, Orange Court House, Culver City, Rochester, Utica, Pine Bush, Carson City, Southold, Blue Point, Juarez, Mineola, Spuyten Duyvil, Pawtucket, Wilmington, Coogan's Bluff, North Beach, Toulouse, Perpignan, Fontenay-aux-Roses, Widdecombe-in-the-Moor, Mobile, Louveciennes. . . . In each and every one of these places something happened to me, something fatal. In each and every one of these places I left a dead body on the sidewalk with arms outstretched. Each and every time I bent over to take a good look at myself, to reassure myself that the body was not alive and that it was not I but myself that I was leaving behind. *And on I went—on and on and on.* And I am still going and I am alive, but when the rain starts to fall and I get to wandering aimlessly I hear the clanking of these dead selves peeled off in my journeying and I ask myself—*what next?* You might think there was a limit to what the body could endure, but there's none. So high does the body stand above suffering that when everything has been killed there remains always a toenail or a clump of hair which sprouts

and it's these immortal sprouts which remain forever
and ever. So that even when you are absolutely dead
and forgotten some microscopic part of you still
sprouts, and be the past future so dead there's still some
little part alive and sprouting.

It's thus I'm standing one afternoon in the broiling
sun outside the little station at Louveciennes, a tiny part
of me alive and sprouting. The hour when the stock
report comes through the air—*over the air,* as they say.
In the bistro across the way from the station is hidden
a machine and in the machine is hidden a man and in
the man is hidden a voice. And the voice, which is the
voice of a full-grown idiot, says—American Can. . . .
American Tel. & Tel. . . . In French it says it, which
is even more idiotic. *American Can . . . American Tel.
& Tel.* . . . And then suddenly, like Jacob when he
mounted the golden ladder, suddenly all the voices of
heaven break loose. Like a geyser spurting forth from
the bare earth the whole American scene gushes up—
American Can, American Tel. & Tel., Atlantic & Pa-
cific, Standard Oil, United Cigars, Father John, Sacco
& Vanzetti, Uneeda Biscuit, Seaboard Air Line, Sapolio,
Nick Carter, Trixie Friganza, Foxy Grandpa, the Gold
Dust Twins, Tom Sharkey, Valeska Suratt, Commo-
dore Schley, Millie de Leon, Theda Bara, Robert E.
Lee, Little Nemo, Lydia Pinkham, Jesse James, Annie
Oakley, Diamond Jim Brady, Schlitz-Milwaukee, Hemp
St. Louis, Daniel Boone, Mark Hanna, Alexander
Dowie, Carrie Nation, Mary Baker Eddy, Pocahontas,
Fatty Arbuckle, Ruth Snyder, Lillian Russell, Sliding
Billy Watson, Olga Nethersole, Billy Sunday, Mark
Twain, Freeman & Clarke, Joseph Smith, Battling Nel-
son, Aimee Semple McPherson, Horace Greeley, Pat

Rooney, Peruna, John Philip Sousa, Jack London, Babe Ruth, Harriet Beecher Stowe, Al Capone, Abe Lincoln, Brigham Young, Rip Van Winkle, Krazy Kat, Liggett & Meyers, the Hallroom Boys, Horn & Hardart, Fuller Brush, the Katzenjammer Kids, Gloomy Gus, Thomas Edison, Buffalo Bill, the Yellow Kid, Booker T. Washington, Czolgosz, Arthur Brisbane, Henry Ward Beecher, Ernest Seton Thompson, Margie Pennetti, Wrigley's Spearmint, Uncle Remus, Svoboda, David Harum, John Paul Jones, Grape Nuts, Aguinaldo, Nell Brinkley, Bessie McCoy, Tod Sloan, Fritzi Scheff, Lafcadio Hearn, Anna Held, Little Eva, Omega Oil, Maxine Elliott, Oscar Hammerstein, Bostock, The Smith Brothers, Zbysko, Clara Kimball Young, Paul Revere, Samuel Gompers, Max Linder, Ella Wheeler Wilcox, Corona-Corona, Uncas, Henry Clay, Woolworth, Patrick Henry, Cremo, George C. Tilyou, Long Tom, Christy Matthewson, Adeline Genee, Richard Carle, Sweet Caporals, Park & Tilford's, Jeanne Eagels, Fanny Hurst, Olga Petrova, Yale & Towne, Terry McGovern, Frisco, Marie Cahill, James J. Jeffries, the Housatonic, the Penobscot, Evangeline, Sears Roebuck, the Salmagundi, Dreamland, P. T. Barnum, Luna Park, Hiawatha, Bill Nye, Pat McCarren, the Rough Riders, Mischa Elman, David Belasco, Farragut, The Hairy Ape, Minnehaha, Arrow Collars, Sunrise, Sun Up, the Shenandoah, Jack Johnson, the Little Church Around the Corner, Cab Calloway, Elaine Hammerstein, Kid McCoy, Ben Ami, Ouida, Peck's Bad Boy, Patti, Eugene V. Debs, Delaware & Lackawanna, Carlo Tresca, Chuck Connors, George Ade, Emma Goldman, Sitting Bull, Paul Dressler, Child's, Hubert's Museum, The Bum, Florence Mills, the Alamo, Peacock Alley, Pomander

Walk, The Gold Rush, Sheepshead Bay, Strangler Lewis, Mimi Aguglia, The Barber Shop Chord, Bobby Walthour, Painless Parker, Mrs. Leslie Carter, The Police Gazette, Carter's Little Liver Pills, Bustanoby's, Paul & Joe's, William Jennings Bryan, George M. Cohan, Swami Vivekananda, Sadakichi Hartman, Elizabeth Gurley Flynn, the Monitor and the Merrimac, Snuffy the Cabman, Dorothy Dix, Amato, the Great Sylvester, Joe Jackson, Bunny, Elsie Janis, Irene Franklin, The Beale Street Blues, Ted Lewis, Wine, Woman & Song, Blue Label Ketchup, Bill Bailey, Sid Olcott, In the Gloaming Genevieve and the Banks of the Wabash far away. . . .

Everything American coming up in a rush. And with every name a thousand intimate details of my life are connected. What Frenchman passing me in the street suspects that I carry around inside me a dictionary of names? and with each name a life and a death? When I walk down the street with a rapt air does any frog know *what* street I'm walking down? Does he know that I am walking inside the great Chinese Wall? Nothing is registered in my face—neither suffering, nor joy, nor hope, nor despair. I walk the streets with the face of a coolie. I have seen the land ravaged, homes devastated, families uptorn. Each city I walked through has killed me—so vast the misery, so endless the unremitting toil. From one city to another I walk, leaving behind me a grand procession of dead and clanking selves. *But I myself go on and on and on.* And all the while I hear the musicians tuning up. . . .

Last night I was walking again through the Fourteenth Ward. I came again upon my idol, Eddie Carney, the boy whom I have not seen since I left the old neighborhood. He was tall and thin, handsome in an Irish way. He took possession of me body and soul. There were three streets—North First, Fillmore Place and Driggs Avenue. These marked the boundaries of the known world. Beyond was Thule, Ultima Thule. It was the period of San Juan Hill, Free Silver, Pinocchio, Uneeda. In the basin, not far from Wallabout Market, lay the warships. A strip of asphalt next to the curb allowed the cyclists to spin to Coney Island and back. In every package of Sweet Caporals there was a photograph, sometimes a soubrette, sometimes a prizefighter, sometimes a flag. Toward evening Paul Sauer would put a tin can through the bars of his window and call for raw sauerkraut. Also toward evening Lester Reardon, proud, princely, golden-haired, would walk from his home past the baker shop—an event of primary importance. On the south side lay the homes of the lawyers and physicians, the politicians, the actors, the firehouse, the funeral parlor, the Protestant churches, the burlesk, the fountain; on the north side lay the tin factory, the iron works, the veterinary's, the cemetery, the schoolhouse, the police station, the morgue, the slaughterhouse, the gas tanks, the fish market, the Democratic club. There were only three men to fear—old man Ramsay, the gospel-monger, crazy George Denton, the peddler, and Doc Martin, the bug exterminator. Types were already clearly distinguishable: the buffoons, the earth men, the paranoiacs, the volatiles, the mystagogues, the drudges, the nuts, the drunkards, the liars, the hypocrites, the harlots, the sadists, the cringers, the misers, the fanatics, the Urnings, the criminals, the saints, the princes. Jenny Maine was hump for the monkeys. Alfie Betcha was a crook. Joe Goeller was a sissy. Stanley was my first friend. Stanley Borowski. He was the first "other" person I recognized. He was a wildcat. Stanley recognized no law except the strap which his old man kept in the back of the barber shop. When his old man belted him you could hear Stanley screaming blocks away. In this world everything was done openly, in broad daylight. When Silberstein the pants maker went out of his mind they laid him out on the sidewalk in front of his home and put the strait jacket on him. His wife, who was with child, was so terrified that she dropped the brat on the sidewalk right beside him. Professor Martin, the bug exterminator, was just returning home after a long spree. He had two ferrets in his coat pockets and one of them got away on him. Stanley Borowski drove the ferret down the sewer for which he got a black eye then and there from Professor Martin's son Harry who was a half-wit. On the shed over the paint shop, just across the street, Willie Maine was standing with his pants down, jerking away for dear life. "Bjork" he said. "Bjork! Bjork!" The fire engine came and turned the hose on him. His old man, who was a drunkard, called the cops. The cops came and almost beat his old man to death. Meanwhile, a block away, Pat McCarren was standing at the bar treating his cronies to champagne. The matinee was just over and the soubrettes from The Bum were piling into the back room with their sailor friends. Crazy George Denton was driving his wagon up the street, a whip in one hand and a Bible in the other. At the top of his crazy voice he was yelling "Inasmuch as ye do it unto the least of my brethren ye do it unto me also," or some such crap. Mrs. Gorman was standing in the doorway in her dirty wrapper, her boobies half out, and muttering "Tch tch tch!" She was a member of Father Carroll's church on the north side. "Good marnin' father, fine marnin' this marnin'!"

It was this evening, after the dinner, that it all came over me again—I mean about the musicians and the dance they are making ready. We had prepared a humble banquet for ourselves, Carl and I. A meal made entirely of delectables: radishes, black olives, tomatoes, sardines, cheese, Jewish bread, bananas, apple sauce, a couple of liters of Algerian wine, fourteen degrees. It was warm outdoors and very still. We sat there after the meal smoking contentedly, almost ready to doze off, so good was the meal and so comfortable the hard chairs with the light fading and that stillness about the rooftops as if the houses themselves were quietly breathing through the fents. And like many another evening, after we had sat in silence for a while and the room almost dark, suddenly he began to talk about himself, about something in the past which in the silence and the gloom of the evening began to take shape, not in words precisely, because it was beyond words what he was conveying to me. I don't think I caught the words at all, but just the music that was coming from him—a kind of sweet, woody music which came through the Algerian wine and the radishes and the black olives. Talking about his mother he was, about coming out of her womb, and after him his brother and his sister, and then the war came and they told him to shoot and he couldn't shoot and when the war was over they opened the gates of the prison or the lunatic asylum or whatever it was and he was free as a bird. How it happened to spill out this way I can't remember any more. We were talking about *The Merry Widow* and about Max Linder, about the Prater in Vienna—and then suddenly we were in the midst of the Russo-Japanese war and there was that Chinaman whom Claude Farrère mentions in *La Bataille*. Something that was said about the Chinaman must have sunk to the very bottom of him for when he opened his mouth again and started that speech about his mother, her womb, the war coming on and free as a bird I knew that he had gone far back into the past and I was almost afraid to breathe for fear of bringing him to.

Free as a bird I heard him say, and with that the gates opening and other men running out, all scot-free and a little silly from the confinement and the strain of waiting for the war to end. When the gates opened I was in the street again and my friend Stanley was sitting beside me on the little step in front of the house where we ate sour bread in the evening. Down the street a ways was Father Carroll's church. And now it's evening again and the vesper bells are ringing, Carl and I facing each other in the gathering gloom, quiet and at peace with each other. We are sitting in Clichy and it is long after the war. But there's another war coming and it's there in the darkness and perhaps it's the darkness made him think of his mother's womb and the night coming on, the night when you stand alone out there and no matter how frightful it gets you must stand there alone and take it. "I didn't want to go to the war," he was saying. "Shit, I was only eighteen." Just then a phono began to play and it was *The Merry Widow* waltz. Outside everything so still and quiet—just like before the war. Stanley is whispering to me on the doorstep —something about God, the *Catholic* God. There are some radishes in the bowl and Carl is munching them in the dark. "It's so beautiful to be alive, no matter how poor you are," he says. I can just barely see him sticking his hand into the bowl and grabbing another radish. So beautiful to be alive! And with that he slips a radish into his mouth as if to convince himself that he is still alive and free as a bird. And now the whole street, free as a bird, is twittering inside me and I see again the boys who are later to have their heads blown off or their guts bayoneted—boys like Alfie Betcha, Tom Fowler, Johnny Dunn, Sylvester Goeller, Harry Martin, Johnny Paul, Eddie Carney, Lester Reardon, Georgie Maine, Stanley Borowski, Louis Pirosso, Robbie Hyslop, Eddie Gorman, Bob Maloney. The boys from the north side and the boys from the south side—all rolled into a muck heap and their guts hanging on the barbed wire. If only one of them had been spared! But no, not one! Not even the great Lester Reardon. The whole past is wiped out.

It's so beautiful to be alive and free as a bird. The gates are open and I can wander where I please. But where is Eddie Carney? Where is Stanley?

This is the Spring that Jesus sang, the sponge to his lips, the frogs dancing. In every womb the pounding of iron hoofs, in every grave the roar of hollow shells. A vault of obscene anguish saturated with angel-worms hanging from the fallen womb of a sky. In this last body of the whale the whole world has become a running sore. When next the trumpet blows it will be like pushing a button: as the first man falls he will push over the next, and the next the next, and so on down the line, round the world, from New York to Nagasaki, from the Arctic to the Antarctic. And when man falls he will push over the elephant and the elephant will push over the cow and the cow will push over the horse and the horse the lamb, and all will go down, one be-

fore the other, one after the other, like a row of tin sol-
diers blown down by the wind. The world will go out
like a Roman candle. Not even a blade of grass will
grow again. A lethal dose from which no awakening.
Peace and night, with no moan or whisper stirring. A
soft, brooding darkness, an inaudible flapping of wings.

Burlesk

Now works the calmness of Scheveningen like an
anesthetic.

Standing at the bar looking at the English cunt with all her front teeth missing it suddenly comes back to me: *Don't Spit On the Floor!* It comes back to me like a dream: *Don't Spit On the Floor!* It was at Freddie's Bar on the Rue Pigalle and a man with lacy fingers, a man in a white silk shirt with loose flowing sleeves, had just rippled off "Good Bye Mexico!" She said she wasn't doin' much now, just battin' around. She was from the Big Broadcast and she had caught the hoof and mouth disease. She kept running back and forth to the toilet through the beaded curtains. The harp was swell, like angels pissing in your beer. She was a little drunk and trying to be a lady at the same time. I had a letter in my pocket from a crazy Dutchman; he had just returned from Sofia. "Saturday night," it said, "I had only one wish and that was that you could have sitten next to me." (*Where* he didn't say.) "The only thing I can write you now is this—after having left the hustling noisy New York works the calmness of a town like Scheveningen as a anaesteatic." He had been on a bust in Sofia and he had taken to himself the prima donna of the Royal Opera there. This, as he says, had given him just the right kind of rakish reputation to find grace with the public opinion of Sofia. He says he is going to retreat and start again a sober life—in Scheveningen.

I hadn't looked at the letter all evening but when the English cunt opened her mouth and I saw all her front teeth missing it came back to me—*Don't Spit On the Floor!* We were walking through the ghetto, the crazy Dutchman and I, and he was dressed in his messenger uniform. He had delivered all his messages and he was off duty for the rest of the evening. We were walking toward the Café Royal in order to sit down and have a beer or two in peace. I was giving him permission to sit down and have a beer with me because I was his boss and besides he was off duty and he could do as he pleased in his spare time.

We were walking along Second Avenue, heading north, when suddenly I noticed a shop window with an illuminated cross and on it it said: Whosoever Believeth In Me Shall Not Die. . . . We went inside and a man was standing on a platform saying: "Miss Powell, you make ready a song! Come now, brothers, who'll testify? Yes, Hymn No. 73. After the meeting we will all go down to call on our bereaved sister, Mrs. Blanchard. Let us stand while we sing Hymn No. 73: *Lord plant my feet on the higher ground.* As I was saying a moment ago, when I saw the steeplejack painting our new steeple bright and pure for us the words of this dear old hymn rushed to my lips: *Lord plant my feet on the higher ground.*"

The place was very small and there were signs everywhere—"The Lord is my Shepherd, I shall not want," et cetera. The most prominent sign was the one over the altar: *Don't Spit On the Floor.* They were all singing Hymn No. 73 in honor of the new steeple. We were standing on the higher ground and I had a good view of the signs on the wall, especially the one over the pulpit—*Don't Spit On the Floor.* Sister Powell was pumping away at the organ: she looked clean and spiritual. The man on the platform was singing louder than the others and though he knew the words by heart he held the hymn book in front of him and sang from the notes. He looked like a blacksmith who was substituting for the regular preacher. He was very loud and very earnest. He was doing his best, between songs, to get people to testify. Every now and then a man with a squeaky voice piped up: "I praise God for his savin' and keepin' power!"

Amen! Glory! Glory! Hallelujah!

"Come now," roars the blacksmith, "who'll testify? You, brother Eaton, won't you testify?"

Brother Eaton rises to his feet and says solemnly: "He purchased me with a price."

Amen! Amen! Hallelujah!

Sister Powell is wiping her hands with a handkerchief. She does it spiritually. After she has wiped her hands she looks blankly at the wall in front of her. She looks as though the Lord had just anointed her. Very spiritual.

Brother Eaton, who was purchased with a price, is sitting quietly with hands folded. The blacksmith explains that Brother Eaton was purchased with the price of Christ's own precious blood shed on the cross, on Calvary, it was. He would like some one else to testify. *Some one else, please!* In a little while, he explains, we will all go down in a body to have a last look at Sister Blanchard's dear son who passed away last night. *Come now, who'll testify?*

A quaky voice: "Folks, you know I'm not much for testifyin'. But there's one verse very dear to me . . . very dear. It's Colossius 3. *Stand still and see the salvation of the Lord.* Just stand still, brothers. Just be quiet. Try it sometime. Get down on your knees and try to think of HIM. Try to listen to HIM. Let HIM speak.

Brothers, it's very dear to me—Colossius 3. *Stand still
and see the salvation of the Lord.*"

**Hear! Hear! Glory! Glory! Praise the Lord! Hal-
lelujah!**

"Sister Powell, you make ready another song!" He
wipes his face. "Before we go down to take a last look
at Sister Blanchard's dear son let us all join in singing
one more hymn: *What a friend we have in Jesus!* I
guess we all know that by heart. Men, if you're not
washed in the blood of the Lamb it won't matter how
many books your name is registered in down here.
Don't put HIM off! Come to HIM tonight, men . . .
tonight! Come now, all together—*What a friend we
have* . . . Hymn No. 97. Let everybody stand and sing
before we go down in a body to Sister Blanchard's.
Come now, Hymn No. 97. . . . "*What a friend we have
in Jesus. . . .*"

It's all arranged. We're all going down in a body to
look at Sister Blanchard's dear dead son. All of us—
Colossians, Pharisees, snotnoses, gaycats, cracked so-
pranos—all going down in a body to have a last look. I
don't know what has happened to the crazy Dutchman
who wanted a glass of beer. We're going down to Sister
Blanchard's, all of us in a body—the Jukes and the Kallikaks, Hymn No. 73 and *Don't Spit On the Floor!*
Brother Pritchard, you put out the lights! And Sister
Powell, you make ready a song! Good-bye Mexico!
We're going down to Sister Blanchard's. Going down
to plant our feet on the higher ground. Here a nose
missing, there an eye out. Lopsided, rheumy, bile-rid-
den, sweet, spiritual, wormy and demented. All going
down in a body to paint the steeple pure and bright.
All friends with Jews. All standing still to see the salvation of the Lord. Brother Eaton's gonna pass the hat

around and Sister Powell's gonna wipe the spit off the walls. All purchased with a price, the price of a good cigar. *Now works the calmness of Scheveningen like an anesthetic.* All the messages are delivered. For those preferring cremation we will have a few very fine niches for urns. Sister Blanchard's dear dead son is lying on the ice, his toes are sprouting. The mausoleum provides a place where families and friends may lie side by side in a snow-white compartment, high and dry above the ground, where neither water, damp, nor mold can enter.

Moving toward the National Winter Garden in a yellow taxi. The calmness of Scheveningen is working on me. Letters like music everywhere and God be praised for his savin' and keepin' power. Everywhere black snow, everywhere lousy black wigs. WATCH THIS WINDOW FOR SLIGHTLY USED BAR-GAINS! MUST VACATE! **Glory! Glory! Hallelu-jah!**

Poverty walking about in fur coats. Turkish baths, Russian baths, Sitz baths . . . baths, baths, and no cleanliness. Clara Bow is giving "Parisian Love." The ghost of Jacob Gordin stalks the blood-soaked tundras. St. Marks-on-the-Bouwerie looks gay as a cockroach, her walls sweet minted and painted a tutti-frutti. BRIDGE WORK . . . REASONABLE PRICES. Moskowitz is tickling the cymbalon and the cymbalon is tickling the cold storage rump of Leo Tolstoi who has now become a vegetarian restaurant. The whole planet is turned inside out to make warts, pimples, blackheads, wens. The hospitals are all renovated, admission free, side entrance. To all who are suffering, to all who are weary and heavy-laden, to every son of a bitch dying with eczema, halitosis, gangrene, dropsy, be it remembered, sealed and affixed that the side entrance is free. Come ye one and all! Come, ye sniveling Kallikaks! Come, ye snotnosed Pharisees! Come and have your guts renovated at less than the cost of ordinary ground burial. Come tonight! Jesus wants you. Come before it's too late—we close at 7:15 on the dot.

Cleo dances every night!!

Cleo, darling of the gods, dances every night. *Mommer, I'm coming! Mommer, I want to be saved!* I'm walking up the ladder, Mommer.

Glory! Glory! Colossius! Colossius 3.

Mother of all that's holy, now I'm in heaven. I'm standing behind the standees who are standing behind Z for zebra. The Episcopal rector is standing on the church steps with a broken rectum. It says—NO PARKING. The Minsky brothers are in the box office dreaming of the river Shannon. The Pathé News clicks like a hollow nutmeg. In the Himalayas the monks get up in the middle of the night and pray for all who sleep so that men and women all over the world, when they awake in the morning, may begin the day with thoughts that are pure, kind, and brave. The world passes in review: St. Moritz, the Oberammergau Players, Oedipus Rex, chow dogs, cyclones, bathing beauties. My soul is at peace. If I had a beer and a ham sandwich what a friend I would have in Jesus! Anyway, the curtain is rising. Shakespeare was right—*the show is the thing!*

And now, ladies and gentlemen, the curtain is rising on the cleanest, fastest show ever produced in the Western Hemisphere. The curtain is rising, ladies and gentlemen, on those portions of the anatomy called respectively the epigastric, the umbilical, and the hypogastric. These choice portions, marked down to a dollar ninety-eight, have never before been shown to an American audience. Minsky, the king of the Jews, has imported them especially from the Rue de la Paix. This is the cleanest, fastest show in New York. And now, ladies and gentlemen, while the ushers are busy squirting and fumigating, we will pass out a number of French post cards each and every one guaranteed to be genuine. With every post card we will also pass out a genuine German hand-made microscope made in Zurich by the Japanese. This, ladies and gentlemen, is the fastest, cleanest show in the world. Minsky, the king of the Jews, says so himself. The curtain is rising . . . the curtain is rising. . . .

Under cover of darkness the ushers are spraying the dead and live lice and the nests of lice and the egg lice buried in the thick black curly locks of those who have no private baths, the poor, homeless Jews of the East Side who in their desperate poverty walk about in fur coats selling matches and shoe laces. Outside it's exactly like the Place des Vosges or the Haymarket or Covent Garden, except that these people have faith—in the Burroughs Adding Machine. The fire escapes are crowded with pregnant women who have blown themselves up with bicycle pumps. All the poor desperate Jews of the East Side are happy on the fire escapes because they are eating ham sandwiches with one foot in the clouds. The curtain is rising to the odor of formaldehyde sweetened with Wrigley's Spearmint Chewing Gum, five a package. The curtain is rising on the one and only portion of the human anatomy about which the less said the better. In life's December when love is an ember it will be sad to remember the star-spangled bananas floating over the sheet-iron portions of the epigastric, hypogastric and umbilical sections of the human anatomy. Minsky is dreaming in the box office, his feet planted on the higher ground. The Oberammergau Players are playing somewhere else. The chow dogs are being bathed and perfumed for the blue ribbon show. Sister Blanchard is sitting in the rocker with a fallen womb. Age comes, the body withers—but hernia can be cured. Looking down from the fire escape one sees the beautiful, unending landscape, exactly as it was painted by Cézanne—with corrugated ash cans, rusty can openers, broken-down baby carriages, tin bathtubs, copper boilers, nutmeg graters and partially nibbled animal crackers carefully preserved in cellophane. This is the fastest, cleanest show on earth brought all the way from the Rue de la Paix. You have the choice of two things—one looking down, down into the black depths, the other looking up, up into the sunlight where the hope of the resurrection waves above the star-spangled banner each and every one guaranteed to be genuine. Stand still, men, and see the salvation of the Lord. Cleo is dancing tonight and every night this week at less than the price of ordinary ground burial. Death is coming on all fours, like a sprig of shamrock. The stage glitters like the electric chair. Cleo is coming. Cleo, darling of the gods and queen of the electric chair.

Now works the calmness of Scheveningen like an anesthetic. The curtain rises on Colossius 3. Cleo advances out of the womb of night, her belly swollen with sewer gas. Glory! Glory! I'm climbing up the ladder. Out of the womb of night rises the old Brooklyn Bridge, a torpid dream wriggling in spume and moonfire. A drone and sizzle scraping the frets. A glister of chryso-

prase, a flare of naptha. The night is cold and men are
walking in lock step. The night is cold but the queen is
naked save for a jockstrap. The queen is dancing on
the cold embers of the electric chair. Cleo, the darling of
the Jews, is dancing on the tips of her lacquered nails;
her eyes are twisted, her ears filled with blood. She is
dancing through the cold night at reasonable prices. She
will dance every night this week to make way for
platinum bridges. O men, behind the *virumque cano*,
behind the duodecimal system and the Seaboard Air
Line stands the Queen of Tammany Hall. She stands
in bare feet, her belly swollen with sewer gas, her navel
rising in systolic hexameters. Cleo, the queen, purer
than the purest asphalt, warmer than the warmest electricity, Cleo the queen and darling of the gods dancing
on the asbestos seat of the electric chair. In the morning
she will push off for Singapore, Mozambique, Rangoon.
Her barque is moored to the gutter. Her slaves are
crawling with lice. Deep in the womb of night she
dances the song of salvation. We are all going down in
a body to the Men's Room to stand on the higher
ground. Down to the Men's Room where it is sanitary
and dry and sentimental as a churchyard.

Imagine now, while the curtain's falling, that it's a
fine balmy day and the smell of clams coming in from
the bay. You step out along the Atlantic littoral in your
cement suit and your gold-heeled socks and there's the
roar of Chop Suey in your ears. The Great White Way
is blazing with spark plugs. The comfort stations are
open. You try to sit down without breaking the crease
in your pants. You sit down on the pure asphalt and
let the peacocks tickle your larynx. The gutters are
running with champagne. The only odor is the odor of
clams coming from the bay. It's a fine balmy day and

all the radios are going at once. You can have a radio attached to your ass—for just a little more. You can tune in on Manila or Honolulu while you walk. You can have ice in your ice water or both kidneys removed at the same time. If you have lockjaw you can have a tube put up your rectum and imagine you're eating. You can have anything you want for the asking. That is, if it's a fine balmy day and the smell of clams coming in from the bay. Because why? Because America is the grandest country God ever made and if you don't like this country you can get the hell out of it and go back where you came from. There isn't a thing in the world America won't do for you if you ask for it like a man. You can sit in the electric chair and while the juice is being turned on you can read about your own execution; you can look at a picture of yourself sitting in the electric chair while you are waiting to be executed.

A continuous performance from morn till midnight. The fastest, cleanest show on earth. So fast, so clean, it makes you desperate and lonely.

I go back over the Brooklyn Bridge and sit in the snow opposite the house where I was born. An immense, heartbreaking loneliness grips me. I don't yet see myself standing at Freddie's Bar in the Rue Pigalle. I don't see the English cunt with all her front teeth missing. Just a void of white snow and in the center of it the little house where I was born. In this house I dreamed about becoming a musician.

Sitting before the house in which I was born I feel absolutely unique. I belong to an orchestra for which no symphonies have ever been written. Everything is in the wrong key, *Parsifal* included. About *Parsifal*, now —it's just a minor incident, but it has the right ring.

It's got to do with America, my love of music, my grotesque loneliness. . . .

Was standing one night in the gallery of the Metropolitan Opera House. The house was sold out and I was standing about three rows back from the rail. Could see only a tiny fragment of the stage and even to do that had to strain my neck. But I could hear the music, Wagner's *Parsifal*, with which I was already slightly familiar through the phonograph records. Parts of the opera are dull, duller than anything ever written. But there are other parts which are sublime and during the sublime parts, because I was being squeezed like a sardine, an embarrassing thing happened to me—*I got an erection*. The woman I was pressing against must also have been inspired by the sublime music of the Holy Grail. We were in heat, the two of us, and pressed together like a couple of sardines. During the intermission the woman left her place to pace up and down the corridor. I stayed where I was, wondering if she would return to the same place. When the music started up again she returned. She returned to her spot with such exactitude that if we had been married it could not have been more perfect. All through the last act we were joined in heavenly bliss. It was beautiful and sublime, nearer to Boccaccio than to Dante, but sublime and beautiful just the same.

Sitting in the snow before the place of my birth I remember this incident vividly. Why, I don't know, except that it connects with the grotesque and the void, with the heartbreaking loneliness, the snow, the lack of color, the absence of music. One is always falling to sleep with the fast pace. You start out with the sublime and you end up in an alley jerking away for dear life.

Saturday afternoons, for example, breaking chain in
Bill Woodruff's accessory shop. Breaking chain all afternoon for a half-dollar. Jolly work! Afterwards we'd all
go back to Bill Woodruff's house and sit and drink.
Come dark Bill Woodruff would get out his opera
glasses and we'd all take turns, looking at the woman
across the yard who used to undress with the shade up.
This business of the opera glasses always infuriated Bill
Woodruff's wife. To get even with him she'd come out
in a negligee studded with big holes. A frigid son of a
bitch, his wife, but it gave her a kick to walk up to one
of his friends and say—"feel my ass! feel how big it's
getting." Bill Woodruff pretended not to mind. "Sure,"
he'd say, "go ahead and feel it. She's cold as ice." And
like that she'd pass herself around, each one grabbing
her ass to warm her up a bit. A funny couple they were.
Sometimes you'd think they were in love with each
other. She made him miserable, though, holding him off
all the time. He used to say: "I can get a fuck out of her
about once a month—*if I'm lucky!*" Used to say it right
to her face. It didn't bother her much. She had a way of
laughing it off, as though it were an unimportant blem-
ish.

If she had simply been cold it wouldn't have been so
bad. But she was greedy too. Always clamoring for
dough. Always hankering for something they couldn't
afford. It got on his nerves, which is easy to understand,
because he was a tight, scrounging bastard himself. One
day, however, a brilliant idea occurred to him. "You
want some more dough, is that it?" he says to her. "All
right, then, I'm going to give you some dough—but
first you've got to slip me a piece of tail." (It never occurred to the poor bastard that he might find another
woman who'd enjoy a bit of fucking for its own sake).

Well, anyway, the amazing thing about it was that every time he slipped her a little extra she'd manage to screw like a rabbit. He was astonished. Didn't think she had it in her. And so, little by little, he got to working overtime in order to lay aside the little bribe which would make the frigid son of a bitch come across like a nymphomaniac. (Never thought, the poor sap, of investing the money in another gal. Never!)

Meanwhile the friends and neighbors were discovering that Bill Woodruff's wife wasn't such a cold proposition as she had been cracked up to be. Seems she was sleeping around like—with every Tom, Dick, and Harry. Why the hell she couldn't give her own spouse a little piece on the side, *gratis*, nobody could figure out. She acted as though she were sore at him. It started out that way right from the beginning. And whether she was born frigid or not makes no difference. As far as he was concerned she was frigid. She'd have made him pay until his dying day for every piece she handed him if it weren't for the fact that somebody put him wise to her.

Well, he was a cute guy, Bill Woodruff. A mean, scrounging bastard if ever there was one, but he could be cute too when necessary. When he heard what was going on he didn't say a word. Pretended that things were just as always. Then one night, after it had gone along far enough, he waited up for her, a thing he seldom did because he had to get up early and she was used to coming in late. This night, however, he waited up for her and when she came sailing in, chipper, perky, a little lit up and cold as usual he pulled her up short with a "where were you tonight?" She tried pulling her usual yarn, of course. "Cut that," he said, "I want you to get your things off and tumble into bed." That made her sore. She mentioned in her roundabout way that she didn't want any of that business. "You don't feel in the mood for it, I suppose," says he, and then he adds: "that's fine, because now I'm going to warm you up a bit." With that he up and ties her to the bedstead, gags her, and then goes for the razor strop. On the way to the bathroom he grabs a bottle of mustard from the kitchen. He comes back with the razor strop and he belts the piss out of her. And after that he rubs the mustard into the raw welts. "That ought to keep you warm for tonight," he says. And so saying he makes her bend over and spread her legs apart. "Now," he says, "I'm going to pay you as usual," and taking a bill out of his pocket he crumples it and then shoves it up her quim. . . . And that's that about Bill Woodruff, though when I get to thinking on it I want to add that light of heart he sallied bravely forth carrying the pair of horns which his wife Jadwiga had given him.

And the purpose of all this? To prove what has not yet been demonstrated, namely that

THE GREAT ARTIST IS HE WHO CON-
QUERS THE ROMANTIC IN HIMSELF.

Filed under R for rat poison.
And what by that? you say.
Why just this. . . . Whenever it came time to visit Tante Melia at the bughouse mother would do up a little lunch, saying as she laid the bottle between the napkins—"Mele always liked a drop of Kümmel." And when it came mother's turn to visit the bughouse and say to Mele well Mele how did you like the Kümmel, and Mele shaking her head and saying what Kümmel, I didn't see any Kümmel, why I could always say she's crazy of course, I gave her the Kümmel. What was the

sense in pouring a drop of Kümmel down Mele's throat when she was so goddamned disoriented as to swallow her own dung?

If it were a sunny day and my friend Stanley commissioned by his uncle, the mortician, to carry a stillbirth to the cemetery grounds, we would take a ferry boat to Staten Island and when the Statue of Liberty hove in sight overboard with it! If it were a rainy day we would walk into another neighborhood and throw it down the sewer. A day like that was a festive day for all the sewer rats. A fine day for the sewer rats scampering through the vestibule of the upper world. In those days a still-birth brought as high as ten dollars and after riding the shoot-the-chutes we always left a little stale beer for the morning because the finest thing in the world for Katzenjammer is a glass of stale beer.

I am speaking of things that brought me relief in the beginning. You are at the beginning of the world, in a garden which is boxed off. The sky is banked like sand dunes and there is not just one firmament but millions of them; the crust of every planet is carved into an eye, a very human eye that neither blinks nor winks. You are about to write a beautiful book and in it you are going to record everything that has given you pain or joy. This book, when written, will be called *A Prolegomenon to the Unconscious*. You will dress it in white kid and the letters will be embossed in gold. It will be the story of your life without emendations. Everybody will want to read it because it will contain the absolute truth and nothing but the truth. This is the story that makes you laugh in your sleep, the story that starts the tears flowing when you are in the middle of a ballroom and suddenly realize that none of the people around you know what a genius you are. How they would laugh and weep if they could only read what you have not yet written because every word is absolutely true and so far nobody has dared to write this absolute truth except yourself and this true book which is locked up inside you would make people laugh and weep as they have never laughed, never wept before.

In the beginning this is what brings relief—the true book which nobody has read, the book which you carry around inside you, the book dressed in white kid and embossed with letters of gold. In this book there are many verses *colossially* dear to you. Out of this book came the Bible, and the Koran, and all the sacred books of the East. All these books were written at the beginning of the world.

And now I'm going to tell you about the technical aspect of these books, *this* book whose genesis I am about to relate. . . .

When you open this book you will notice immediately that the illustrations have a queer pituitary flavor. You will see immediately that the author has forsaken the optical illusion in favor of a post-pineal view. The frontispiece is usually a self-portrait called "Praxus" showing the author standing on the frontier of the middle brain in a pair of tights. He always wears thick-lensed spectacles, Toric, U-31 flange. In ordinary waking life the author suffers from normal vision but in the frontispiece he renders himself myopic in order to grasp the immediacy of the dream plasm. By means of the dream technique he peels off the outer layers of his geologic mortality and comes to grips with his true mantic self, a non-stratified area of semi-liquid character. Only the amorphous side of his nature now possesses validity. By submerging the visible I he dives below the threshold of his schizophrenic habit patterns. He swims joyously, ad lib., in the amniotic fluid, one with his amoebic self.

But what, you ask, is the significance of the bird in his left hand?

Why, just this: the bird is purely metaphysical—a quaternary type of the genus dodo, having a tiny, dorsal aperture through which it delivers homilies on the nature of all things. As a species it is extinct; as an eidolon it retains its corporeality—but only if maintained in a state of equipoise. The Germans have immortalized it in the cuckoo clock; in Siam it is found on the coins of the Twenty-third Dynasty. The wings, you will observe, are almost atrophied—because in the pseudo-catalepsy of the dream it does not need to fly, it needs only to *imagine* that it is flying. The hinges of the bill are slightly out of order as the original ball-bearings were lost while flying over the Gobi desert. The bird is definitely not obscene and has never been known to foul its nest. It lays a speckled egg about the size of a walnut whenever it is about to undergo metamorphosis. It feeds on the Absolute when hungry, but it is not a carrion bird. It is exclusively migratory and, despite the vestigial wings, flies incessantly over great imaginary tracts.

If this is clear we can now go on to something else—to the peculiar object swinging from the author's left elbow, for example. With due humility I must admit that this is a little more difficult to explain, being an image of great subjunctive beauty haunting the scar tissues of the hind brain. In the first place, though contiguous to the elbow you will note that it is not suspended from the elbow. It lies at the junction of fore arm and upper arm asymptotally—that is, a symbol

rather than a precise ideological concept. The numbers
on the lowest pan correspond to certain Runic devices
which have resulted in the pragmatic invention known
as the metronym. These numbers lie at the root of all
musical composition—as imponderable mathematic.
These numbers lead the mind back to organic modalities
so that structure and form may sustain the elegant perpetuity of logic.

This much clarified, let me add that the conical object in the background must necessarily be capable of
only one interpretation: laziness. Not ordinary laziness,
as the Pauline doctrine would have it, but a sort of
spasmic phlegm induced by the leaden fumes of pleasure. It is hardly necessary to specify that the halo above
the conical object is not a quoit nor even a lifesaver,
but a purely epistemological phenomenon—that is, a
phantastikon which has taken its stance in the melancholy rings of Saturn.

And now, dear reader, I wish that you would make
ready to ask me a question before I file this portrait
away under *P for petunia*. Won't somebody please
testify before we go down to have another look at that
dear dead face? Do I hear some one speaking or is that
a shoe squeaking? It seems to me I hear some one asking
something. Some one is asking me if the little shadow
on the horizon line might be a homunculus. Is that
right? Are you asking me, Brother Eaton, if that little
shadow on the horizon line might be a homunculus?

Brother Eaton doesn't know. He says it might and
again it might not.

Well, you are right and you are wrong, Brother
Eaton. Wrong because the law of hypothecation does
not permit of what is known as doing the duck; wrong
because the equation is carried over by an asterisk

whereas the sign points clearly to infinity; right because all that is wrong has to do with incertitude and in clearing away dead matter an enema is not sufficient. Brother Eaton, what you see on the horizon line is neither a homunculus nor a plugged hat. It is the shadow of Praxus. It shrinks to diminutive proportions in the measure that Praxus waxes great. As Praxus advances beyond the pale of the tertiary moon he disembarrasses himself more and more of his terrestrial image. Little by little he divests himself of the mirror of substantiality. When the last illusion has been shattered Praxus will cast no shadow. He will stand on the 49th parallel of the unwritten eclogue and waste away in cold fire. There will be no more paranoia, everything else being equal. The body will shed its skins and the organs of man will hold themselves proudly in the light. Should there be a war you will please rearrange the entrails according to their astrologic significance. The dawn is breaking over the viscera. No more logic, no more liver mantic. There will be a new heaven and a new earth. Man will be given absolution. *Filed under A for anagogic.*

Megalopolitan Maniac

Imagine having nothing on your hands but your destiny. You sit on the doorstep of your mother's womb and you kill time—or time kills you. You sit there chanting the doxology of things beyond your grasp. Outside. Forever outside.

The city is loveliest when the sweet death racket begins. Her own life lived in defiance of nature, her electricity, her frigidaires, her soundproof walls. Box within box she rears her dry walls, the glint of lacquered nails, the plumes that wave across the corrugated sky. Here in the coffin depths grow the everlasting flowers sent by telegraph. In the vaults below the river-bed the gold ingots. A desert glittering with mica and the telephone loudly ringing.

In the early evening, when death rattles the spine, the crowd moves compact, elbow to elbow, each member of the great herd driven by loneliness; breast to breast toward the wall of self, frustrate, isolate, sardine upon sardine, all seeking the universal can opener. In the early evening, when the crowd is sprinkled with electricity, the whole city gets up on its hind legs and crashes the gates. In the stampede the abstract man falls apart, gray with self, spinning in the gutter of his deep loneliness.

One name branded deep. One identity. Everyone pretends not to know, not to remember any more, but the name is branded deep, as deep within as the farthest star without. Filling all space and time, creating infinite loneliness, this name expands and becomes what it always was and always will be—*God*. In the herd, moving with silent feet, in the stampede, wilder than the greatest panic, is God. God burning like a star in the firmament of the human consciousness: God of the buffaloes, God of the reindeer, man's God. . . . *God*.

Never more God than in the godless crowd. Never more God than in the early evening stampede when the spine rattling with death telegraphs the song of love through all the neurones and from every shop on Broadway the radio answers with megaphone and pick-up, with amplifiers and hook-ups. Never more loneliness than in the teeming crowd, the lonely man of the city surrounded by his inventions, the lost seeker drowning in the common identity. Out of desperate lonely love-lack is built the last stronghold, the webbed citadel of God formed after the labyrinth. From this last refuge no escape except heavenward. From here we fly home, marking the strange ether channels.

Done with his underground life the worm takes on wings. Bereft of sight, hearing, smell, taste he dives straight into the unknown. Away! Away! Anywhere out of the world! Saturn, Neptune, Vega—no matter where or whither, but away, away from the earth! Up there in the blue, with firecrackers sputtering in his asshole, the angel-worm goes daft. He drinks and eats upside down; he sleeps upside down; he screws upside down. At the maximum vitesse his body is lighter than air; at the maximum tempo there is nothing but the spontaneous combustion of dream. Alone in the blue he wings on toward God with purring dynamos. The last flight! The last dream of birth before the bag is punctured.

Where now is he who out of endless nightmares struggled up toward the light? Who is he that stands on the surface of the earth with lungs collapsing, a knife between his teeth, his eyes bursting? Vulcanized by sorrow and agony he stands aghast in the swift, corruptive flux of the upper world. With blood-soaked eyes how glorious it is to behold the world! How bright and gory the empire of man! MAN! Look, there he is rolling along on his little sledge, his legs amputated, his eyes blown out. Can't you hear him playing? He is playing the *Song of Love* as he rolls along on his little sledge. In the coffee house, alone with his dreams and a revolver under his heart, sits another man, a man who is sick with love. All the clients have gone, save a skeleton with a hat on. The man is alone with his loneliness. The revolver is silent. Beside him is a dog and a bone, and the dog has no use for the bone. The dog is lonely too. Through the window the sun streams in; it shines with a ghastly brilliance on the green skull of the lovelorn. The sun is rotting with ghastly brilliance.

So beautiful the winter of life, with the sun rotting away and the angels flying heavenward with firecrackers up their ass! Softly and meditatively we march through the streets. The gymnasiums are open and one can see the new men made of stovepipes and cylinders moving according to chart and diagram. The new men who will never wear out because the parts can always be replaced. New men without eyes, nose, ears or mouth, men with ball bearings in their joints and skates on their feet. Men immune to riots and revolutions. How gay and crowded the streets are! On a cellar door stands Jack the Ripper swinging an axe; the priest is mounting the scaffold, an erection bursting his fly; the notaries pass with their bulging portfolios; the klaxons going full blast. Men are delirious in their new-found freedom. A perpetual seance with megaphones and ticker tape, men with no arms dictating to wax cylinders; factories going night and day, turning out more sausages, more pretzels, more buttons, more bayonets, more coke, more laudanum, more sharp-edged axes, more automatic pistols.

I can think of no lovelier day than this in the full bloom of the twentieth century, with the sun rotting away and a man on a little sledge blowing the *Song of Love* through his piccolo. This day shines in my heart with such a ghastly brilliance that even if I were the saddest man in the world I should not want to leave the earth.

What a magnificent evacuation, this last flight heavenward from the holy citadel! Looking downward the earth seems soft and lovely again. The earth denuded of man. Unspeakably soft and lovely, this earth bereft of man. Rid of God-hunters, rid of her whoring progeny, the mother of all living wheels her way again with grace and dignity. The earth knows no God, no charity, no love. The earth is a womb which creates and destroys. And man is not of the earth, but of God. To God then let him go, naked, broken, corrupt, divided, lonelier than the deepest gulch.

Today yet a little while Progress and Invention keep me company as I march toward the mountain top. Tomorrow every world city will fall. Tomorrow every civilized being on earth will die of poison and steel. But today you can still bathe me in God's wonderful love lyrics. Today it is still chamber music, dream, hallucination. *The last five minutes!* A dream, a fugue without a coda. Every note rotting away like dead meat on the hooks. A gangrene in which the melody is drowned by its own suppurating stench. Once the organism feels death within its grasp it shudders with rapture. A quickening which mounts to triumphant agony—the agony of the death rattle, when food and sex are one. The whirlpool! and everything that is

sucked into it going down with it! The wild, unknow-
ing savage who began at the circumference in pursuit of
his tail drawing in closer and closer in great labyrinthine
spirals and now reaching the dead center where he
whirls on the pivot of self with an incandescence that
sends a blinding flood of light through every gutter of
the soul: spinning there insane and insatiate, the ghoul
and gouger of his soul, spinning in centrifugal lust and
fury until he sputters out through the hole in the center
of him; going down like a gas bag—vault, cellar, ribs,
skin, blood, tissue, mind, and heart all consumed, de-
voured, blottoed in final annihilation.

This is the city, and this the music. Out of the little
black boxes an unending river of romance in which the
crocodiles weep. All walking toward the mountain top.
All in step. From the power house above God floods
the street with music. It is God who turns the music
on every evening just as we quit work. To some of us
is given a crust of bread, to others a Rolls Royce. All
moving toward the Exits, the stale bread locked in the
garbage cans. What is it that keeps our feet in unison
as we move toward the shining mountain top? It is the
Song of Love which was heard in the manger by the
three wise men from the East. A man without legs, his
eyes blown out, was playing it on the piccolo as he
rolled through the street of the holy city on his little
sledge. It is this *Song of Love* which now pours out of
millions of little black boxes at the precise chronolog-
ical moment, so that even our little brown brothers in
the Philippines can hear it. It is this beautiful *Song of
Love* which gives us the strength to build the tallest
buildings, to launch the biggest battleships, to span the
widest rivers. It is this Song which gives us the courage

to kill millions of men at once by just pressing a button. This Song which gives us the energy to plunder the earth and lay everything bare.

Walking toward the mountain top I study the rigid outlines of your buildings which tomorrow will crumple and collapse in smoke. I study your peace programs which will end in a hail of bullets. I study your glittering shop windows crammed with inventions for which tomorrow there will be no use. I study your worn faces hacked with toil, your broken arches, your fallen stomachs. I study you individually and in the swarm—and how you stink, all of you! You stink like God and his all-merciful love and wisdom. God the maneater! God the shark swimming with his parasites!

It is God, let us not forget, who turns the radio on each evening. It is God who floods our eyes with shining, brimming light. Soon we will be with Him, folded in his bosom, gathered up in bliss and eternity, even with the Word, equal before the Law. This is coming about through love, a love so great that beside it the mightiest dynamo is but a mosquito buzzing.

And now I take leave of you and your holy citadel. I go now to sit on the mountain top, to wait another ten thousand years while you struggle up toward the light. I wish, just for this evening, that you would dim the lights, that you would muffle the loudspeakers. This evening I would like to meditate a bit in peace and quiet. I would like to forget for a little while that you are swarming around in your five-and-ten-cent honeycomb.

Tomorrow you may bring about the destruction of your world. Tomorrow you may sing in Paradise above the smoking ruins of your world-cities. But tonight I would like to think of one man, a lone individual, a man

without name or country, a man whom I respect be-
cause he has absolutely nothing in common with you—
MYSELF. Tonight I shall meditate upon that which
I am.

Louveciennes;—Clichy;—Villa Seurat.
   1934–1935.